THE FUGITIVITIES

THE FUGITIVITIES

JESSE McCARTHY

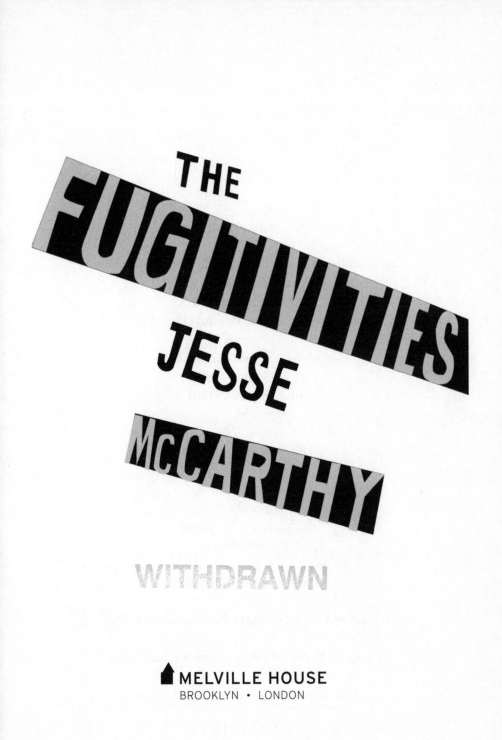

MELVILLE HOUSE

BROOKLYN · LONDON

The Fugitivities

First published in 2021 by Melville House Publishing
Copyright © Jesse McCarthy, 2021
All rights reserved
First Melville House Printing: June 2021

Melville House Publishing
46 John Street
Brooklyn, NY 11201
and
Suite 2000
16/18 Woodford Road
London E7 0HA

mhpbooks.com
facebook.com/mhpbooks
@melvillehouse

ISBN: 978-1-61219-806-4

Library of Congress Control Number: 2021932777

Designed by David Ter-Avanesyan/Ter33Design

Printed in the United States of America

1 3 5 7 9 10 8 6 4 2

A catalog record for this book is available from the Library of Congress

For my mother and fathers,
and all the foremothers and forefathers
who keep us in flight

They said a whale swallowed Jonah
Out in the deep blue sea
Sometimes I get that ol' funny feelin'
That same old whale has swallowed me
—J. B. LENOIR

Le voyage est une suite de disparitions irréparables.
—PAUL NIZAN

THE FUGITIVITIES

PART ONE

My best allegiances are to the dead.
—GWENDOLYN BROOKS

Your letter came today. I brought it with me to the Luxembourg Gardens and read it on the shaded path behind the tennis courts. Are things going very differently from the way you imagined? Or is it that your writing has changed since you moved? You sound more American now, I think. But there's something else too, a sadness that you haven't shared with me before. I'm glad that you found an apartment, and, if I read you right, a new friend. I liked the image of you and Isaac painting the walls, and of the group of black girls playing double Dutch on your street in the evening. I understand you're worried that they might soon disappear, but could Brooklyn really change that suddenly? I would have written sooner if I didn't keep falling behind at work. I get so distracted staring at the screen. Does it happen to you? I'll be clicking and tapping along and the whole thing weirds into daydreaming. I think it's the other half of my brain playing tricks on me—the part that wants to write songs. Sometimes I get into a panic, interrupt whatever I'm doing and throw down scads, a flurry of notes that I hope I might finish someday. Not even songs, just spots of emotion flaring up, like Sailor Moon in her ecstatic transformation. It's funny how I used to fantasize about being swept up in that tornado of light. I wrote something the other day that made me think of you. It's about the river by my grandfather's house. The smell of its mossiness. The cold licking at my ankles. Those spirals of snail-colored water under the neat lines of the poplar trees along the départementale. It reminded me of those ripples of river grass in the Tarkovsky film that we talked about at the café around the corner from Le Champo. I miss those days when we were always together. I guess I should worry about you—or tell you that I do. You say that maybe you're drinking too much, waking up suddenly in bars not knowing where you are and stumbling outside to hail one of those yellow taxis that have televisions in them now so that you don't have to look out the window. That many times when you wish you would pass out, you don't. I feel like

I can see you slumped in a musty back seat, hear the droning rush, and feel your loneliness as the car takes you over one of the great bridges, and for a brief moment you feel everything drop away. Like the city all around you is a distant star. I know better than to tell you what you need to do. But don't forget that you promised we'd keep writing, even in our delayed, interrupted way. Remember all the things you promised to tell me, and the stories we've only half told each other. I have my moments, comme tout le monde. I never told you about them, maybe because there would be too many other things to say. But I think that's what these letters are for. To make up for lost time with an unavoidable slowness, like a station where we always know we'll bump into each other. I wish I could tell you why I think of you when I think of my river. Or the smell of rain along the footpath behind our house. I would say it entirely in images like one of your favorite poets. But I can't right now. I still have two open reports to file and my mother needs me to help her with the telephone company. They're tearing up her street to install the fiber-optic. I'm going to Strasbourg tomorrow. I'll be sure to write you again from there if I can. I'm bringing your letter with me and will read it again on the train. I want to travel with it a while, stretch these words across space and time, unfold, read, refold. I want to hold onto you, to this.

—A

1

Perspiring, dizzy with heat and exhaustion, Jonah stopped at the corner of Underhill and St. Johns and plunked down the armchair he had trundled through the leafy streets of Park Slope, along the wide sunbaked extension of Flatbush Avenue, and, at Grand Army Plaza, around the imposing monument to the "Defenders of the Union," where bronze charioteers looked out over the construction of a condominium tower. The rich folk in the Slope had a habit of throwing out nice furniture in the summer, and he was determined to furnish his new apartment. The haul had been pretty good so far—a "reclaimed-wood" bookcase, a banker's desk lamp, a vaguely Oriental side table—with the only downside being that the crib now had the eclectic air of a showroom.

He was about halfway down the block when he took note of the commotion surrounding a double-parked Grand Cherokee directly across from his building. The vehicle was loaded down with equipment for living: a cream leather sitting chair crammed in at an angle, trash bags full of clothes, a plastic crate stuffed with video-game accessories, assorted lotions and hair products. Foodstuffs, cooking appliances, a bottle of Crisco, remained stranded on the sidewalk awaiting transport. A man carrying a stereo unit emerged from the brownstone across the street and hollered. At the boom of his voice, a somber boy in a durag, one earbud pendant, looked up. At the man's side stood a little girl with beaded braids, wearing a backpack; she saw Jonah and ducked behind her father's knee. "You heard him, go help your father," shouted a woman from the front passenger side, where she must have been trying to find more room. Her gaze passed over Jonah, assessing and dismissing in one sweep, before turning to the stoop as she called out the girl's name in a high sweet voice.

It took Jonah a moment to understand what he was seeing even though it was the simplest thing in the world. The expression on the face of the man carrying the stereo was concentrated and severe. He arranged the equipment in the back seat, then turned to go back in for whatever remained. The boy still stood curbside, staring blankly at nothing in particular. They would have been neighbors, but as it stood, Jonah was only a straggling stranger who happened to be moving in while they were moving out. There was no trace of sadness in the boy's face, no trace of fondness or regret for the street he was leaving, only an intimation that fairness was something he had never known and never would.

The scene stuck in Jonah's mind as he struggled with the chair up two flights of stairs to the apartment. Isaac was in the living room unpacking his records. Jonah shoved crumpled newspapers and packing materials out of the way and set the chair in the corner facing the window with the fire escape, then dropped his exhausted body into it. Focused completely on his own task, his roommate barely registered Jonah's entrance. The brother had more records than a DJ. Isaac wasn't actually that involved in the music scene; mostly he just listened to a small handful of albums on rotation. When they had first moved in, Jonah would find him there at all hours, sitting on the bare floor in the unfurnished room with his back up against the wall, one leg outstretched, locked in deep concentration, now and then murmuring a word or two, nodding his head in solemn agreement with the sound.

"Folks next door are moving out," Jonah said as he watched his friend digging through the crates, meticulously arranging his collection, unfazed by the room's stifling heat. Everything had to be strictly alphabetical—his Main Source record, with its splash of atoms, he held aloft momentarily

6

like a rare talisman, before sliding it in next to Madlib and Mahalia. That was Isaac, cool as a fan.

"Oh yeah . . . it's gonna flip."

"I feel like I should say or do something, you know . . . and then I'm standing there looking a fool with this vintage armchair in the middle of the street . . . like I'm a harbinger of doom or some shit."

"Yeah, I don't know, man. It's like the migration all in reverse. Same old story though, chief. Black folk moving out, white folk moving in . . . you know the deal. They stay on top like an apostrophe."

The conversation moved on to a recent television show, dropping the issue without acknowledging they were doing so, though both were eager to change the subject for reasons they didn't yet feel they could share. There would, in any case, be no conclusions to *that* conversation, and the concrete reality they shared was the next day's dawn commute to another training session in Canarsie.

Jonah had met Isaac one month earlier at the orientation assembly for a teacher-training program at the Canarsie High School auditorium. They were around the same age and had followed the call to fill the ranks of the city's teaching corps, decimated by decades of decay and demoralization that had driven the most qualified teachers out to better, wealthier, and whiter districts, where the parents were on the right side of the law.

He found himself among a hundred or so would-be teachers crammed into the school's gymnasium. There was no ventilation and like the rest of the educator corps, Jonah sweated into his interview attire as he tried to make sense out of the raucous commotion, the bleating cell phones, the shouted orders and pleas for attention. A team of young folk in matching polos circulated frenetically through the rows of folding seats thrusting documents into people's hands. A beleaguered administrator shouted into a microphone until the hive cooled to a bearable hum. A series of officials took to the mic to enumerate rules and policies. They made frequent use of the words "rigorous" and "compliance." The intimidating legalism culminated with a deadline to report to the Department of Education on Court Street for fingerprinting.

Something about the way the brother seated next to him kept his quiet made Jonah think he must be there to teach math. After a quick glance and a hesitant pause, Jonah turned to him and they settled on an awkward dap. Jonah commented on the heat and the hectic crowd. If the teachers were this bad, Isaac said softly, he hoped the students would be saints.

When the teacher orientation broke for lunch, they went out together in search of a bite. Jonah was thinking sandwiches, but Isaac seemed to ignore that proposition and they ended up gravitating to a Crown Fried Chicken. After waiting in line and getting their orange trays with menu items #1 and #2, they secured a table of their own with a view looking out onto a set of mid-rise housing projects arranged like Tetris blocks along a stretch of Ralph Avenue. Over wings, Isaac mentioned that he had split up with his girl and needed a place. Jonah was living in a hostel and needed a permanent roof over his head too. They agreed to join forces and they were already discussing neighborhoods and rent when they returned to the gymnasium to fill out more forms.

The gears of metropolitan bureaucracy did their thing, and Isaac and Jonah were duly anointed with stamped (or photocopied) city certificates asserting their aptitude for pedagogical instruction in the public schools. A week later they were signing a lease. The rent was steep but between their two salaries they could afford a place within walking distance of Prospect Park. They would live together, but they would be working far apart; an obscure lottery system determined which schools they would actually serve in. When the numbers came up, Isaac was directed to a school in Brownsville—*Never Ran, Never Will*—and Jonah to a school in Red Hook, a neighborhood he associated mainly with *On the Waterfront*.

It wasn't until they were living together, going through some of the same experiences, that Jonah really got to know his new roommate. Isaac's folks had fled the chaos and violence in Detroit for the suburbs of Richmond where he grew up a little more isolated but a whole lot safer. It was the trade-off people had to make—the lucky ones, those who already had something going, a minister in the family, a funeral-home director, a mother who had broken into one of the public school systems. They took advantage of the affirmative-action door jimmied open ever so briefly after the riots, raised *Reading Rainbow* kids, and never looked back. That was basically, Isaac told him, how he'd ended up everywhere, in that sweet spot where admissions officers were always hunting for precisely his demographic, the ones who had been afforded all the benefits of a better zip code, but who would also color in the brochure and the website appropriately.

Jonah wondered, as he always did, how his own ambiguous but affluent upbringing would go over. A black dude *from* Paris? But his new friend was unimpressed, if interested. "That's cool. A brotha from *Paree*. They got barbecue over there?" Isaac had a line for everything, but nonetheless this underwhelmed curiosity pretty much summed up the attitude he held generally. Isaac had been all over the US, on school trips, to visit friends and family. But he had never left the country. He wasn't opposed to the idea; he simply never had the means, certainly not to go somewhere on his own. One time, his junior year of college, he had been on the verge of visiting a girlfriend in Jamaica, but they had broken up a few weeks before he was set to go. Now Jamaica was out of the question. Next chance he got, though, he was hoping to use his first paid vacation days as a teacher to go somewhere else in the Caribbean, maybe Trinidad or Barbados. "Frenchman, you gotta teach me to use them words the way you do," Isaac would say, screwing up his face. "L'amour, les misérables, les incompétents. Love them French horns, too. I knew a football player in high school named Terrence who played the French horn. He wanted to go to Virginia State and play for the Trojans, but he got injured in a practice senior year. He ended up dropping out and going into the military. Haven't heard nothing since."

In spite of the disparate slots and different ladder rungs Isaac and Jonah had alighted on, everything they learned about each other confirmed how significantly their trajectories converged once they graduated with their degrees. Jonah had attended an elite private college in New England, and

Isaac a public university in North Carolina. Yet they both knew former classmates who had started more lucrative careers in consulting or banking or found prestigious internships with distinguished institutions and nonprofits, while they were both now engaged in something like charitable work, in "giving back," as people said.

On balmy evenings, they'd sit with beers in the front room and share stories about hallway incidents. When Jonah was buying, he walked over to Flatbush to purchase one of the new floral microbrews; when Isaac was buying, it was always Miller Time. It was a mellow ritual. They listened to Isaac's favorite records, originally his mother's. There had been some tension around his acquiring them. Isaac had started a small collection of his own during his senior year of high school. When he came home from college over spring break of his freshman year, he wouldn't leave his room for days. He threatened not to go back and eventually showed his mother a note from the school therapist. They talked about it, and she made a deal with him. If he would go back to school and get his education, he could take some of her own records with him. It was, he said, just one of many ways in which she'd probably saved his life.

The poor righteous teachers sat back in their bougie furniture and talked about "the situation" as they half listened to the plush tones of the Emotions or seventies-era Bobby Womack. There was always music in the air. On Sundays, Jonah awoke to the Clark Sisters ringing all down the hallway and into his room. The scratchy records somehow thickened things, popping softly in the air while they bantered until Isaac, without interrupting his train of thought, switched them out.

"The situation" was everything and nothing in particular. Even though the friends almost never agreed on why, or what, it meant, or what was to be done about it, they agreed and mutually reinforced each other's opinion that something had gone fundamentally wrong. It was in everything. Language and manners, gestures and traditions, entire understandings could be hollowed out overnight. Things had gotten weird, glitchy, like the looping video of the second plane. Twisted creeps were coming out of the woodwork all across America. Berserkers armed with gleaming shotguns and tubes of K-Y Jelly slaying Amish schoolgirls. "Active shooters," in the new parlance, burning holes in the bodies of fellow college students cowering under their desks. Wars and shadow wars multiplying, mutating without a semblance of purpose. The inferno of Katrina. Corpses floating through the Ninth Ward. The Malebolge of the Superdome. The death of the oceans. Texaco dumping crude runoff in the rainforests of Ecuador. Jihadists slitting throats. Ice caps collapsing. Narco wastelands. The interfaces taking over. The death of the heart. Everywhere and in everyone, the situation was drawing out the worst; the sickos were gaining the upper hand.

On paydays, Jonah and Isaac walked to a new soul food joint on Franklin Avenue, run by a West Indian woman who had anticipated the changes coming to the presently less gentrified parts of Crown Heights. Isaac was offended by the lack of white bread stuck to the bottom of his wings, but the sauce wasn't bad, and over drinks they talked politics and traded gossip, arguing fiercely about the importance of various music critics they had, in reality, only just discovered.

In the dark on the walk back, they'd swagger, partly on account of the rum and sugar, but also because they felt the eyes of the battered neighborhood watching, and even though not a finger or even a holler was ever raised in their direction (although occasionally it seemed it might happen, and plenty of adventurous white kids, especially white girls, had gotten robbed in the area since their arrival), they knew with unspoken certainty that they were alien to these corners and that no amount of Garveyite pleading would ensure their safe passage should things take a different turn.

Early in the mornings, hungover or not, they left the apartment together, walking in hurried silence down to the subway station at Grand Army Plaza, where they split with a nod and took trains in opposite directions. The subway platform was quiet at those hours, and it wasn't uncommon to have to wait fifteen or twenty minutes before an arrival. The inbound trains coming from East New York and Flatbush on Jonah's side were always packed with black and brown faces. White folks started boarding in numbers just one stop farther in the Slope. The cars were so packed by then that they were often left stranded at the edge, with their wet hair slicked, earbuds in, staring icily at the compressed accordion of bodies. But before the crunch, in that precious time before the thundering clatter rolling up out of the tunnel announced itself, Jonah would head to the abandoned stretches of the platform where he could sit on the last bench (unless a homeless man was slumped there) and feverishly compile notes about the previous day in a teacher's journal that the school administration had recommended he start keeping.

In his first weeks as a new teacher, the thing that struck Jonah most about the students were the tattoos. They all had them. Gangs, he'd figured at first, or the usual rituals of adolescence. Boyfriend-girlfriend, signs and blessings for courage, fearlessness, spirituality. There were plenty of those. But they were not the most common ones. Those were the markings of death. Names and nicknames of friends, schoolmates, brothers, sisters, cousins. One of them Jonah recognized from screen-printed T-shirts he had seen students wearing in the hall. The face, name, and lifespan of a kid who must have been sitting in a classroom with whoever had filled Jonah's role the year before. This grim reaping, everyone agreed, was nonetheless a measure of progress. Things were far better than ten years earlier, in the terrible early nineties, when the death count had been much higher and even the school's principal of twenty-six years, Mr. Daly, was shot and killed in a burst of crossfire while out looking for a student who had been bullied. R. J. 1982–2000. Wade Never Forget 1980–1997. Antoine 1984–2004. Krystal R.I.P. in Heaven 1985–2001. Jermaine Noah Howard 1980–2002. The most beautiful, and the saddest, inked along a forearm in tightly bound cursive simply read, "Peace To All My Brothers Who Passed Away."

Teaching was, among other things, a high-wire act. Jonah learned to walk the wire, often by falling painfully from it. The hours of instruction sometimes felt like battle. Something about the collective charge of restless minds made endings, no matter how calculated, feel sudden and abrupt. The students rushed back out in a vortex, a few strays always lingering, sometimes out of curiosity, or kindness, oftentimes for protection. There was no silence like that of the classroom when one stood at the desk alone, wiping down the blackboard, gathering one's papers in a quiet shuffle.

The long commute home from Red Hook required a transfer from a bus, since the trains didn't run there. When Jonah got home, he often found Isaac as drained as himself. They'd barely be able to speak to each other, unless to relate what often sounded like war stories. Jonah hadn't necessarily expected his job to be what it was, but now he was knee-deep. Almost without realizing it, he spoke more to himself than to anyone else, and he did so in the pages of his journal. The weeks passed, and as he grew more practiced in the form, more accustomed to the rhythms of his own mind, the number of pages scrawled in haste every morning on the subway platform multiplied. So much so, that, more than once, he looked up in a jolt of panic to see the doors jamming shut in his face.

Lesson planning helped, but it could not save them. That was the conclusion that kept resurfacing in his notes as the days began to resemble each other more than they differed. He held a pivotal but tenuous role in the lives of the kids who came to him from the housing projects that sat between the long-defunct waterfront and the elevated tracks over the Gowanus canal. A stabbing incident involving a transfer student less than a month after his arrival concentrated these thoughts into an indissoluble fear. He felt it leeching his courage every morning as he approached the high walls and metal cladding of the school's fortresslike frontage. Once he got past the metal detectors and up the grand staircase, his classroom was at the end of the hall, a corner room on the fourth floor, which meant it got light and even a glimpse of the harbor where, though you couldn't see it, Lady Liberty watched over the endless rounds of the Staten Island Ferry.

He wasn't afraid for himself. What he feared was becoming attached to a student who might lose their life, or spend years in prison, or who might never leave these same blocks that formed everything they knew, and that they might not want to. The fear was that he would fail to reach them, founder in showing them how to remain on the narrowest of rising roads, the slim chance that maybe, if they went against everything, the most powerful forces in society and the most intoxicating impulses of puberty, if they persevered with unwavering tenacity and a near-military discipline, there was a chance they might slip through the bonds. This fear could be crippling.

The infernal contradictions between his hopeful expectations and the downward spirals of aimless and angry students deepened. He was locked in a struggle, but against whom? It felt like it was against *them*, the students who went off like bottle rockets without warning, were fine one minute, spazzing out of control the next. But it wasn't them, and he knew it. He told himself it was their parents. Or it was the administration; the school principal with her perpetually gleeful greetings and frizzy hair who had clearly decided she would rather be liked than respected. But that wasn't the truth. Nor was it the brand-new Barnes & Noble Classics he had purchased that sat untouched on the "reading shelf" he had set up along the back wall. It was none of those things, and yet in a way it was all of them. Everyone knew the rot had reached the core. Knowing didn't make a difference to what could be done. The acronyms, the tests, the teaching staff themselves; everything changed except for the thing they were all supposed to be achieving. The unspoken game was how to get credit for sweeping dirt under a rug. But then why should he have expected anything else?

From his pedagogical instruction, Jonah knew that he was never supposed to have a favorite. He knew it was unethical to think in those terms. But he did have a favorite. B., who usually came in with a hoodie, kept to herself, and pretended to be asleep at her desk. It had taken Jonah months to understand that she was too smart for the class. He hadn't connected the dots until she turned in a free-writing assignment not long after the Christmas break. It was an essay about discovering her aunt's fatal overdose. She wrote it in longhand with a glossy purple pen. Her prose was elegant and fluid. When Jonah handed her the paper and she saw the letter grade, she lit up. He told her it was exceptional, that she was talented, and he asked her if she had thought about going to go to college. She said she wanted to study fashion. He gave her a copy of *If Beale Street Could Talk*, and in the following weeks she would show up early to class every day and read alone at her desk, still wearing her puffer coat and cradling the book defensively like a treasure.

The possibility of her failing had never entered Jonah's mind. So, when B. stopped coming to class around Easter, he was genuinely shocked. Was there something more he should have done? Had he done all that he could have? If he were doing a better job with his classroom management would she still be there? He tried to hold the students in his mind in a loosely individuated whole, a kind of buzzing abstraction. But when bad things happened to them—and they did with alarming frequency—their fragile lives suddenly became very real and singular, unbearably so.

As the weeks passed, the possibility of her recovering or making up assignments and getting a passing grade faded and then finally evaporated entirely. Jonah thought he might not see her again at all, and he was told by other teachers that this was something that sometimes happened, and that one simply had to accept it. But at the very end of the year, on a bright summery day with light streaming in through the corner windows, B. appeared in the doorway after class and asked to speak with him. She apologized for her absence and told him the outlines of what he understood was an account of sexual assault. It might have been exceptionally allowable to give her a hug, but he did not think he could, so he told her gravely and emphatically how sorry he was and asked her if there was anything he could do to help. She told him not to worry about her. That she was more confident in her future than ever before. She said she had suffered more than anyone would ever be able to make her suffer again. She said she was sorry to have failed his class. He told her she hadn't failed. That so many people, and he first among them, had failed her. She told him not to blame himself. She wasn't angry anymore, she said. She said nothing could hurt her now. "Don't worry about me—Imma do for myself," she said. He told her it was a brave thing

15

to say, that he was proud of her resolve. She said she was going to make her own way in the world, like she always knew she would have to. She thanked him for the novel, and said that Tish was her, that she had never connected with someone in a book like that before. He was going to say how pleased he was that she enjoyed the reading, but her friends were calling to her from the hall. She dabbed her eye, smiled, picked up her schoolbag, and hurried on her way.

2

Teaching had not allowed for much in the way of frivolities but going out to film houses to lose himself in the dark was a vice Jonah couldn't shake. As long as he stayed in Brooklyn the unfavorable equation of public transport and distance usually led him to adopt the path of least resistance: ordering takeout and watching something random online. But in Manhattan, he gravitated toward indie screen institutions like Cinema Reggio down on Twelfth Street, with the old-fashioned marquee that reminded him of the rue Christine. One evening that spring, he ducked into the Reggio, mostly to get out of a sudden downpour. They were screening a restored print of Charles Burnett's *Killer of Sheep*—according to some critics, read the lobby notice, it was the greatest black film ever made but virtually unknown outside the indie film world, having disappeared from most screens for decades. He went to purchase a ticket.

Unmistakable. The lanky boyish shag of hair, the reedy voice, the thin delicate hands extended in Italianate gestures. The vendor working the booth was his former college classmate, the wild Cubano from B Dorm. Octavio Cienfuegos. In this serendipitous instance, Octavio was occupied with finessing the elderly couple in line ahead of him; the old man, visibly overwhelmed, was writing down his email address for the Reggio newsletter. Unbeatable discounts, exclusive VIP screenings, not to mention the privilege of supporting the seventh art—Octavio dispensed his assurances with charming conviction and more than a little free association. Once the couple had given up their email and fled in polite haste, Octavio seemed to just as swiftly become a statue again, an inscrutable Pierrot, his gaze fixated on a point somewhere in the middle distance, so that when Jonah got up to the counter and knocked on the glass, he nearly jumped.

"Oh shit! Oh, *shit*! Jonah? Qué bolá, asere?"

Octavio was visibly high.

"Nothing much, man, just come to see a movie. How the hell you been?"

"You see I'm working, right! Listen, Jonah, normally man, *for you*, you know I would hook you up, but I haven't been on the job so long, you know how it is, give me a few weeks, I'm gonna have my way around here, I'm seeing things *already*, man, I'm telling you, the way they run this rig, it's por la izquierda, you wouldn't believe it. Next time you come . . ."

"No worries, man," Jonah said. "I wasn't looking for the angle. I make decent money now, anyway. I'm teaching."

"Okay, Teach—get those tax dollars, but don't be a stranger, come see me after the film. Seriously. I'll be off by then. I want to talk to you. Some strategies I've been working on. Knight moves. Avanzadas. I'll explain. You gotta catch the flick, pero socio, find me later, okay? If you don't see me, just chill, don't ask around. Sometimes I duck out, you know, but I won't be far."

This conspiratorial tone and its implied precautions proved entirely unnecessary. After the film, Jonah found Octavio waiting for him outside in front of the theater. He was standing unperturbed under the marquee. The rain still coming down hard and blowing in sideways had left him soaked on one side, as if he had been standing there for a long time. Octavio handed him one of the cinema's upcoming events calendars to use as an impromptu umbrella. Jonah accepted it with thanks, and they ran, splashing, over to Heathers, a nearby bar, where Octavio was well known, and, as he put it, had "standing." Under Prince-purple fluorescent lighting, they reacquainted themselves with college anecdotes and a debate over whether *Killer of Sheep* was truly the greatest black film ever made. Without hesitation, Octavio said it was commendable but in no way superior to the best of Micheaux. Jonah hastily agreed, vaguely recognizing the name, though he had never actually seen a film by that director. Octavio had always already seen every-thing—working the Reggio "internship," which meant little pay and a lot of free films, certainly helped. Not that he needed rent money. He was living with his parents in the city to save money while he applied to art schools.

The job itself was a soft take. Do whatever management said needed to get done, be a jack-of-all-trades. He would fix the marquee, sell popcorn and tickets, and assist Benny, a Mexican dude from Aguascalientes, who cleaned all the surfaces and the bathrooms, and mopped the lobby. The Reggio management was Sal, a cigar-smoking Bensonhurst man built like a bouncer and notorious for his gator-skin loafers and low boiling point. Octavio put his Cuban heritage to good use when they hosted the Latino Film Festival, doing Q&As and the like. As long as Jonah kept a low profile, Octavio volunteered to sneak him into the festival when it came around.

Jonah found himself drawn to the air of intelligent mischief that he recalled admiring from a distance in college. Octavio was the kind of guy who cut it close and knew, maybe a little too well, that he was attractive, and that the relation between those things allowed for certain kinds of movement in the world, slippages and maneuvers available only to some. This meant that when he had an idea, he acted on it immediately, seemingly intuitively, although because the hidden ratio of calculation and impulse remained masked it was impossible to tell whether plans or impulses led the way, only that the end result was that he enjoyed a remarkable knack for merging with whatever currents were around.

So, when Octavio texted Jonah one evening in May to say that he had an idea that would change their lives, Jonah agreed to meet him the very next morning without giving himself cause to question the possible reasons or portents. The school year was in its last few weeks, and because Jonah still needed to make his way to Red Hook and Octavio was in Manhattan, it was suggested that they meet at the crack of dawn in the Financial District, where they could catch a ferry taxi over to the Brooklyn waterfront. The trip over, Octavio said, would give him all the time he needed to explain himself, and Jonah would get to class on time.

That morning, Jonah got up in the blue darkness and left the apartment while Isaac was showering and took the train to downtown Manhattan. The Fulton Street station hadn't reopened yet, so he got out one stop higher, grabbed coffee at the first Starbucks he saw, and headed down on foot. A good third of the district was still being excavated and repurposed. Construction workers cried out to one another over the chorus of chattering rock drills. Thunderous loads of concrete barreled into the tumbril of Mack trucks to be carted away. American flags were draped on machine pieces, decals adorning the countless work helmets of men whose booming Jersey voices seemed to hang and ring out longer in the dusty air. Forty stories above him floated the largest flag he'd ever seen, billowing out behind a crane operator, the long boom turning like a clock hand, sweeping across the brightening sky and over the massive hollow below.

Jonah crossed below City Hall in the shadow of the Woolworth Building, mostly east and south again, into the blue veins of New Amsterdam. He toyed with visions of the same streets in the first century of their existence, festooned at their ends with sail and riggings. The disembarked European tribes staking out street corners, scrabbling like dogs trained for the fight. The clank of continental commerce and the groan and shudder of titanic construction. Black dock workers signaling with their eyes and a nod of the head to the runaways not yet secure on the landing. Looking for agents on the path to the North. Those others had walked here, those persons whose cherished names and things had gone misremembered, unrecorded, or just overlooked, trapped in fine layers of archeological sediment, entire cities of the dead murmuring under the blab of the pave, like the African burial ground he had read about, discovered underneath a parking lot.

He imagined the perspective of someone who had worked in these environs for a living, maybe as a customs inspector. The comedy of summing up exhausted voyages, transoceanic in scope and plagued with a litany of troubles, all taken in under a looking glass, done up in fine penmanship, arranged for the benefit of the custom's house master, who requires neat columns on the page.

One hundred and fifty years later, the commercial ocean recalibrated and danced about him. Somewhere above the sea-level streets, the diversity-trained, indefatigable, and ruthless agents of white-shoe firms huddled in their war rooms, ready to think outside the box, to dismantle and repackage the world at will. In the blink of an eye, a tinkering of margins could send spasms across the globe, tremors registered in cable-news crawl picked up and translated into sports analogies by the screaming bald guy on *Mad Money*, another indefatigable prognosticator in the wilderness of mirrors.

Jonah passed the lines at the Dunkin' Donuts where black workers wearing hairnets took orders, looking tired of building someone else's civilization. He watched Bangladeshis manning their outposts in the early traffic, poking at hot dogs under their blue umbrellas. The storefronts were already open for business: gadget shops with their galaxy of cellular components; luggage vendors; and shoe stores with loafers 20 percent off. Above them, in a tinted haze, rows of high office windows transecting the sky in every direction conveyed a degree of the gray mystery of the general enterprise, as if the whole system generated a sweat, a mist burning off a dark river down which one had already been sold, without the friction of a public auction, and better yet with one's tacit consent, the human cargo happily surrendered, as though the end of all historical troubles and aspirations, centuries of subsistence, of slavery, of colonialism, of empire, of industrial totalitarianism, had contracted to the dim radiance of this null surface.

Jonah caught sight of Octavio ahead of him as he neared the water. He recognized the gait, the slim frame nimbly jaunting past some corporate art on the corner of Water Street, his presence made noirish by an orange-and-white Con Edison ventricle siphoning off steam that turned lavender, then green, in the traffic light. They went under FDR Drive and Jonah caught up just as they were turning on to the pier. Octavio swiveled and extended an arm in embrace without entirely arresting his motion, as though anticipating and absorbing the momentum of the encounter. They exchanged swift and somewhat severe greetings, before resuming the march down to the water. A foghorn sounded. At the far end of the dock, a water taxi was tying up. It was packed with business types all jockeying for positions at the exit. When the chain rope was pulled aside, they came pouring out in droves like extras from a Buster Keaton film. Octavio looked upon the scene with an enigmatic grin. When the commuters had disembarked, they made their leisurely way onboard.

The sun was hoisting itself over the deck of the Brooklyn Navy Yard. They stood at the prow of the water taxi, the spray of the East River prickling Jonah's shirt as his tie snaked in the snapping wind. The roar of the motor and the flapping gusts nearly covered their voices, so they ended up howling two feet away from each other, like floor traders caught in a five-hundred-point drop. Jonah had to concede the genius. He certainly wouldn't do it on an everyday basis, but this was a hell of a way to commute to Red Hook for work. Octavio gazed south to the Verrazzano Bridge lying like an open parenthesis on its back.

Octavio's impassioned hollers overcame the diesel motoring.

"We need to go south!"

"What, you want to get off in Sheepshead Bay?"

"No, I'm talking farther south, all the way south. Think big picture!"

"What, Florida?"

"No, man. I'm talking farther out. Past the Caribbean."

"You want to go to South America?"

"To Rio."

"Rio. If you want sand and bikinis, why not Orchard Beach?"

"Tss! No seas tan bruto . . . perdónalo dios, el caballero es flemático."

"You're losing me. Why Rio?"

"You remember my girl, Barthes?"

"Barthes?"

"Maggie Reynolds. Brunette, soccer team, she was the year above us. We both took lit theory our junior year. Every time she spoke, it was 'Barthes this' and 'Barthes that.' I used to tease her. The name stuck. Anyway, we had a thing, right, it was going pretty well too, but then we had to break it off when she decided to leave the city to work with favela children in Rio through one of those GlobalGiving NGO-type things. Anyway, the point is I have a plan. We go down there, we find her, we say what's up, you know, and she gets us connected down there—she'll have the whole place figured out, all we gotta do is take it all in. And she can put us up, I mean, she wouldn't refuse me; we have history at this point, I'm talking *romantic* history!"

"Yeah, I'll bet," Jonah scoffed. "You want to go all the way down to Brazil to rekindle a flame. That's romantic, that's cool, man . . . Maybe that'll be impactful on your life, but why do you need to bring me along? I'm not trying to play third wheel. Are you suggesting we're going to get work with Barthes's NGO or something like that?"

"Think bigger. We don't go to Rio, we *begin* in Rio. We take on South America! Brazil! Argentina! Bolivia! Peru! The Andes! The Amazon! The Southern Cone! I'm saying, let's get the hell out of here! It's about having connections on the ground, man. Once we do, we make our own NGO. Needs Getting Obliged. Anyway, who needs a reason? This country is terminal—it doesn't deserve saving. I wouldn't wish a life in Castro country on anyone. But if you think Miami is a paradise you're out of your mind! It's a drugged-out swamp with a Gucci store. A resort-world run by reactionaries, real estate barrons, and cartel lawyers. The population is lunatic ex-Batistas and a mezclado of non-white refugees who basically do all the shit service jobs in the tourism hustle where the overlords launder their money. Come on, man, don't act like you don't know what I'm talking about—it's the same everywhere. New York is a joke, a punchline in a tired Diceman routine. Have you listened to the way people talk? The writing is on the wall. We have to get out of here, see something else before it's too late! How can these people *live*—how can anyone live when it's like you can't breathe half the time?"

"But, so . . . what? You want me to just drop everything I'm doing and fly off with you," said Jonah, watching the terminal pier come into view. "I think I know what you mean, but even if I agreed, I'm not sure running off somewhere else solves anything. Plus, I can't just abandon my students."

The water taxi slowed, coming around the bend into the part of the waterway that fronted the ruins and relics of the Gowanus. There was a plan, much discussed at Jonah's school, to have large tracts of it converted into a furniture superoutlet. Furniture for the massive influx of white graduates fleeing the suburbs their parents had fled to, not for the kids in the Red Hook Houses, who had never gone anywhere, who had survived, and who now sat in Jonah's classroom daydreaming about driving a foreign supercar, or having enough money to buy a pair of limited-edition sneakers, or nodding off because of their meds or because they only ate one hot meal a day in the school cafeteria.

"Who knows what is important? All my life, I feel like people have been telling me what is important," Octavio was saying. "Everybody has a theory. God is important. Making money is important. Saving the environment. Ending racism. Changing health care. The church. It's Marx, or the Media. But none of those things ever felt important to me. People just *say* they are. Barthes and all her friends and all of us—all of us. Come on, man, you know it's all bullshit. Everyone wants what people have always wanted. They want to win. Why you think they sent us to that school? They only care that you're successful. Famous and successful. To do that, you need to be someone other than yourself. So now you get good at simulating. You hide all your feelings and beliefs and desires, which you didn't even know in the first place, and soon you can't tell the difference. But it's easier to believe in the you that does well in interviews, the you as corporate candidate, a good team player who knows how to display leadership and integrate criticism and bring the right kind of energy to the project and smile like the diversity hire they all hoped that you would be. And you must be right about everything

because all these people want to be your friends, and you des‿
more money in one year than your parents made working hard in ‿
And that's if it all works out, and odds are sooner or later it won't. Hov
we be part of any of this shit, honestly? Look at you. I mean, you're doin‿
good. But tell me the truth. Dime la verdad. Do you want to be a teacher
for the rest of your life?"

Jonah looked out at the hazy undefined Brooklyn skyline, the endless
tumble of warehouses and cranes that made up the Red Hook waterfront.
The rest of life appeared sprawling and unknowable.

"I don't know. Probably not, I guess," he said at last.

"So what are you doing here? What is anyone doing? Work? Nobody
believes in work anymore! It's all a joke. A scam. You make a latte. You sign
people up for forty bucks a month for free wireless and explain 'features'
to them. You make a website that takes like two hours and charge for two
hundred because these morons think making their Flash site is like building a cathedral. You look for things on search engines and add numbers
to spreadsheets, then make new spreadsheets. You do all of this as part of
an internship for which you are not paid, or only enough to pay for the
commuting costs to get you back to your desk. Maybe you get the right kind
of soy milk-substitute for the head of production and you feel gratified and
tell yourself you're getting ahead when they take a minute to gasp about the
latest episode of *America's Next Top Model*. No matter who you are or what
you do or where you are, you spend the better part of your earthly hours
staring at a computer screen and waiting to be free again. Period. Nobody
works—they're tethered, bothered, harassed by tasks, all kinds of mindless
drudgery. But in truth, the only people who work are immigrants and men in
construction. Everyone else is either a technocrat or serving the technocrats.
Why play these corny games? I say out. Out! Let this place go to pieces.
Life is too short. Ask anyone. If you had time and money, what would you
do? Their answer: travel. Get away from it all. There's nothing to figure out
here. Nothing to solve. Get out! That's all that matters."

Jonah got off at the pier. He had assumed Octavio would follow him, but when he turned around, he saw that his friend was still standing on the deck and sending him an indecipherable sign. The lanky figure cupped his hands to his mouth. "Think about it!" Octavio shouted something more after that, but whatever it was got swallowed by the chugging growl of the ferry as it reversed course across the greasy waters.

Jonah turned into the pastoral calm of Red Hook's cobblestone streets. Little clumps of greenery and dandelions sprouted in the curbside. He passed old cable drums and warehouses with marine outfittings, their bricks glowing warm and pinkish in the sun. The kneading sensation under his dress shoes kept him awkwardly amphibious, dipping in and out of his thoughts, pausing to bask momentarily whenever a salty summery gust came in off the wharf. Despite ambling, he arrived at the school early enough to find his classroom still empty. Through the windows he watched as morning light poured down over the harbor and the island city. Octavio was over there somewhere now, walking among the skyscrapers. It was, just then, the wrong feeling, and he was aware of this without being able to shake its significance in his heart. Manhattan had never looked so alarmingly beautiful.

3

Summer had arrived, bringing with it hydrant games, daylong cookouts, and heated brawls. The first Monday after school let out, Jonah spent the day wandering uptown. He walked through Central Harlem, heading west. He stopped to see the cathedral where James Baldwin's funeral had taken place and then popped into a café across the avenue. He ordered coffee, secured a small table in the back, and ostentatiously pulled out his copy of Baraka's The Dead Lecturer. He seemed to be the only person there without a laptop. But his mind wasn't really in the poetry. It was on Octavio's offer. His phone vibrated with a text: Isaac in "the city" (code for Manhattan), wondering what he was up to. Jonah texted back saying he should join him uptown.

Whenever Isaac arrived somewhere, people took notice. The way the brother moved, like Morris Day, you knew what time it was. Entering the coffee shop, he gave the place a once-over, looking mildly irritated. A young couple stepped gingerly around him, offering an unnecessary apology. Only black men can unnerve a whole room so effortlessly, generating a sudden surface tension with only the faintest outward ripple. Jonah smiled. The waitress came by with fresh coffee, and Jonah launched right into it.

"Listen, man, I've been thinking. Octavio wants to go down to Brazil, and he thinks I should come along."

"You buy your ticket?"

ot yet, I'm still trying to figure out what I can afford."

Huh. Why?"

"Because there's nothing left! New York is dead, it's moribund, practically a Connecticut suburb at this point. It's getting to be like you can't breathe. And it's only going to get worse. The wars are never gonna end. The street shit is never gonna go away. And we're still young but it won't last forever, and I want to see more, you know, see the world before . . . before it's too fucking late and the whole thing is underwater or whatever."

Isaac considered this without skepticism or keen interest.

"Well, shit, man. You're Mr. International over here. If the shit appeals to you, go for it."

"I don't know, I mean it's crazy on one level, but what if I regret not doing something that I'll probably never be able to do again?"

Isaac looked past Jonah. For a moment he was completely still, even statuesque. Then he sat back in his chair and let out a loud breath.

"Listen, J., I think you alright, you have a good head on your shoulders— but you know Octavio is crazy, right? I mean, don't get me wrong, he's a great guy, but he's got a . . . man, I don't know . . . he's got this restlessness . . . that you'd best be mindful of. I'd say he needs you to go with him just to keep him from doing some crazy shit that will get him killed down there."

"Yeah, I know . . . I know what you mean. But I can handle it."

"You can handle it."

"I can handle my own."

"I don't doubt it—I'm just saying, with Octavio, it ain't about to be just a walk in the park . . . and to be honest it sounds like he probably has his own reasons that got nothing to do with you. It's like GZA says, 'I gotcha back but you best to watch your front.' That's your problem right there. Don't get me wrong, I like Octavio. But you know how he is. Trouble finds him. I'm talkin' some outlandish diplomatic-incident type shit. Brazil? Nigga, you be lucky just to make it to the airport."

Octavio and Isaac had met a couple of times, usually at whatever bar

Jonah had invited them both out to. In theory they should have vibed well, but more often than not Jonah found himself trying to mediate and preempt miscues between the three of them, the minefield of perceived slights or challenges that masculine conversation cannot seem to avoid. This often meant that even if he didn't fully perceive himself to be doing so, he was taking sides. Music was especially unforgiving territory.

As a New Yorker, Octavio felt a homegrown entitlement to hip-hop, a fierce pride that could abide no pretenders, and he brought up his favorites with a defensiveness that they didn't need. Isaac respected, even appreciated, the depth of Octavio's knowledge. But that was as far as he was willing to go. Because there wasn't nothing in the world like being born to it. Cradled and raised in it. He never missed an occasion to remind them that the real home of the music would always be the South. They heard about it all the time because apparently Isaac had never loved and understood what made him Southern until he got to the city. As he saw it, Octavio was like an ambassador of the city. Isaac had talked with Jonah separately about his problems with some of the black administrators at his school, the ones he sensed would have called him country if they could say it to his face. Who kept an attitude but played like it wasn't nothing, like they could afford to deny what they were made of, like it wasn't all those dusty front porches and tiny one-room churches across the South that their families had made their way through and left people behind in. Like the South wasn't the lifeblood that made everything how it was in the first place. He was always complaining to Jonah about the way they talked, the way they leaned over you with their corporate-seminar lingo. Isaac said he hadn't seen a square mile so ignorant, so dissonant and confused about how to live, as the core of the rotten apple between the bottom of Central Park and Canal Street. He wouldn't dispute Octavio's claims to NYC's hip-hop bona fides. But as far as he was concerned, the South was never wrong when it came to the sound. New York didn't know shit about drop-tops and candy paint. And there would come a day when the South finally had its say. When all that funk leaking out of Houston and Atlanta would bubble up like an unstoppable lava. Rising up out the Louisiana low-rises of Calliope and Magnolia. Pumping the full repertoire of low life into every nook and cranny of George Bush's patriot-acting U.S.A. Flooding it with criminal hieroglyphics and underworld lore cooked up in dank bedrooms and basements. Exorbitant odes to pimpology served up on mellifluous flows. Mortuary tales of the long drug wars of the nineties rattling a trunk on the outskirts of Memphis where a box Caprice with a pint of Crown Royal in the dash creeps through the twilight bumping Tupac's "Lord Knows." That bass turned all the way up, soaked in so much pain it slows the heart.

Despite their territorial and musicological disputes, Isaac and Octavio got along all right enough, and in certain moments Jonah even felt a spark of mutual understanding between them that *he* was fundamentally left out of. Sometimes they would suddenly lock in and start trading bars, flipping back and forth, sometimes pulling from tracks that he recognized, or thought he recognized, and sometimes breaking out into a mutual hilarity that Jonah couldn't parse. On the other hand, now and then Octavio would go out on a fiery tirade, causing people to stare and bartenders to call for the bouncer, and Isaac would always refuse to move, shake his head, directing a look squarely at Jonah like *this your man,* disowning any association with either of them. For Jonah they read like devastating verdicts on him as a person, throwing into question how he carried himself along and across the color line, a potential laser beam that could appear at any time, snapping subtextual lines of force together with sudden, icy coherence.

Isaac would switch off sometimes, his whole frame of mind gone to a place where he was only half in the room, following the scene from afar. Jonah could tire of Octavio's high-strung energy just as easily. But he also felt a special closeness there. They shared a fanatical love of film; besides, Octavio's eccentricity appealed to him, he interpreted it as an assertion of defiant personal freedom. It did not occur to him that Isaac might resent that very freewheeling quality as something he could not afford himself.

And this hairline fracture running beneath the surface of things extended to an unnamed reserve between Isaac and Jonah. It was never a resentment exactly, although Isaac hinted once that he might well have gotten his much tougher assignment, in a much rougher part of the city, on account of his dark skin—though of course it would be impossible for him to locate exactly when or by whom this calculation had been made. Isaac would just say stuff like that. "Color just has to be navigated, bro, it's sad but we got to face that shit." He told Jonah that it was like a student going to a math exam with formulas programmed into his advanced calculator. Like a cheat code that allowed you to skip certain levels, defeat seemingly impossible bosses. For Isaac it had nothing to do with sincerity, or even character. It was more of a naturally expected thing, like a weather pattern, something he felt he'd been primed his entire life to see and to recognize whenever it came across his path. The light-skinned ones. Always on their way, somehow effortlessly floating upward, buoyed by currents seen and unseen, sliding past the glass doors and showing up on the other side and waving back, always insisting everything was the same, even though everything was different—for them.

Isaac appeared to brood and consider the general mess of things. He was always the type who took his time while he searched for the right thing to say—so that when he had framed it for himself it ended up coming out blunt, not because he was imprecise, but because his tone always had an intimidating air of Solomonic judgment baked in. Tell it plain. That was his instinct, his way of keeping shit real.

"So you think I should go?" asked Jonah.

"I didn't say that. But I do think you've already made up your mind."

"And I can't convince you to come with."

"Shit . . . there you go."

"What? You're always talking about how you hate the city."

"Look, J., I'm an American. This is where I belong. I think you're used to existing between cultures. It's good for you. Traveling is a natural extension of that. But me, I got to fight on the home front. I know it's not glamorous, but it's real. It's real to me."

Isaac took a sip of his coffee. His composure was unwavering.

"You're not bored with this place? I mean, the same shit, the same violence, the same stories over and over?"

"Bored? I'm not bored. It's the rest of the country that's bored. They've all been shocked into numbness. We live in a blasé culture right now. Straight up. Turn on the TV any time, day or night, and prove me wrong. It's a way of protecting ourselves against something. I don't know what it is. But that's exactly why I need to be here. Someone has to fight back. And the truth is, it doesn't help anything, you leaving. You run away from your teaching, but also your friends, your people. I mean, call me old-fashioned, but I still believe in the struggle, and not in some bullshit flag-waving sense. I mean in that you build yourself around a community and take responsibility for it, own it, make a good old-fashioned contribution."

"I know what you're saying. And you're not wrong. But don't you ever feel suffocated? Like, it's too big, too vast for anything we do to count? Like the atmosphere is poisoned? It's not in one thing or one group of people. It's everywhere you look. And there's this feeling of 'Fuck it, man!' Just get out. See something new, be somewhere else."

"I see it another way, J. I mean for me, it's all right here. You can live a whole life right here in Harlem and never know the half of it. I mean, look at Albert Murray. My man is still living right here in the Lenox Houses. I don't need to go find the rest of the world, let the rest of the world find themselves . . . I'm trying to fuck with this music shit, and this is where it's at here, now, and it's about us, like it's always been, and the only place you can find the realness is in these same streets. In our history, J. There's so much richness we have that no one has even touched yet."

"Yeah, there's richness, and you know what we do with it, we throw that shit away like it don't mean nothin." We both know what happened in New Orleans. Gave this country our culture and they let us drown on live television! They Wolf Blitzer you and then it's so long, folks. Moving like

32

piranhas. Feed on the body and they're gone. No one cares about our losses, and you can't make them.

"Hey man, Kanye said it." Isaac leaned back with his arms folded. "The president don't care about black folks. Like we didn't know already. So yeah. You right, so far as it goes. But who needs they opinion anyways? I don't need George Bush to care—I don't need none of these fools one way *or* the other. The way I see it the culture stands for me and I can stand on that. What you so upset about anyhow? Our shit has survived bigger storms than this. Our shit is official. Always has been. Official down to the bone gristle. Made outta gutbucket bayou back-porch church sweat and grease all up in it. Built hand to hand. Built outta nothing and no way. They tried to lock us up but we did it anyhow. Did for this country. And did for us. I seen niggas bounce back straight outta county and make that shit sound like a cool million. You understand what I'm saying. I ain't 'bout to start feeling sorry for myself now. Shit, with what ma dukes been through? Her mother, her grandparents? No hope, just run away somewheres? Is that what you gonna tell the kids you teach?"

Jonah, already defeated, interjected anyway: "I don't know *what* I'm teaching them. I don't know that anything I can teach them would even make a difference."

"You lying, bro. You know they watch and listen to every word come out your mouth. You just mad because you don't really want to be there."

Jonah winced and failed to make any reply. Isaac, seeing that he had hit a nerve, shifted away as if to indicate he wouldn't dwell.

"Listen, I'm just saying. How you know what's around the bend? What if the best days for New Orleans is yet to come? What if we only just getting started—only just starting to get the conditions we need to make this place really work out the way it's supposed to? You talking all this apocalypse. Everywhere I go it's the same racket. I got these *Wall Street Journal* dudes on the subway, breathing on me and shit, yakking about how we're under attack by 'Islamofascists,' whatever *that* means. Every Asian kid in the country is convinced it's the black kid done jacked his spot in college when we got more brothers in jail than finished the twelfth grade. Meanwhile everybody mad at the war. But only cause the Iraqis not takin' the ass-whooping and quick drive-by they was supposed to. So I'm not buying none of it. Maybe we're all just a little screwed-up right now. Maybe we grew up thinking we were special. Turns out we ain't. Now the whole world gotta catch hell, and even the Dixie Chicks ain't safe? Nah, I'm not having it. Say you're right, and we are the undertakers for this doomed country, and yeah, even this doomed planet. Well, a pallbearer should try to get the damn funeral right. I ain't running nowhere. And I'm not complaining neither. I got to build from what I know. I love my people, I love our music, the whole thing, man, my everything. Imma stand on that."

The coffee shop was filled with light bouncing off simmering coffee pots. The wide steel fan in the corner shuffled sticky air without providing any relief.

"Let's get out of here," Jonah said. "You want to go for a walk?"

"Sure. I don't mind heading down the West Side, but let's go up first so we can take that path, you know, the one that goes through the campus."

They walked together up Amsterdam Avenue along the outer ramparts of Columbia. The weather was cooling off into evening; fit young students jogged by or stood around laughing in small huddled groups. They cut into the main section of the campus and sat down on the steps facing Butler Library. The sun was going down to Union City. Warm rays bathed the library's massive frontal colonnade, catching the light like a massive neoclassical grill. They stared across the patchy turf where commencement tent poles had bruised the grass below the pantheon chiseled into the facade: Homer. Sophocles. Plato. Aristotle. White teeth. Washington's fake smile. Harvested out the mouth of his slaves. Jonah lit a cigarette.

"You know something?" Isaac said.

"What's that?"

"This is the only place, I mean it's the only thing, that could ever make me wish I were white. Nothing else. And I'm not saying I do. But I've felt it before. Man, when you first lay your eyes on a nice college campus, and you see the girls reading on the steps, and everyone's got this flair about them, like they belong there, like they've always belonged there. I look at it, and I wish, man, I wish I could feel that."

Jonah knew inexactly what he meant. He said nothing.

4

June was moving closer to July and Jonah still hadn't given Octavio an answer. It wasn't like Jonah was doing anything that required him to be in New York, but Isaac wasn't wrong in questioning why Jonah should spend money he didn't really have. Surely he could do something. When he wasn't writing in his journal now he was scribbling out a loony screenplay for a secret-agent spoof movie about black underground radicals with a plan to set up a revolutionary resistance base in Paris that gets foiled when they discover a time machine that would allow them to control the future but that they end up using against each other instead in a series of backstabbing leggy entanglements with white women. He would pitch it as Solaris meets Austin Powers, preferably to be directed by Melvin Van Peebles. He thought about asking Isaac to collaborate. Maybe he could do the soundtrack? But when Isaac did catch him typing away furiously in his room one evening, Jonah lost his nerve and made up a story about a set of school reports and self-assessments.

Summery days full of hypothetical promise flowed by uneventfully, until one morning Jonah got a call from his father in Paris. In a strained and uncharacteristic voice, he instructed Jonah to pack an overnight bag and meet him the next day at the airport rental lot in Newark. His father's brother, Vernon H. Winters, had died of a heart attack at his home in Pleasantville, New Jersey. He was flying home for the funeral, his father said. Home was a word he rarely used.

Jonah didn't know his uncle Vernon. "Vern," as his father referred to him, was unmarried and childless (a striking anomaly by family standards), and he and Jonah's father hadn't gotten along. But then, his father didn't seem to get along with anyone. Toward Uncle Vernon, though, Jonah suspected his father of harboring some degree of envy. Vernon was considered the successful sibling in the Winters family. He had worked his way up at a local division of Honeywell, one of the biggest employers in South Jersey. The only time Jonah had met him was also the first and only other time Jonah had been down to Pleasantville. It was for his grandfather's funeral. His uncle was one of the pallbearers, and he stood out to Jonah because he had never seen old-fashioned conked hair before. He remembered his uncle's long, thin frame, his severe expression, the sweat dripping down at his temple, and his thin mustache, wet with tears. Jonah was still a boy then, and had been completely overwhelmed by the event, by all the faces of family that he didn't know, by the rawness of the emotion and the clamor of the church, and also because it was the same week Tupac was killed in Vegas, and the two events had become linked as a period of deep confusion and mourning in his mind. Now it was Vernon's turn to be put to rest, and it would be Jonah's father shouldering the box of his estranged older brother. Jonah would take the train out to Newark and then they would drive the rest of the way down to Pleasantville together.

The next morning, he packed and made his way to Penn Station. In the New Jersey Transit lounge, swirling crowds of commuters struggled against the stale ventilation, dodging and slipping around ragged drifters, counterterrorism units patrolling in military fatigues, and deceptive low-pressure zones where bodies people had given up on lay slumped against the side of a wall or sprawled on the steps under faux mosaics memorializing the old Penn Station, the one modeled on the Baths of Caracalla that they tore down in the sixties. It occurred to Jonah that Vernon, as the older brother, must have walked through those grand archways as a boy, holding his parents' hands. Madison Square Garden, where Spike Lee watched the Knicks play, now stood in its place.

Once he was in the frigid railcar, everything was efficient and swift. Only a few minutes from departure, they were rolling under the Hudson in a tunnel built under conditions he could scarcely fathom, but which must have cost untold lives for every yard he now traveled. The train banked up over the meadowlands and refineries and trucking depots around Secaucus, stopped in the brick carcass of downtown Newark, and then proceeded to the gray terminal complexes of the airport.

His father was waiting in the rental-lot complex. He was calmer than Jonah expected, as if the situation brought a kind of neutrality to their relationship that made it easier for his father to be around him. It helped that his father had logistics to keep him occupied. They got in a midnight-blue Ford Focus, looped through the interlocking airport clovers, and merged onto the Jersey Turnpike.

After they settled into the road, Jonah's father told him to reach into his travel bag and pull out a stack of CDs.

"Which one you want me to put on?"

"I don't own no jive records, boy. Just put one in. We gotta have *something* to make up for this bullshit ride they gave me. Five times I told them over the phone, I want a Lexus and I ain't payin no goddamn fees. Now Avis tells me all they have left is a Ford Focus. They got me paying for this golf cart when I was supposed to show up pushing a Lexus. Jonah, I'm telling you. Why you think I left this messed-up country in the first place? Why I left? Because a Nee-gro can't get a fair deal. I mean how—how? And see, they know I gots the mo-nay. They just want to ruin my day a little is all. But I ain't gonna let em. Boy, you listening to me? Don't ever let them ruin your day. Give an inch, and they will get you everytime. Not a thing, not a damn thing changed since I left. Rental man tellin me this the best-selling car in America. Like imma take advice *from you*— the guy grinning in my face cause he clocked in on time at the Liberty Hertz rental desk this morning."

"How 'bout this right here?" Jonah ventured.

A smile, the first he had seen since they had left the lot, beamed back at him.

"Okay. Now you talking."

As they pulled out of a tollbooth in the southbound lanes, the familiar piano chords of one of the Gap Band's Greatest Hits sent *soul-stirring* tremors through the little Ford. They nudged along for a while in heavy traffic, canyoned between big rigs, barracuda-grilled SUVs, Hummers fresh off the assembly line and ready for Baghdad beyond the Green Zone or a P. Diddy video shoot. *You light my fire* . . . The traffic thinned as they passed the gaslights and townships of the Jersey midlands with their names blazoned on the water towers . . . *I feel alive with you, baby* . . .

His dad was suddenly saying, "Your uncle Vernon could get down, boy, ooohhhweee, Jonah, when he was liquored up, like the time he started dancing at our wedding reception. Lord, I can see it now, like it was yesterday. He had your grandpappy's funky chicken legs, and he could work them things too. You had to see him out there, puttin' moves on 'em." Jonah saw a wet line on his father's cheek. The Band harmonized, urging someone not to *keep running in and out of my life.*" Jonah lowered his window a crack and squinted at the road ahead. Warm soupy gusts of chemical fumes and car exhaust buffeted the soulful audio-love inside. They were hurtling toward the prickling points of holding tanks, pharmaceutical plants, the megalith forms of malls and factory-discount outlets, RKO-style radio masts rising into irradiant haze. Everywhere and nowhere, isolated suburban lights winked like fireflies as they sailed down the trunk roads of the Garden State through the summer dusk.

Pleasantville was a residential community that fed off the perpetual transit of gamblers, criminals, and retirees passing through on their way to Atlantic City. His father had booked a room for them in a budget motel in the shadow of the casinos. But with the roads increasingly snarled in beach traffic, they decided to take a break and stop for dinner at the Walt Whitman Service Area outside Cherry Hill before making the turn on Route 40 that would take them toward the ocean. Over fried chicken and curly fries, his father started loosening up.

"You know Vernon never married?"

"Yeah, I know."

"But he had a woman. I'm talking back in the day. Before you were born. Wonderful woman named Evelyn Jones. One of the strongest, most beautiful women I ever seen. You would have liked her. I know she would have liked you. She was so damn smart. Her and Vernon met at night classes at Atlantic Community College. She came from poor folks, at a time when Atlantic City was beginning to decline, but she was doing good, you know, and she had a smile that just . . . it just had you wide open soon as she walked in the room. And your uncle Vernon was gone on this woman. But, you know, she was very proud . . . She had that poor working pride, tough as nails, boy. She wouldn't bend, and she never asked for help. Always figured things for herself, did things her own way. And that was okay with Vern, but what happened was she was so proud, she wouldn't say when she wasn't well. They had been seeing each other almost a year, and Vern is in the bathroom and sees some blood in the sink. Come to find out she'd been sick for months but hadn't allowed that she was, didn't want to bother him about it and figured neither of them could afford the doctor. Well, Vern loved this woman, Jonah. He says, 'You have to see the doctor. I'll pay for it.' Finally, he convinces her to go, and you know what, she has a cancer, but now they got it too late. And she got real sick, and Vern took care of her and then moved with her to be by her family. She died the same year. Like that. Wilted and all shriveled up . . . it was terrible. Your uncle, he never really recovered from Evelyn. In fact, he kind of retreated from the whole family, kind of like me, but in a different way. Threw himself into work. I would hear sometimes about a woman here and there, but it never lasted more than a few months. A few times I think because he was abusive, wasn't treating them right. Didn't treat himself right either. You know, I wasn't so surprised when I heard. He's had a lot of problems the last few years, gained a lot of weight, always seeing doctors. Tellin' him he has to exercise and all that. We had so many arguments about him needing to get better that I finally just gave up. I didn't want you to be around his troubles. For a long time, I was angry at him for having put the family through such concern about his well-being, for his refusal to get better, but as I flew over here, I got to thinking that maybe his depression went deep. For him, there was no light at the end of the tunnel. It was like he only had that one love, and that was it. And that loss came between him and the world, and between us, and now . . ."

His father made a gesture to finish the sentence. They sat for a while in silence, watching the crowds circulate through the eatery line with their trays.

His father snapped back into logistical mode. "Come on, I want to get us to the motel early so you can get a good night's sleep. I want you up and sharp for the service tomorrow."

The following day, under the beleaguering Jersey mugginess of an overcast summer's morning, Jonah and his father joined the rest of their kinfolk in a long shimmering line of wide-crowned brims, flitting fans, tie clips, pocket squares, brooches, impeccable footwear, peppery wafts of cologne and grand-motherly jasmine, that overflowed the parking lot and spilled over onto the corner of Elm Avenue. Muted gasps of delight rose in the air as cousins and elders exchanged strong effusive clasps. As with all large families, a peculiar energy hovered over any Winters reunion, and it gained in strength now, as the reunited prepared to enter Mount Zion Victory Baptist Church for Vernon Winters's homegoing.

Since the time of Grandfather Earl's passing, they had multiplied consider-ably. Jonah had no idea he had so many cousins, aunts, folks who had driven all the way up from Florida, from the Carolinas, from DC and Baltimore, down from Mount Vernon and New Rochelle. And Vernon was beloved by the people of Pleasantville. A city councilman, members of the local school board where he had donated heavily to after-school programs; even two or three white folks showed up from the Honeywell office and were greeted just as warmly.

The whole service, Jonah was in a daze. The minister spoke. The siblings gave testimonials. They sang "Lord Keep Me Day by Day" because it was known to have been one of Uncle Vernon's favorites. The piano and the choir led the assembled, old folks and young, family and friends, neighbors and coworkers, in sending Vernon Winters home.

I'm just a stranger here And I'm traveling through this barren land

Rapturous vowels thundered around their heads and the rolling march of foot stomps charged the air with the acknowledgment of the one whose journey was won, who watched them now, from a building not made by hand.

Then it was announced that a young lady, Jonah's cousin Esther, would line a hymn she had practiced for the occasion: "A Charge to Keep I Have." Little Esther couldn't have been more than sixteen or seventeen, and her range and tone weren't perfect or even sweet exactly, but she laid it out. Everyone was on their feet and called back to her. *Go 'head.* They clapped her on. *Lord, Jesus.* The voices raised the hymn together until its unearthly roar was only praise and the praise took the body before it took the voice.

To serve the present age, My calling to fulfill

From out her tiny frame, songful Esther moaned the lines with utter ferocity. No one could deny. She was there with him, and she brought the church with her in her singing. Jonah felt all the hairs on his neck stand on end and the shivers run down, and he saw that even his father was crying.

O may it all my powers engage. To do my Master's will!

Esther stretched it out. *Mmmhhhmmm. Yes, Lord.* She stretched it out. She left nothing, allowed no one to feel they were not hand in hand with the one they had come to see off to the other world. *Somebody give Gawd some praise for that one,* someone shouted. And the church gave forth.

When the pallbearers emerged, the sun had broken through and glinted off the chrome trim detailing the hearse, and off the waiting Cadillac Escalades and Lincoln Town Cars and the sunglasses of so many men in dark suits you would have thought a statesman were passing through. They had lined the street and spilled over into the parking lot of the Rite Aid, which faced the church. Uncle Vernon was buried just a few minutes away in the family plot at Greenwood Cemetery, a modest burial ground between Washington and Martin Luther King Jr. Avenues. They had a spot for him next to the elders, Earl and Liza, who rested together. After the burial, there was a reception at his aunt Ella's house, and Jonah found himself pressed into a near-continuous embrace as paper plates piled high with a seemingly never-ending procession of sweet potato pie and oxtail and fried chicken and peas and greens and all the cake you could eat to feed the riotous laughter, tale-telling, well-wishing, and greetings and goodbyes. It was moving and exhausting all at once.

When they finally left a little after midnight, Jonah's father, who'd had a bit to drink, asked him to drive, which he did, rolling very precisely within five of the limit at all times, the music soft and no words between them, all the way back to Atlantic City. When they got to the motel, instead of getting out of the car, his father rolled down the window and lit a cigarette. After a moment, Jonah took one from his own pack, and they sat that way in the motel parking lot, looking like a couple of gangsters. Jonah's father looked like he had something to say, and Jonah waited for him to say it. Finally, his father took an envelope out of his coat and placed it on the dashboard.

"This is for you, from Vernon. He left you and all your cousins, each and every one of them, a portion of what he had, what he made for himself. That's a remarkable thing. A great gift, and I don't want you to take it lightly. There are a lot of ways to go about life. No matter which way you go, you're gonna need money. And, more importantly, you're gonna need to know how to handle money. When he was sick, your uncle decided to make some decisions about what he wanted for after he was gone. And he wrote it all out. Take that envelope, it's yours. I have no control of what you do with its contents. But as your father, I'm asking—no, I'm telling you, son, think on it. Think on it careful now. Remember, this man worked hard for that money. Nothing came free to him in life. Nothing comes to no one free."

With that, his dad stepped out of the car, leaving Jonah with the envelope. He thought about opening it there but felt no rush to do so. He exited the vehicle and locked it for the night, then headed toward the waterfront.

The boardwalk was eerily vacant. Down the shoreline, the lights of the Taj Mahal loomed in the murky distance like an anglerfish. A woman rolled by in a Power Chair, indifferent to his gaze. He had walked a bit down the boardwalk before he gave up and headed back inland. On Atlantic Avenue, he came to the Breezy Point, a tiki-themed joint just off the strip. It was almost as devoid of people as the boardwalk. The lounge area had big bay windows facing the Econo Lodge Riviera, and he took up a seat there. Kanye West's "Gold Digger" was playing at a tepid volume on speakers behind the bar. A suite of large, muted television screens were running SportsCenter highlights, while the screen farthest away, at the end of the bar, showed a news story about a unit of marines getting ambushed in the Korangal Valley. A waitress appeared to take his order. A Braves tomahawk was visible above her tiki-themed apron, and she had a tattoo of an ankh on her inner wrist. She was too attractive for Breezy Point, but perhaps not attractive enough— or, rather, light enough—for the casino floor, especially at the Taj Mahal.

"What can I get you?"

"Do you have something not too floral but not too bitter—actually, forget it, do you have Budweiser?"

"Is that a question or an order?"

"Maybe both?"

She smiled forgivingly and walked away, leaving Jonah to turn his attention to the envelope in his hands. Inside there were two separate sheets. One was a letterheaded set of instructions to get in touch with Rhonda Rollins, a Philadelphia-based attorney. The other was a plain paper letter autopersonalized to his attention, evidently formatted in an outdated version of Microsoft Word. As he looked these over, the waitress returned with his beer. He thanked her and looked around. As far as Jonah could tell, he was her only customer. He could tell, too, that she was watching him examine the materials in his hands. It didn't matter. He took a sip and began to read.

To my nephew, JONAH WINTERS,

If you are reading this, I have passed. Attached to this letter, you, like all of your cousins, will find instructions with my lawyer for how to retrieve the inheritance I have left you. Since I love all of you equally, it is my wish that you all receive equal shares. Since there are many of you, this means nobody is going to walk away with a fortune. I do feel it's best this way. I would have liked to leave you each $10,000, but with the tax and the lawyers and fees that must be paid, it could not be that much. Instead, you are each receiving $6,500. Whatever you may think, this is a very great deal of money. If you are wise, any one of you can use it to build a company or start a family or get an education. Yet these are not conditionals. Only YOU can decide how best to use these funds. I believe in hard work, and I hope all of you do too. I believe in education, and I hope all of you will try to go to college and make your parents proud. I also believe in offering a helping hand. And so I want to leave you, instead of with more instructions, with a little story, a true story from my childhood.

When I was a boy, your grandfather (my father), Earl Winters, worked in the casinos in Atlantic City. It was a grand destination back then, not the seedy place it has become. But back then, things for us were also harder. In the summer, me and my brothers used to pick up white folks at the Steel Pier and push them around in rickshaws for a nickel. I went to the Indiana Avenue School, which was for colored students only. I liked school, but I was often in trouble. When we'd get into trouble, sometimes we'd have to go sit or stand in the hallways with the school janitor, a big man everyone called Pop. One day, because I had been bad, I was sent to "cool it," and I found myself sitting with Pop and talking. He wanted to know what was bothering me. I told him these kids were bugging me, that I felt stuck here. And he said, "Well, you can't let these things get you down. You can't let things stand in your way." He said, "You know, if I'd been that way, I never would have become a ballplayer." Well, I had no idea Pop had played ball. But Pop's real name was John Henry Lloyd, and he was one of the greatest baseball players to ever play the game. He was a real legend back in the days before Jackie Robinson, when black folks played in the Negro League. I was stunned.

"And now you're here?" I asked him. I was a kid, so I didn't know any better, and that must have hurt him the way I said it. But he wasn't bothered by it at all.

"Sure, I'm here," he said. "But I've also been there. I did those things. I set those records. I heard the crowds shout my name. No one can take from me what I done. Where I've been. What I seen. And even if all the records of all my games were lost, and nobody even remembered my name, God would know, and I would know, and I am well with him. You see boy, time is like God's great wax cylinder. He keeps track of everything, and what I've done and who I am are fixed that way for good, like a line engraved in God's hand." Pop had huge hands, and after that talk, he got up and took my little one in his, and he walked me back to class. To this day, I have not forgotten that. Make your lives whatever you will with where my helping hand will take you. Don't go making excuses. Work hard. Do something righteous with your life.

Faithfully,

Your Uncle Vernon

They drove back to Newark the next day and dropped off the car at the airport lot where they had picked it up. His father was very agitated now, and he ended up arguing with the clerk about the cost of the rental. Then suddenly it was time to part, and they were hugging warmly, Jonah assuring his father he would stay in touch. He felt a sense of relief once he was on the train heading back to New York, but when he did finally reach Penn Station, a terrible sense of emptiness overwhelmed him, a void in the midst of the surging crowds. Back at his apartment, he found Isaac eating takeout and listening to records. They talked a bit about the funeral. Isaac's grandparents were still living in Detroit.

"So I guess you haven't gone through it like that," Jonah said.

Isaac looked away toward the window with their fire escape. When he answered, it was without looking back and in a tone of voice Jonah hadn't heard before.

"Nah, I been to a lot of funerals. Too many."

Jonah had willingly let his phone battery die on the trip and hadn't charged it for days, so he assumed he would have a million messages and reminders waiting on him. It turned out, apart from reminders to pay his phone bill, the only one trying to reach him was Octavio, who was trying to get him to confirm he was down for the trip to Brazil. He must have left thirty messages ranging from one word to rambling non sequiturs to just random background scratches and a huff.

"So what's the word?"

Because Jonah hadn't replied, Octavio had followed with, *"I'm going to assume this is a no."*

Jonah rang his number, not expecting him to pick up.

"Yo. Why've you been avoiding me?"

"I had some family stuff to take care of. I'm in, actually. Let's do this."

Jonah could hear Octavio's voice change from grim to glorious as he first sputtered disbelief before whooping his enthusiasm.

"Alright, then, alright," said Jonah, trying to calm his friend down. "So when we leaving?"

"How's July 1?"

"'Til?"

"Open ticket."

"Open ticket?"

"Yeah man, we come back when we're done, not when we feel like we're supposed to. I can even get us tickets through my friend's mom, who's a travel agent. You good to pay me back?"

"Yeah, I'll cut you a check next I see you. When can that be?"

"There's a launch party for a literary journal this Friday," Octavio replied. "A couple friends are in the first issue."

Jonah could imagine the kind of time he'd have. Literary parties were infamously the worst gatherings of any kind in New York City. You could guarantee zero dancing, stilted conversation, nasty sexual tension, quipsters, conservative outfits, liberal politics, and much playing at being adult. There would be enough booze to get everyone seriously sloshed, but not enough of a good atmosphere for anyone to willingly want to be there. Token minorities were de rigueur.

"I don't know. Could be a drag."

"C'mon, man, these parties are for networking. I'm doing you a favor. Plus, you're the one who wants to be a writer. It'd be good for you to meet real ones."

Octavio's dig was a shot that should not go unchecked, but he didn't have the energy to take up the fight. Besides, a night out would take his mind off the funeral, the money, the command of little Esther's voice, the solemn charge to keep.

"Alright then," he said. "I'll be there."

5

In New York everything that matters occurs as part of a "scene." Octavio had made inroads in the film scene and these networks overlapped significantly with the adjacent literary one. Jonah would pick him up after his shift got out at the Reggio, and they would fortify themselves at a local dive before making an appearance at an apartment in cozy book-lined apartment in Cobble Hill or Fort Greene or a chic loft in Tribeca. One of the bigger events of the season was the launch party for a new lit mag with a radical name and a sleek green cover. Octavio was tight with one of the founding editors whom he had known from his school days. The comrades funding the publication and staffing the key positions on its masthead reflected the city's superconducting private school to Ivy League pipeline. The word on the street was that the most talented writers would be gravitating to its pages, attracted by the considerable sums on offer for fairly predictable content and by the "hot" interns prominently featured on the magazine's elegant, minimalist website.

The launch took place at the magazine's new offices, located in a refashioned Greenpoint warehouse right on the East River. Octavio and Jonah rolled up a little after eleven, entering into a scene that was sumptuous and well attended. The guests were balkanized into tiny groupuscules, each in their corners, accentuating the negative space of the floor plan, which in city psychology was also, of course, a supreme assertion of luxury.

All around the open cross section of the loft were the faces of the sad young literary men, each in their own way terribly preoccupied with the unbearable whiteness of being. Jonah knew them. Not personally, but almost by osmosis; and he felt a measure of ironic sympathy for their plight. They had self-consciously constructed themselves as a force for good. They had good politics, went to good schools (where he had first crossed paths with the tribe); they were good readers of the best reviews (which they hoped to emulate and rival), copies of which further advantaged a vintage mid-century credenza. They all wanted change and hated racism: principally in politics, and geographically in the vast hinterlands (starting in Long Island and New Jersey). The greatest shame of all was the racism in their own families. Sometimes, a good few drinks in, they wanted to confess those unpardonable horror stories in hot breathy convulsions that Jonah had some practice in compassionately, but firmly, evading.

He felt for them because what could be wrong with them, really? They wanted what he wanted, more or less. To see good ideas and good art triumph, especially their own. The only problem was that the ascendant power blocs didn't seem to care a whit what they said. Those with the real power—the consulting firm types, the I-Bankers, the DC apparatchiks and the math majors gone to Wall Street that they knew from college—wanted art, if they ever thought about it at all, to be a larger, more expensive version of a desktop background. They were too busy rigging up massive systems that would liquidate the old printing-press jobs to worry about what was being said by the last cohort to have them.

The sad young literary men were the most despised men of their time. They held a declining share of even those few perches they had once held like grand viziers in the days of the Plimptons, the Mailers, the Updikes; when shuttling between mistresses in Connecticut and dipping down to Greenwich Village to drink with famous war correspondents was all in a day's work. Most of the top jobs in their circles were held by women now, and the proclivities associated with fashionable narcotics were starting to be scrutinized and sometimes even openly deplored. There was still money, of course, but without status it was an enfeebled collateral glare. They formed, ironically enough, a genuinely besieged class; and presumably in their minds they constituted an oppressed one too, since whatever largesse and goodwill among the Midtown Maecenases remained was reserved strictly for identities that would appear charitably treated upon its disbursement. Since they would never be in that number, the spoils of a wilting branch had to be fought over ever more bitterly. It was the main reason such events were to be avoided. Over a shitty mixed drink, the knives come out: friends and colleagues cruelly humiliating each other while desperately trying to appear relaxed and popular. There was no direct danger to Jonah in this; he would be safely ignored. Unless he spoke up. But to what end? It was perfectly typical for him to spend a great deal of these tense soirées finding ways to say nothing at all.

Instead, he listened. To the cornered woman agreeing overenthusiastically; to the political argument; to the chopped ticker-tape phrases indexing the fait divers of industry gossip. Apparently, African child-soldier narratives were trending and there was speculation that one of them might snag a Pulitzer. The perennial topic, however, remained real estate. And on this point, there was much woe. For it is a truth generally observed that everywhere white money moves, it does so in the same settler-colonial pattern. Like so many before them, the sad young literary men had attempted to desert from the advancing army. They had crossed the river and set up camp in the desolate streets of postindustrial Brooklyn, only to find like *Dances with Wolves* that the army was close on their heels. Within a few years, the frontier would be closed. The chill of enclosure and amenities would dominate this once savage ground. It would be ready for unparalleled comfort, saplings and lit walkways, constant surveillance, delivery of goods and services, yoga studios, the good life in all of its passionless expenditure. The sad young men would have to decamp to a farther zone or give up the struggle and put their trust funds into homesteads of their own, get tattoos, strollers, take comfort in ethically sourced and shockingly expensive garlic scapes. Of all the seven and a half billion people in the world—who else carried such a burden?

On the other hand, didn't they, on balance, have a rather desirable existence? The things in this apartment *were* expensive and they *were* pretentious. But they were also nicely made; they looked cool, better yet they looked right. Hadn't Jonah, in truth, been trying to make his own apartment look essentially just like it, only on the cheap? And couldn't he, if he made the right connections, perhaps at this very party, have a loft of his own one day? Sure, it would mean living in a place where he'd have to turn the stereo down at ten o'clock or have the cops called on him for a noise complaint. And the cops might even be called on him as he was trying to enter the building, if, say, he decided to wear a hoodie. And it would mean having to listen to *This American Life* and other boring but *important* shows on NPR in order to make small talk over Pabst Blue Ribbon and hummus. But wouldn't that possibly be worth it?

Even in its decline, there was a lingering aroma of achievement in this lettered world. Its nicer and more adult clothes; its confident intelligence and cosmopolitan circulation. It would snugly envelop his life, like a boutique-hotel bathrobe, making it richer and ready to be enjoyed discreetly, without the loud vulgarity that some other lifestyles would necessarily require. And naturally he would bring to it just enough of a mocha touch, the crucial note, so that his own contribution would be immensely and inevitably appreciated, perhaps without him even having to try that hard. With the right glasses (those being naturally the correct accessory), he might pull off a move like his father had in the art world—propping himself up on the stepladder of white guilt and taking the journey for all it was worth.

Jonah was drinking steadily, standing next to Octavio, doing his best to look interested and supportive as they talked to Sasha, an attractive reader for the magazine. The three were comparing college experiences, and Sasha was explaining the "rapey" social scene and how many times she had blacked out at parties. They had moved on to a vividly confessional discussion about antidepressants and feats rumored to have been accomplished under the influence of Adderall when Jonah excused himself to make an expeditionary foray back to the beverage lineup.

By now he was three or four drinks in, operating with a pleasurable motion that felt more graceful than it looked. On his way back to Octavio, a curator from a swanky Chelsea gallery thought she recognized him. She wanted to know what he was doing these days. "Teaching," he said.

"That's great!" she said. And since it was clear she had made a mistake and that he had nothing to offer her, she immediately broke off, leaping like a salmon toward whoever had the real pull, maneuvering adroitly across the trench lines of her possibilities.

Jonah needed to get some air. Smokers were directed back to the landing and up an extra flight of stairs that opened to an expansive rooftop. The view was tremendous. Midtown in profile. Power suit lines cutting into the darkness, the whole fabric softly pulsating. There wasn't anyone around. Jonah lit a cigarette and walked to the far ledge.

He thought about Uncle Vernon's letter, what Octavio was saying about cutting out altogether, and what Isaac meant about making oneself responsible to something here, *now*, where it mattered.

His life was absurdly gifted with choices, and here he was, lonely, drunk, growing increasingly bitter. Just then, he felt a tap on his shoulder.

"Excuse me, do you have a light?"

The man asking must have come across the rooftop without a sound. He had what Jonah thought was maybe an Australian accent and fine, pale features that made him suspect the high station and poor diet of English boarding schools. His eyes appeared preternaturally fatigued.

"Yeah, I got you."

"Thanks, mate, so kind. I've been dying for a smoke, and I can't seem to find anyone who does. My god, it's ridiculous, you'd think at a launch party in New York . . ."

"Yeah, times change."

"So, what do you do?"

"I, uh . . . I teach."

"Oh, I see—like in bad areas type of thing?"

"Yeah, something like that. You?"

"I'm an editor at Minos Press."

"Oh. Nice."

"Yeah, I was in banking for years, and then I thought, '*What am I doing?*' You know? I've always loved books, loved reading. So I changed it all up and now I'm practically running the place. Hit the jackpot. You know Esteban Riocabo?"

"I haven't heard of him."

"You will."

"Oh."

"He's going to blow up, mate. Huge, and I'm the one that got him for us at Minos. The thing is, it's all about timing. It's a prestige economy, and what you do is you wait until these writers die, you know, and then their value explodes, right through the roof, man. He's dead, plus he's Latin American, like Uruguayan Mexican, so it's got all the mystique built in. The edge becomes the product, the whole package. Practically markets itself, really."

"Sounds like a good setup."

"Best thing about it is that we bought all the material, and now we can just trickle it out whenever we want, control the buzz around it and so forth, extend the life of the brand, so to speak, so it keeps generating revenue long-term. I expect we'll get about a decade's worth of earnings out of it by the end, if not more. Ah, it's a bloody great view, isn't it?"

Riocabo's editor gestured toward the scintillating skyline and aspirated violently on his smoke as Jonah pondered the view.

"Right, got to be off, then. Thanks for the light, yeah?"

Jonah watched him flick the butt in a high arc toward the street, and then the editor slicked his fingers through his hair as he marched resolutely back to the stairwell and down to the business below.

When he got back to the party, Octavio and Sasha were nowhere to be found. He made himself another drink, downed it, and drank another. People were staring; he didn't give a damn. He was going to get faded, and this shit was free. The luminaries of the literary world and their sour complexions felt as alien and irrelevant as the savage customs of some obscure tribe whose way of life only really tells you how you read your own, how you think, and what you care about—or what you don't care about. An ethnography of rarefied social gatherings in New York City could make an interesting volume someday. Or maybe it wouldn't.

He stumbled out into the night. Traffic honking, hipsters yelling on Bedford Avenue coming at him, nice white couple out on the town. Racist bastards. He hailed a cab and hoisted himself inside. Too hot. The West African up front asked too many questions. "Ay, yo, open the window! Turn the radio up, man! I said turn that shit up!" Hot 97, Funk Flex playing throwbacks. RIP J Dilla tributes still pouring in. Dilla dead at thirty-two. All that Motor City soul leaking out, all that warm fuzz on the tracks he blessed . . . so many things lost and found in hours of head-snapping beats, all those years knocking Tribe, *Illmatic, Only Built 4 Cuban Linx, Uptown Saturday Night*, scattered mixes taped off the radio, the nineties boom bap, with its Christmas chimes, clunky rhymes, and fat piano licks, blowing smoke over the yellow Discman with the skip protection, practicing gangster gestures with the earphones in . . . *Can it be that it was all so simple then?* . . . Mecca to Medina. Harlem to Brooklyn. Queensbridge. Exodus of the Afrocentric Asian. The Sunz of Man. Trife Life. Wu-Tang. The Chef. *Shine like marble. Rhyme remarkable. Time is running out* . . . Ay, man, I said turn that shit up! Rush of lights and blasted air like a wind tunnel . . . we moving. Through the night. Like Gladys. Singing "The Way We Were." *Can it be that it was all so simple then?* . . . What happened? What happened to all that was and all that was supposed to be? All that beauty. What did it all mean? And how would it ever all get remembered? My Nigga! My Nigga! *Time is running out* . . .

The cab hit the bridge, and the clunk knocked him back like a slug to the chest. He drank in the sheet of lights slashing from all sides now, the effect nightmarish, like the strobe of a muted television in another room. A swelling breathless rage seemed on the verge of splitting him apart. Then they were in city traffic again, lurching ahead violently in breakneck spurts. At a slow corner, he had the car pull over, ready to be sick. The cabbie demanded money. *Give him the money. Blood-thirsty vampires. Just needed another drink anyway, whatever was left. Whatever.* So many things incoherent. Like this other man sleeping behind the fucking Citibank planter. He entered another bar. Pricey, glossy sign, beefy arms. A Gorgon manned the cobra-headed taps. Music crashed overhead. Television aspirants, underage girls on safari, squealing, blurting obscenities, ordering Jell-O shots that cost twice what the Mexican barback would make in an hour washing their vomit off the floor later as they passed out in private cars on their way back to the upper echelons that flank Central Park. And then this moronic automaton shoving him out, ready to swing. Outside again, colder than before. Everyone in the street a sad clown. Everything *ugly.* Shrieking homeless man. Poor bastard shoving his raggedy-ass Rocinante under the aquiline noses of the Abercrombie & Fitch flagship. Pale mannequins floating in the twinkling windows. Unbothered as this wretched man, reeking of filth, howls and pounds his fists against the glass.

He was leaning heavily against a wall, breathing hard. Screaming into his cell phone. But there was no call in progress. Who was he dialing? Did he get her digits at the party? Sasha? He sat down in a damp cool place. Next thing it was like his head was leaking. Slush. Toppled, flattened out. The blur was general for some time, he had no idea how long.

A man appeared towering over him. For a moment he was sure it was Uncle Vern, but that couldn't be. Was it his father? No, it was Phineas! It was the jazz pianist! The genius of Phineas watching over, up above his head, playing sweet music in the air. And it was all rhythm. Rhythm! Flowing in time like a river. Like the whole frame, conceived in motion. America, a mighty river rhythm. World moving, pulling everything into its fated direction, debris digested, every broken limb jigged up, dead matter as welcome as the live, as likely to proliferate unspeakable wastelands of ruin as to float the delirious chandelier of a paddleboat. A river rhythm swallowing belly-up even its sucking countercurrents, its bubbling froth nurturing settlements of moss, loosely girdled banks soused in green shades, the long-bearded current animating the living underbelly right down to the bottom. Nothing on solid ground. Everyone floundering, everyone grasping like looters for whatever might be at hand. Not only the poorest but even the richest families in the land busy making a raft for themselves, doing their best to paddle along, facing the wilderness, knowing nothing of where they are, knowing nothing of the way back. Only the slaves holding a tattered map to join the sundered worlds—their vision grown deep. And here was one. Could it be? Yes, Phineas standing overhead, astonishingly tall, like some warrior god of Meroë enrobed in a pulsating sheet of blue light.

"Either he can walk and he goes with you, or we're booking him."

"You bastards! I didn't *do* nothing . . . I'm innocent . . . tell them they can't take me . . . tell them I have *rights* goddamnit . . . I'm a teacher!"

"Look, we don't want to waste our time, but he needs to get off the street."

"I understand the situation, sir, but it's okay, he's with me. I take full responsibility for him. Got my car right around the corner, he won't bother no one, I promise."

"You understand normally we would have to take him in . . ."

"Sir, I understand that perfectly, but I can assure you I can handle my baby cousin. You know how the kids is these days. Ain't like back in the day, right? Hey, you guys probably too young to even recognize me, but, you know, I used to ball back in the day . . . Yeah, in the league, check this one out right here, always keep it in my wallet."

"No shit, hey, check this out."

"So listen, Imma get this young fella home, and we're all good here, right?"

Phineas, sweet Phineas, always in time, just a little behind the rhythm so that it carries you ahead, carries you away until the level is passed, and the flood is everywhere, and the flood is all things.

6

Nathaniel Archimbald placed the boy on the couch in the living room with a pillow under his head. He went into the kitchen to make some energy drink. In the sink a frying pan streaked with grease lay stranded like a supertanker. No matter. Doing dishes, for Nathaniel, was a pleasing exercise, an operation that allowed him to ventilate his mind, to see before him those magic hands splendidly at work, the rhythm and practiced improvisation like smooth handles on the dribble. When he returned to the living room, the youngster was lying on the rug. *Now how in the hell did he end up on the damn floor?* The kid looked too clean to be a dopehead, dressed in that eccentric preppy style he often saw downtown or in Brooklyn. He found a teacher's ID in the wallet, though that hardly proved anything in New York City.

Nathaniel lightly touched his shoulder, not too hard, but with enough pressure to make sure the boy would feel his hand through his coat.

"Hey, kid."

The boy moaned.

"Look at me."

Jonah turned over, his face nearly plastic from dehydration.

"Where the fuck am I?"

"You in *my* house. So let's get one thing straight. You follow my rules. And I only got three. Rule number one: Watch your mouth. Only person that cusses in this house is me. Keep that up, and you'll find your way out my door with my foot in your ass. Rule number two: This ain't a flophouse. Don't mess with none of my furniture. You get yourself together and stay off my rug."

Jonah sat up. The full force of head-spin and nausea hit him with a wrenching dizziness. "Okay, okay," he said. "What . . . what's rule number three?" he asked, swallowing back a hint of bile rising in his throat.

"Rule number three: When I ask questions, I better get straight answers. I saved your ass from a long night in the Tombs—you can thank me later. For now, we gon' get you back on your feet so you can go about your business. And while we're doing that, you best keep in mind that you a guest in my house. I did you a favor, so you better do as I say. Don't give me no lip, and *don't* get any ideas. Here, take this Advil. Bathroom is down the hall on your right."

Jonah returned feeling less nauseated. His head raged with pain, particularly behind his eyes. There were other pains on his body too, bruising pains he'd have to locate later. His large host offered him a tall, greenish beverage.

"What is this?"

"That there is the good stuff. I call it Nate-o-rade, it's a secret recipe. Gets you squared away quick, never lets me down."

"And who are you?"

"Nathaniel. You can call me Nate. You're Jonah."

"How did yo—"

"Cause I'm Kojak, black. It's called photo ID. In your wallet."

"Right, sure. And you make your own Gatorade—you into fitness and stuff?"

"Fitness? Man, I learned to make this shit before Gatorade even existed. I was a pro athlete, fourteen years shooting hoops in the league. Didn't you notice?"

Nate gestured at the photos and plaques on the wall. Jonah had vaguely registered the museum-like clutter but hadn't mentally brought the content into focus. Now he stood up gingerly and gazed around the room. There his host was, in a Celtics jersey, suspended in midair, going for a layup, a defender with outstretched arms trailing behind him; and there, dribbling with spiderlike angularity; standing with fans and celebrities, holding a trophy of a man helping his teammate up.

"What award is that?"

"Teammate of the Year. Got that during my final year on the court."

"And when was that?"

"A long time ago."

"Why did you leave? You don't look that old."

"Blew out my knee. Any other questions?"

"What do you do now?"

"Coach."

"A lot of ballplayers seem to go right into coaching."

"This is more of a new development. I went overseas for a while after I retired."

"Where did you go?"

"France."

"No shit! Oh, sorry . . . I guess what's funny is that I'm from Paris . . . well, kind of. I mean, I'm American, but I grew up there."

"No shit? So what you back in New York for?"

"My life was too easy, I guess. I was just watching movies all day. I sort of had a girlfriend, but, well . . . it's complicated."

"Sounds cushy. Why did you leave?"

"I don't know. I mean, I do—but it's hard to explain."

"We got time."

As the young man got to talking, Nate examined him closely: the lightness in the eyes, his bony frame, the odd accent. *Jonah.* An errant prophet washed ashore. What had overcome him to pick this boy up and bring him home? Was it his spiritual thing, his compassion? Was it refusing to see another young brother get taken to jail like that? Whatever the reason, Nate concluded that Jonah's appearance was significant, a crosscurrent in the flow. It was instinctual; there was something about the young man that made him want to know more. He let Jonah talk (the brother loved to talk), and now he was going on about the situation he had left in Paris. And the things he was saying convinced Nate in the rightness of his thinking. Because the words spoken in his living room were taking him back, way back, across the ocean to that same city, to that place and time in his life that he could never entirely forget, but that he thought, at least he had once, that he'd left behind for good.

⊁⊰

When Jonah spoke, the words rushed out of him and Nate struggled to keep pace as the young teacher bolted through sentences like hopscotch boxes, quick in his form, leaving a pattern in the air that was easy to see but hard to follow.

He told Nate about the work of a projectionist, the one who operates behind the scenes to bring the movie to light. There was always a moment before a screening when Jonah was alone. He would catch himself scheming, coming up with some fantastic occurrence that might indefinitely prolong his stay in the funk of the little booth. It was a space of half-lights, murky and warm. He enjoyed threading the film quickly and efficiently through its zigzag of sprockets and gates. If something went wrong, the film could get caught, a nightmare scenario that any projectionist worth their salt would prevent at all costs. Only when the picture was up could he feel his blood relax, and his mind begin to idle. In the booth he could see and not be seen. The eyes reached out across the dark where the stories rose and fell in the alphabet of variable light. A dry oven-like heat radiated from the lamphouse. The fractious chatter of rotors and film reels generated a gentle dharmic drone. The bulky frame of the mid-century projector loomed overhead like a mammoth lately fossilized; one of those vanished beasts that went down to drink of cool water at the Seine, whose bones came up when they dug out the tunnels of the Métro.

Jonah had taken the job fully aware of how it would look. Film was on its way out; the fact that it was dying gave it an old-world authenticity that

made it all the more attractive. He had been aware from a very
that everything cool was archaic, defunct, retro. If it had har
dials, all the better. It was a way of styling yourself as not entirely ᴏɴ ᴅᴇ
with the futurists, the programmer dorks who had grown up friendless and
who had since secured their revenge by ascending to positions of unfathomable power and wealth. They still couldn't dance, but it didn't matter.
They were remaking the entire world in their image. They wrote the code
and the rest would have to follow it. Like them, Jonah had been born just
early enough to see something of the previous world before it disappeared,
enough to have a nostalgic attachment that was useful only insofar as it
could be converted into quaint mementos of that lost world, notes of tasteful
decay or bygoneness. Landing a gig as a projectionist seemed like the most
successful thing he could have done, at least in that regard.

But the job wasn't necessarily as easy as it looked. In the tiny Parisian
movie houses, the projectors were cranky old machines, and one needed a
nimble hand just to keep them going. The film came on platters like shellfish.
He shucked them, holding the strips up like X-rays, pinching them carefully
along the sides, looking for damage and dust, for splices or punctures along
the soundtrack. There was an absorbed solemnity to the work. The ultimate
test was in motion; he waited for the cue marks on the flying filmstrip, those
bright cigar burns in the corner, enjoining the projector to bring two pieces
of the story together. His heart rate slowed as the moment to change reels
approached. He imagined a single frame on its Z-shaped voyage, around the
big platter, up to the roller, then down to the film gate, where the intermittent
sprocket held them, one by one, twenty-four times every second, each slice
of light a still picture, like the frozen gestures of the saints projected daily by
the sun through the oculi of the cathedrals.

One evening, he learned that his assignment was to project a documentary
about an obscure jazz pianist. He had never heard of the film or the director
or its subject; likely it had screened once at Deauville before getting dumped
on them by one of those obscure cultural functionaries who followed the

seasonal junkets across the globe. The titles scrolled, and the name of the subject appeared in a bold, modern font: *Quiet Genius: The Life and Music of Phineas Newborn, Jr.*

He checked his watch and called down to the office. They were ready. He set the action in motion. The film leader wound through the reel, sending a crazed scribble across the screen. With a soft pop, the picture came up.

Jonah squinted in the viewfinder and sharpened the focus. With a sudden self-conscious check, he realized he was looking into the grain of a black man's skin, right about his neck. He looked up from the viewfinder at the face staring back over the shadowy rows. On the screen he took in the man's smooth brown facial features, boyish, shy, an aristocratic demeanor and a faint trace of anxiety in the expressive eyes framed by a pair of thick, horn-rimmed glasses. A fine trace of sweat glistened on his brow. *Phineas.* The musician gazed down at his instrument, the flight of keys reflected in his lenses.

Just then the senior projectionist, a man named André, came in to check the feed on the projector.

"Salut, Joe," said André.

He called Jonah Joe, like so many other French people did—happily and over Jonah's objections. His passport read Jonah Raymond Winters. His parents sometimes called him Ray, and sometimes J.R. Joe was the diminutive of Joseph, not Jonah. André didn't seem to care.

André snapped some technical questions at him as he patted his rail-thin body down in search of tobacco. He wanted to know if Jonah knew anything about *le grand jazzman.* Without hesitating, Jonah lied. It was a reflex—he always lied if asked about something he didn't know about black culture. He knew they would never dare to call him on it. André invited him to come down to the lobby for a drink once the picture was up and running. Jonah quickly explained that he wanted to keep a close eye on the feed, which, truthfully, had been somewhat finicky that week. André appeared pinched, or simply baffled, and abruptly left.

Jonah trained his eyes back on the screen, where Phineas was now playing piano. From time to time, the camera cut to focus on his hands. Massive black fingers filled the screen, rising and falling on the ivories. A heavily accented voiceover described a tumultuous life in decline, a squandered talent. A montage sequence revealed the musician's unraveling, falling prey to inebriation, predisposed to mental breakdown. Still photographs drifted in hesitant suspension. Down and out in New York, Memphis, Philadelphia. In this sequence, there was no music, and the only sound in the theater was the flutter of the projector itself.

The movie ended with an interview, a coda of sorts. An interviewer with a thick Italian accent asked, "Mr. Newborn, you have many fans here in Europe. Tell us about your first solo European tour. What did you think of it?" Now Phineas spoke, and his granular Southern voice reached out and seized hold of Jonah in his booth.

> Well, I always did dream of arriving one day in a city. Some place far away from America. Some place where nobody would know my name and I wouldn't know nobody else and I could just be who I am, the finest pianist that ever came out of Tennessee. When I recollect those days, what I think of is how fast everything happened at that time in my life. Like I was no more than a little flea caught up in some mighty circus. That's how I think on it now. But you can't imagine the feeling, at the time, what it was to make that trip. Where I was coming from. I remember arriving in Europe. I can see it clear as yesterday. Boy, I knew I had arrived, too. I'd made it, and with a recording contract to my name. And over there, the women and the men all dressed so nice, but best of all nobody asked me my business like I had none. And no "colored" water fountains. I could walk down the swankiest boulevard just as tall as the next man. I really felt so blessed to be alive. But you know, I think maybe it's always like that when you arrive for the first time in a city, the shock of things could be different. Like hearing Bud Powell for the first time. See, I never think of a city without

thinking of music. For me there's no Paris without hearing Bud. So every new city is an opportunity to change your ear. You might catch the light in the trees more. The rhythms of life arrive with a strange off-kilter sensation, and the artist has to try and make something of this new arrangement, to catch the changing signs of the new world in their flight.

Could you tell us, Mr. Newborn, what year was this?

That was nineteen hundred fifty-eight. I had released *Phineas' Rainbow*, and the people at RCA wanted me to do a European tour to promote the album abroad.

What about your early life? You had a difficult relationship with your father, yes? Could you tell us some things about that?

My father was a musician. But my father used to say, "You got to walk the valley by yourself." I truly believe he hated the idea of me getting into music like he did, but I never had it in me to give something up if I liked it, and I loved playing music from the day I was born. I'd say I got my stubbornness from him. Sure, between us, it wasn't always easy, you know? But it wasn't in him to back down, to give up, to settle. He was the one who told me, "You just remember, boy, none of your forefathers never jumped off no slave ship." He was a tough man. Had to be. Born down in Georgia in the Reconstruction. A terrible time, and we see how it still is. The whites were stringing black folk up in trees and they might set you on fire for any damn thing. When I was a boy, I remember folks talking about Elbert Williams. He had started working to help the blacks vote in our area and before long they found his body face down in the Hatchie. Well, I never thought about it as something that *could* change. Other than music it was all I knew. Father was a music man, a drummer known all round Memphis. Made a name for himself good enough that he figured mine should be the same as his. I remember how him and Tuff Green would come stomping through the house after a night at the juke and my mother would cuss the both of them out till they were forced onto the porch. They would keep on hollerin' back and forth for hours it seemed and I lay awake listening through the walls. They might be playing off the banister or a chair with a wooden spoon or just clapping their hands and that was better than transistor radio. Sometimes they would get to singing an old blues number or a jug-band tune. That was like water to me and I took to it. Beale Street was right there in my house. Jelly Roll was my little night music. My father he trained me to follow in his footsteps and work in his band. But I knew that I wanted to make my own way and to do that I would have to be better than good and get noticed out east in the big cities. So I put my two little hands together and I prayed. I asked the Lord if He would only let me I was going to become the greatest piano player Memphis had ever seen.

You mentioned Jelly Roll Morton. Who are some of your other influences?

How much time you got? Art Tatum, Oscar Peterson, Ellington. The great Ahmad Jamal. But of them all, I most admired Art Tatum. The only smart thing I ever heard a critic say—and this was a white critic, mind you—he said,

"When you listen to Art, you feel like a bird-watcher who stumbles across a sky full of kingfishers." That stayed with me. Now, you know, Art was very nearly blind. From birth, I believe. But he could see music clear as sunshine. Far as I know he never practiced, never needed to read a sheet of music. He just sat down and played. It was like the notes were there for him all the time, like he could see them all at once. As a musician, you didn't want to go up after him. It wouldn't make sense. He didn't leave nothing for you. Anything you could think of he already knew it, and he had the sweetest rhythmic understanding of the instrument I ever heard. No one, I mean no one, could play like Art. I don't believe anyone ever will.

What about yourself? What is unique about your style?

Let me play you something, let's see . . . You hear that? That's Billy Strayhorn. See, I can get that color because Strayhorn is a genius and he's in love with the sound. Then all I need is for the keys to be ready, and then you've got to be ready for them. That ways you bring kindness to the hammers as they fall. You keep them yearning at all times. That's why the sound you hear is what we call lush, the way Billy wanted it. Now I could be playing in Rome or Los Angeles, it don't matter; when I'm ready, I'll always be sitting right there in my old house in Whiteville, Tennessee. Where you can hear the locomotives of the L&N goin' down the line and the voices of my aunties and uncles talking about the rent man and cooking up the fish fry. To me that's what style is. It's the presence that lives around the notes, the part of your playing that tells the listener this is how my music sees the world, how it lives in it. It's like what happened one night when I was playing a gig in Copenhagen. After the show, I see these two cats with horns waiting for me; it was Albert Ayler and Don Cherry. They had come to see me play so I invited them up. And I'll never forget this, Albert came on the bandstand and started doing a spiritual. And I heard this sound. It had that unbroken fire, the way before you become known, when you're still practicing, woodshedding as we like to call it, there's this naturalness, this fearlessness, before you're discovered by the commercial world and they put you in that whole mess. Well, I could hear it in the man's sound, all that love. And to me, it was like the Word came back, and I had that feeling of when I was very young and my parents would take us on Sundays to church. And it's this feeling you get in a Baptist, holy-type church, when everyone feels the Spirit in the room, and people become happy, they call it. And some people even speak tongues. But it's this feeling of the Spirit holding the room, and it happened that night with Albert too. He took hold of us. And I felt his Spirit, the world of the ancestors talking to us through him. And that's really what our thing is all about. Getting to that place where the sound touches you, and the shadows of the valley flicker, and you're moved, touched by the source of things, the love that brings all things back.

～

Freeze-frame. That was the effect if he had to describe it, Jonah said. He was aware that the lights had come on, the cinephiles dispersed, the theater

71

returned to entombed silence. But as he placed the film reels carefully back in their cases, he could feel the lingering presence of Phineas, his troubling voice and troubled genius shifting him off foundations he hadn't even known were there, something newly moving, like a pendulum at the instant when it has finally passed the point of its maximum amplitude. He hastily jotted down his hours and slipped out.

On the rue Christine, the air felt clean and cool. It was late in the afternoon and people strolled languidly, pausing to consider café terraces and their perennial cast of dilettanti. Sounds and images from the film trickled in his mind and mingled with anxieties that had followed him since his graduation. Folks had warned him that, after college, if he wasn't careful, he could be led into a dead-end job, that if he didn't keep his eye on the ball, he could be knocked off the course of professional and personal advancement and fall behind his peers, that it was too easy to lose all the hard-fought gains that a college education had provided, particularly (although he felt it didn't need to be repeated as endlessly as it was) for a young man like himself. One had to advance decisively.

This attitude (firmly adopted by his kinfolk) held a very dim view of the kind of reasoning that would consider an internship as a projectionist's assistant in a Parisian art-house movie theater an acceptable postgraduate term of employment. The suspicion was, depending on who he asked, that Jonah was either spoiled or a damn fool, or both. He didn't have a good counterargument. It *was* easier to view life than to experience it. At work, he sat in the dark, watching; at home, he flipped open his laptop and watched his friends' life-pages proliferating, streaming at an ever-increasing frame rate.

His own life, up to that point, had been, by most counts, "interesting," special, even singular—though to him it seemed primarily a matter of cushioned apartness. Boyhood brought to his mind mostly an impression of innocence suspended in a kind of fin de siècle phoniness, an unlikely life of privilege. The details he retained most vividly were sheltered and

oddly abstract. The tinkle of pickup sticks; the loving rotundi
Burton's voice; clots of Nestlé powdered cocoa and the vibran
of multipack breakfast cereal. At the time, it had seemed to him like an
ideal upbringing. It could have occurred just as easily in one of those rare
and famous wealthy black American enclaves that his father liked to crack
awkward jokes about. But a black American in Europe? That was a weirder
story, not without precedent, but not entirely relatable either. It was his
father, Jonah said, who was the architect of this strange situation, who
provided the illusion and snatched it away. "Remember this, boy," he'd say
if Jonah upset him. "You're living a life other kids just like you don't have.
You have no idea how good you have it, you never will."

Confronting one's history was important. His father talked a great deal
about history and power. The limitations placed on men by its cruelty; the
force of hatred in the world, which was oppressive and could strike anywhere
at any time, which he should be prepared to face down as a special condition
because it would inevitably target him. This was the most terrible vision.
That history would come looking with special prejudice *for him*. Sooner or
later he would confront a penalty, and it would be his responsibility to prove
that he was not going to allow that penalty, however unjustly imposed, to
hold him back. That he would use the extraordinary good fortune of his
upbringing to make something great of himself and serve others, in spite
of the inevitable swerve of history that would come looking for him and all
who were darker than him, with intentions that were not to be trusted but
nonetheless grimly confronted, surmounted with grace, without complaining,
without under any circumstances allowing *them* to see the hurt.

Often, history was taught through the television, which brought its
lessons—sometimes, and sometimes not, involving darker people—into
the living room. But in his father's explanations, they all were versions of
the same thing: the great contest between the forces that tried to pit man
against man through hate, and the forces of quiet dignity that tried to

resist this, but often failed and often paid a terrible price. The more terrible price was paid by women, who generally bore the scars of this great cosmic conflict twice over, and who were the ones left to tend to the wounds caused by male chaos, to weep at funerals, to care for and raise neglected children, to survive and patch together the human family while making a life for themselves as best they could.

On such occasions, his father adopted a tone of ancestral teaching, as if (despite his rather limited schooling) his paternal mission consisted of imparting the ways of the world from the standpoint of successes and failures not only his own but of mankind generally. His voice, always grave at the outset, could shift, depending on his humor, revealing unsettled edges like a graveled road. He was fond of marking dramatic pauses with a flick at the base of one of his blue packets adorned with an Asterix helmet. The little kick liberated a cigarette, whose consumption was momentarily deferred until oratorical triumph dictated it should be plucked and ignited to his satisfaction.

Through the gauzy spread of tobacco fumes, the Japanese television set transmitted the revolution in newscasting, a never-ending global drama beamed directly into the living room. Riots, earthquakes, rafts of the dispossessed, Ethiopian famine, the space shuttle, Nelson Mandela, Morgan Freeman, Michael Jackson, Whitney Houston. He remembered his father explaining the Berlin Wall coming down, the throng of fists and scarves and gloves parading, a chorus rising and roaring to garbled cheers and astonished weeping, a white man with a sledgehammer whacking away as slabs of gray matter yawned open. "You see, son," his father said, "this is what freedom means. Taking it into your own hands, making the arc of history bend to your will. Hell, that's what all great men want, and it's what all great artists do—*if*—if they have the *opportunity* and the God-given ability to meet the challenge that's in their path."

Jonah's father believed strongly in the greatness of art. He also believed, and for a time had convinced enough other people with the right connections, that *he was* an artist. He had come to this realization while studying for a degree in business communications. If he had learned one thing from those classes, it was the importance of seizing on opportunistic timing in a volatile market. He was well aware that, to some extent, he had taken advantage of a moment, after the assassinations of the sixties, when white liberals felt guilty about race relations and wanted to be seen endorsing, supporting, and promoting radical black art. This awareness didn't imply pure cynicism on his part. Especially in the early days, he had brought genuine anger and frustration to his work, and its expressionist élan reflected something bold and unnerving that caught the eyes of gallerists and the art press alike. He nurtured an Afrocentric brand and ran with the dashiki crowd, admired Ron Karenga, flirted with Islam, even seriously considered converting, but couldn't bring himself to give up swine. He also came to doubt (or confront) the reach of his abilities, seeing them for what they were, talents not gifts, unusual but not immeasurable, not genius beyond compare.

He liked to tell the story of an important showing of his work at a reputable gallery in Paris in 1977. He was particularly proud of a mixed-media portrait, a mural of sorts, that he called *Homage to Barbara Jordan*, which depicted the congresswoman as a towering figure of justice in the act of indicting Nixon, who appeared as a grotesque, pale gnome in the corner, part of his face spray-painted over with graffiti. The crowd at the opening gave it rapturous attention and adulation, and he basked in this glow, right up to the moment when he noticed, or came to the end of a long failure to notice, that he was the only black person in the entire room. "If you ever find yourself doing something and you're the only one there—you better check yourself," he would warn Jonah in his sternest voice.

His father was, according to himself, black in the right place at the right time. But it still felt wrong, like a bad joke. Like he was getting the pretend version of what he had grasped at all his life. Yes, he had faked it when he had to, in order to rise; but now that he really wanted it, or rather wanted to be real *in* it, every vernissage he showed up to was full of the wrong people, even though they were the same people from the years before, the ones who were always thrilled to see him, wanted him to drink at their tables, pose for pictures with them, and never gave a damn about a thing he had made.

It could have led to despair, and for a brief and turbulent time, it seemed it would. But his father was able to convert these frustrations into a desire to get over, to get the most, and his social connections blossomed accordingly. He was even more successful once he made it obvious and plain to them that he was scheming, that he was a needy and somewhat fraudulent hustler taking advantage of their thirst for his "urban" sensibility. It only made him more glamorous, more real, and a stream of increasingly prestigious "minority" and "diversity" fellowships, residencies, and keys to chateaus were never more than a phone call away. His plot against the white art world quickly turned into something of a perpetual-motion machine, as he dragged his family with him from position to position, always in search of a place where he could maximize his quality of life at minimum cost. The family bounced around overseas from one art-world metropolis to the next: London, Berlin, Paris.

Berlin Jonah remembered as gray blocks, gray skies, and snow. Deep drifts under the linden trees on Hölderlinstraße. And the beautiful girl, very blonde and porcelain, whom he met sledding somewhere in a forest clearing, her image set to rest at the very back of the mind like a snow globe waiting to be shaken. If he closed his eyes, he could remember the sound of her name, but not the name itself. He might not have remembered her at all if she had not formed an early taste of some unspeakable gulf between desire and detachment, something bitter, a cool remoteness that frightened him. Those were strange days, when the TV spoke in a foreign tongue and rosy-cheeked boys like cutouts from Kinder chocolate commercials stopped cheerfully to interrogate him, touching his hair, laughing. The girl and her sky-colored eyes had questioned him too, that day in the woods, not with any overt hostility, but with distance, as if he had appeared like a comet, a sight from another world.

When his father announced that they were moving to Paris, the change meant nothing more to him than another, hopefully more temperate city. On the overnight train he dreamt that the girl was hidden in his father's suitcase. He joined her there, and, in the darkness of the sealed luggage, she played with his hair. He told her to stop and slapped her. The trunk flew open, and she fled, vanishing into the silence and whiteness of German forests. He woke near dawn. Their carriage was flooded blue. The train clacked and screeched, gently rocking across the exchanges of a rail yard. Outside, the little balconies and the slate rooftops of Paris faced the pale sunlight.

They moved into an apartment on rue de Tocqueville, an unglamorous part of Paris near the rail yards, Jonah said, where switching tracks formed long radial chasms bisecting the Périphérique before sweeping out into the dreary suburbs to the north. The neighborhood shared the name of the little Square des Batignolles that stood beside the Pont-Cardinet station. If the weather was good, Jonah spent long afternoons in the park, where time was marked by the rumbling of the trains and the clean, cracking report of Pétanque players punctuating the gravel lots. A carousel turned, radiating a ragtime or an old song by Barbara, a sad woman who looked like a bird and sang like one too. Sometimes the race-car man had a set of wooden-pedaled soapboxes. If he was there, for five francs you could hurtle along into a halo of glory like Ayrton Senna, racing the commuter lines out of Saint-Lazare. That childhood experience of Paris, Jonah said, was impossible to evoke clearly. It had a shimmering, confectionary weightlessness; and yet it was also dense, a plenitude accumulated imperceptibly, like the leafy dust sagging in the green awning of the crêpe stand.

On the evening of the Phineas Newborn screening, he had come across an accident as it was unfolding on the boulevard Saint-Germain. A woman on a scooter had been struck by a small delivery van that had pulled out hurriedly into her lane. The woman was on her back in the street, and a small crowd had gathered around her. Passersby stopped, dumbstruck, some putting their hands to their mouths, others looking around anxiously or reaching for their phones. The woman was wearing a navy-blue business jacket, and Jonah could see her dark hair coming out of her helmet, which rested motionless on the pavement. It was impossible to tell if she was conscious. A wail came pulsing up the boulevard. Police arrived and began diverting traffic. With the traffic stilled, the plane trees appeared even more majestic, their crowns basking in the evening light. As the ambulance neared, some bystanders began to move again, but others just arriving now stopped, transfixed. The paramedics crouched over the woman's body. There was a shout, and a man in a light-blue shirt, holding a phone to his ear, ran up the sidewalk. He was sweating heavily, and everyone understood. He knelt over her, talking into the helmet and turning periodically to consult with the medics. And then Jonah could see a small heaving in the woman's chest. The man held her wrist. The medics brought out an orange canoe with straps and a pillow. The driver of the van hid his eyes with his hand.

Jonah waited a bit longer. Then, feeling vaguely irritated with himself, he turned and left the scene hurriedly. It was overwhelming, the touch of human stuff, the queer vastness of it colliding all around. Everyone knew all of it could, in the space of one head-on smash, come to a full stop. That there was a day, a definite one somewhere still in the future, full of the same buzz and pullulation of other people living and going on, when it would be someone else in some version of that crowd looking on at him, lying there, watching him exit the play with no more difficulty than the energy it took him to turn and walk away.

The accident had caused him to backtrack, reversing course along the opposite side of the boulevard as the summer evening deepened. At the Odéon intersection, looking more miserable than ever, Danton thrust his arm out over the loiterers assembled at the base of his socle. Jonah turned off the boulevard into the medieval passageways running down to the Seine. He passed art galleries with garish and austere baubles. Tourists fumbled with their digital cameras. At the angle of the rue Jacob, he thought he heard a piano playing. But it was only a waiter storing his silverware. He pressed on into the quiet streets. On the rue Bonaparte he passed the cobbled courtyard of the École des Beaux-Arts and its Greek statues, and then the Tunisian greengrocer where he sometimes bought clementines in the winter. He kept thinking of Phineas. That image of Phineas Newborn at his piano, staring down at his own hands.

He arrived at the crossroads near the statue of Condorcet. To his right, the Pont des Arts stretched across the Seine to the Louvre. The bridge was peppered with young professionals and students. They lounged against the railings or formed circles around cheap bottles of wine and beer, laughing and rolling cigarettes. Dealers roamed their periphery looking for sales. Street vendors with key chains, plastic gadgets, and bottled water, button-holed tourists trying to pose for each other with a romantic view. A column of jolly Americans dressed in khakis and polo shirts rolled by on Segways, traversing the scene like a vaguely alien but benign patrol force.

Paris at the dawn of the new millennium. The softness of its way of life, its affordance and assumption of the artful enveloped them all like a delicate and indefinitely antiquated movie set. It was, Jonah said, almost sickeningly beautiful. He stood in it as one who had neither a place nor no place in it. He hadn't done nothing to nobody. But really, he had done nothing, could do nothing, other than grow more like the city around him. Become a waxy walker in the museum of nostalgia, a curious prop, seemingly borrowed from another set for the tourists to ponder with disinterested bewilderment.

What was *he* doing? Elsewhere life was happening, moving in some fateful direction. It might ultimately be catastrophic, but it was moving all the same. The decisive meanings would be discovered and won or lost there. His college friends, armed with their degrees, were moving to Brooklyn or out to Silicon Valley, where the future was being encoded as a set of calculably diffusive effects presided over by a sempiternal abstraction devoted to watching, recording, and taking a cut. He knew he wanted no part of that. But what alternative vision did he have? These thoughts obsessed him as he walked back across the city to the rue de Tocqueville.

His bedroom was full of movie posters, most of them rolled up in tubes in a corner leaning against his desk. He got them for free on the job and had more than he knew what to do with. He had seen so many films, too many. Art films from small European countries that were younger than he was; obscure westerns that only the elderly came to watch, and usually dozed off to. Even the glorious Isabelle Adjani who stormed across the screen in her avenging genii, her Emily Brontë, her Adèle Hugo, her Camille Claudel; even Adjani's achingly romantic poses looked somehow hollow to him now. He was tired of watching. What was he really looking for? What did the watching conceal? He loved the movie theater; he loved working in the booth, feeding the reels and watching the platters turn. But how long would any of it last? What did it have to do with him? It came back to the same thing. The movies were his way of hiding. And he knew it. He just hadn't had the courage to admit it. Somehow Phineas had said it for him. Reached something vulnerable, something that was broken but not forgotten in the life that held the music forth like an instrument that played his unknown past and spoke of unknowable futures.

Phineas. Newborn. His voice was still going in Jonah's mind, tinkling as it receded like a caboose. How far back did one have to go to understand a man? He had seldom found a single word to fit his own question mark. Was there a way to the inner directness of the thing, the things that he had never found he could say? Shades of history and cries of a people. Was that what Phineas had finally moved into the light? Fear of the missed life. Like that of the Ex-Colored Man discovering one day he has chosen the lesser part? There was only one way to find out. Get out ahead of it. Complete a turn toward whatever was out there that he had yet to know. Grasp and hold. Or be held.

It was time to get real. Get a real job, deal with the real world. New York was a place where you figured some shit out, where whatever people could handle could be found, along with a good dose of whatever they couldn't. The force of a decision brought with it a fresh inlet of perspective. His room, when he finally got home, looked entirely different, Jonah said. The things in it were no longer just the haphazard accumulation of restless days. They formed an image of his life up to that point. The nobody he saw there bothered him.

He stared at the map on the wall over his bed. It was a gift from his mother. A Mercator projection, the Earth squared to the tidy scale of one to five hundred thousand. In the corner above the legend, the Air France Pegasus reared up with the national colors flaming in its mane. Air routes sprang from the world's magnetic poles—Paris, London, New York—and sailed off in falling parabolas to distant cities, crossing the time zones. Underneath the map was a wide and low bookcase that ran the length of the wall.

He pulled out a novel by Aragon and read the first sentence. It was as arresting as he had remembered. Arna had given him the book and he had promised her he would read it. He flipped through the pages, pausing over her elliptical notations. It was long and he had put off finishing it at some point without giving himself a reason for doing so. He could perceive now that it wasn't anything about the story or the style that had failed to enthrall him. It was something in the sadness of the fate gripping its characters that he wanted to avoid resolving. It was the implication of her deciding this particular story was one they ought to share. He had concealed this to himself and chalked it up to distraction. But the truth was that he was afraid to read too far, to accept an ending that her intelligence had absorbed, reflected upon, and deemed cautionary.

7

Arna Duval Fignolé. A name redolent of fronded colonial mysteries, some obscure relay between la France hexagonale and the American South (perhaps if it had never sold Louisiana to Jefferson after defeat at the hands of her revolted slaves), a combination that, for one reason or another, Jonah associated with Arna's equally unusual areas of expertise, such as how to knot a cherry stem inside one's mouth; how to split matchsticks into figurines; how to carry anime jingles with a boyish whistle before lapsing into an awkward, hissing laugh.

Despite these talents, Arna wasn't exactly popular, Jonah told Nathaniel. Outside of school, she wasn't easily reached. Jonah would call the landline. If her French father answered they would exchange the usual greetings, and then he would receive (crystallized in the impersonal politeness of French conversation) the default declaration that his daughter was unavailable. But if her American mother answered, it was another story. He would be quizzed on everything: school, his parents, weekend plans. Her mother spoke in high bursts of spirited Southern drawl that had been amusingly livened by a distinctly Parisian chirrup full of assumed common sense about the way things are done. If it was her mother, he would gladly talk all evening, because he knew it meant, sooner or later, she would pass him along. There would be a "Hey, hold on," and through the receiver the plink and clatter of the kitchen would yield to the thudding of footsteps and the snapping of coil on the cord as Arna yanked the phone back to her room.

In art class, he often sat behind her. The uniform-blue smock was tied in a bow at her back; her hair was the color of a chestnut you find in the yard and pocket for safekeeping. She was the beginning of poetry, and the idea of it spread contagiously to his tender nerves, like the smell of a face drawing near. Overnight, he was Lermontov. The great Russian poet, Jonah explained, whose very name (even if he was unsure how to pronounce it) had suggested the dashing sound of what poetry ought to be, and of all that it promised to do. Every sonnet smoldered, even the formidable Séyès lines of the composition books could not regulate them. The finest lyric achievements of an evening were delivered up the rows to Arna's desk the next morning. With respect to these strenuous developments, Arna maintained perfect inscrutability and a distanced cool.

While his fevers swirled inward, Arna was slowly but surely expanding her vision outward, primarily through her admission to the circle of the beautifully scarved elite, who gathered in the nearby Parc Monceau to smoke hashish after classes. One afternoon, after much pleading on Jonah's part, she allowed him to join her at a small gathering in a high-ceilinged apartment on rue de Téhéran where she taught him privately how to heat a stick of Moroccan hash with a lighter and fritter its crumbs into a bed of rolling tobacco. Hashish was Arna's oblique answer to poetry. She had accessed a different portal to knowledge, one she wanted to know of through her body, and that she had somehow, seemingly without his being able to detect when or how, confidently claimed as new territory for exploration. While he pretended to watch music videos on a television fitted into a Louis XV cabinet, she moved lithely from one body to another, laughing tipsily, then suddenly entwined in voluptuous and cryptic gestures. There were no rules, at least none he could detect; sometimes she was kissing boys, sometimes caressing girls.

Jonah worried that his wallflower inhibitions would mean losing Arna

to the dizzying new world she had so swiftly, and apparently effo[ ]
integrated. But, miraculously, even as he remained outside the inner circle,
his skin color had come to take on new meanings, some of them positive,
or at least it was made clear to him that his presence added something cool
and desirable, like a prized and rare accessory. Most importantly, from
his perspective, it ensured his continuing access to certain invitation-only
parties at country houses in the "Island of France," that green Merovingian
radial marked by all points, no less than half and no more than one hour's
distance from the bell towers of Notre Dame.

To get there, Arna and Jonah had to prearrange rides. Things started in
the back of seat of a Peugeot in whispers, a joint passed around furtively,
burning at the lips. Circumflex accents in tight sweaters caught the eye and
legs brushed together in the woozy sway and tip of the car, touching off
tactile collisions. Sometimes there was "free" kissing, in that it didn't count.
In the gardened manor houses, all vaguely alike, someone always put on the
same album by the Doors, and Jim Morrison's oracular pronouncements
licensed and promised a time in which anything could happen, and would
happen, under the sign of eternal youth. The aroma of hash and spilled
Malibu liqueur, of being seventeen, caused a permanent tilt, so that there
was only the possibility of bodies moving toward each other or falling away
into various degrees of paranoia. In the tense, hermetic daze of the country
house and its many attic rooms, skin and color were complicating assets,
and Arna took it upon herself to act as a kind of chaperone, keeping her eye
on him, teaming up when necessary, so that he, too, could fleetingly let his
guard down and succumb to the ambient goal of pursuing new sensations.
She allowed him to kiss and to discover the surface of her body, only, or
mostly, above the waist. She gave him hints of desire, but he understood
that it was also an act of generosity, a tacit sign of the compact that she was
engaging in to protect them both. In the morning, the stone houses were
always incredibly cold. Three and four under extra blankets, they lay in

bed virtually naked and feverishly hot. He listened to the birds sing in the blue darkness, unsure whether the spell had broken, how much longer they might touch that way before it was time to go.

With Arna things were never official. They weren't "going out," but they also agreed that theirs was a special kind of friendship. They haunted the record stores behind the Pantheon, watched Hitchcock flicks on the rue des Écoles, and posted up in cafés, bantering about movie stars and music and the hookup scene. Arna's hair was short like a boy's. She should have been a member of the group of girls from the good families, but those girls hated her. She was a transfer student and the shape of her eyes and her skin tone was held to be suspicious. Behind her back they called her "a Mongol" and the rumor was that Arna was a gitane. One afternoon as they waited in line for the bus, a group of girls got a chant going. Arna walked away, presumably to cry, but she reappeared moments later with a jar full of filthy water that she tossed in a girl's face, causing an eruption of hysteria. On one of their first hangs, Arna showed Jonah an impressive knife from her father's collection, a lissome folding blade. She liked to play with it over lunch after slicing vertices from her Camembert. It was Arna's idea to carve their names into the green plank of a park bench where they met sometimes after school. Their special friendship, which was always something more, but also less, went on this way until the afternoon Arna came over to the rue de Tocqueville.

Jonah had invited her before. This time she accepted. It was midweek and his mother had left her usual note reminding him she would be working late. They sat on the living room floor watching MTV Europe. MC Solaar, Massive Attack, heart-stopping Lauryn Hill, watery flashes of Kurt Cobain. Arna half watched as she flipped through a *National Geographic*. She was wearing her evergreen track shorts with the Adidas flower, and a white tank top. A new show came on, and they decided to move to his room. Arna sat on his bed, poring over an article on whaling in Iceland. He followed along over her shoulder. Her hair smelled like wet wood in the sun, like the bark of a tree hit by a sprinkler in the summer. She flicked through the pages for a while, then, with a sigh of boredom, stretched out on the bed. He picked up the magazine, pretending to read in silence. Arna said something muffled into the pillow, and he heard her pull off her top and flounce back down. He waited a moment, then put the magazine aside and lay down next to her carefully, as if afraid of waking her. At first, when she touched him, he thought it must be an accident, but then he saw that her other hand had slipped under the elastic of her shorts. She stopped and gave him a long serious look. Then she rolled over, pressing herself on top of him. He felt her heat as she placed his hand. "I want to get this over with," she said. When it started, he felt like her body was squirming away. They thrusted in contradictory motions, meeting in tense shocks. When he shuddered, she jerked away violently. He apologized and she did not answer. They stayed that way for a time, breathing. At one point, he feared she was crying, but she wasn't. When she got up, she wiped the back of her thigh with his T-shirt. Suddenly, there was a sound at the front door. Arna bolted. Within seconds, she was somehow dressed again, her backpack slung over her shoulder, saying something to his mother with a quick laugh of surprise in the front hall as she slipped out onto the landing. Jonah went to the balcony. He watched her cross the street in a dash, walking, then running, as she turned the corner and disappeared.

That was the early summer of their graduation, as Arna was preparing to leave for England and he was waiting to go off to college in the States. She asked to meet him the day before she was set to go. They met for a coffee not far from the school, but ended up walking for almost an hour, down along the river and then through the hot, dusty Tuileries Gardens crowded with tourists. Arna was going to study politics, philosophy, and economics at Oxford, a compromise with her father, who had wanted her to follow the family tradition and attend one of the grandes écoles in Paris but consented to let her go abroad as long as she promised to return and not to study anything frivolous.

They ended up standing in the proscenium by the ticket booths at the entrance of the Métro station at Concord. The pneumatic gates of the turnstiles whooshed and clattered. Against the wall opposite the ticket booths was an old indicateur d'itinéraires, one of those connecting boards that lights up when a steel node is pressed down next to the label for a destination. Punch in Mairie des Lilas and a string of pale, green dots illuminate your trajectory across the city. Jonah and Arna took turns pressing possible destinations. The board lit up, dutifully, colored bracelets radiating outward in crossing paths.

Jonah had hoped at least for a warm farewell. Instead, they struggled to find things to say. Arna was distant. It became clear that there was too much they hadn't acknowledged over the years. As if they had crossed some threshold, run afoul of the obscure bylaw that states that past a certain point of ambiguity in a relationship, the real one can no longer be recovered. The realization felt strange, because the possibility that they would become vastly different from each other had never really occurred to him before.

Arna said she thought it would be a good thing to have some real distance between them. He quickly agreed. She gave his shoulder a gentle, playful nudge. Sweaty faces were streaming past them out of the tunnel. He thought to kiss her, but the jostling of the crowds, the heat, the noise, it was all so overwhelming that they briefly hugged instead.

It was Arna's idea that they should correspond, and he enthusiastically co-signed. They kept in touch "across the pond" while attending university. Though there was no positive sign of the romance that had made their friendship special, the letters, which increased in volume over time, took on increasingly intimate hues. He knew a good deal of what was going on in her life—at least, the portion she wished to share with him.

Jonah said he only saw Arna in person once during college, however, around the same time the following year back in Paris. On that occasion she was in town for a few days and said she could only do coffee. They met at one of the large corner-sweeping brasseries by Courcelles. Even though it was a little windy, they sat on the terrace in rattan chairs, not facing each other, but side by side, oriented outward toward the traffic of the boulevard and beyond it, the high gates sealing off the cool verdant mass of the Parc Monceau and the plump facades of the grand villas overlooking its "English" gardens.

Arna told him she was seeing someone, a guy who went to the London School of Economics, who played in a band and was studying to be a human rights lawyer. She spoke well of him, without particulars, but added that she wasn't sure it was going to work out on account of her plan to take a post-graduate fellowship with the Directorate-General for Regional and Urban Policy under the European Commission. In theory, it was based in Brussels, but in practice she would travel almost the entire time, all across the Union, gathering statistical data and meeting with local and regional political actors to gauge various measures of compliance. She would essentially be "taking the temperature of the European project," as she put it. Once people could see the numbers, she explained, recalcitrant populations that were being manipulated by local politicians would realize the many benefits that they were ignorant of or took for granted. She had learned at Oxford that a totally politically integrated Europe was now only a matter of time, possibly less than a decade away, and it was crucial to martial more popular support for the supranational conception of citizenship that it would entail. She was animated about her looming professional debut, and it struck Jonah, as he in turn explained to her something about his dismay at the decline of the film industry, that their conversation in person was far more formal and stilted than in their letters.

"Ack, I'm sorry. I hate it. This will just take a sec."

"No worries."

She was responding to a text message. *From the guy,* Jonah thought, although it would turn out that she was actually making plans with her mother. Jonah reflexively felt in his pocket for his own phone. He had text messages from his parents too. His father wanted to know if he had seen the latest news about the torture scandals from the war. He had heard about them, seen a handful of the images. But it was the last thing he wanted to think about just then.

In college, a friend had urged him to join a small group gathered in a dorm room to watch the beheading of a Jewish journalist. He had gone to check it out, and then, as the tape began, excused himself. It wasn't only the gore that he sought to avoid. Or even the dissociation of being a random onlooker watching this snuff film from Karachi on a laptop in snowy western Massachusetts. There were those who whispered that, like the September attacks, this was one of the signs of the coming "clash of civilizations." Jonah didn't have the courage to face that bleak possibility, nor could he imagine what confronting it would require. He hated conflict and didn't have the stomach for it, even if it was inevitable. But he also, more reservedly, couldn't comprehend the self-evidence of that phrase to many of the students around him. To him, if anything, there was a clash of barbarisms, and the barbarians could be found just as easily in Columbine, or Howard Beach, as in Baghdad. What truly made the video impossible was the foreknowledge that there would be so many more like it; that this spewing taste for cruelty and hatred was just the beginning of a long death-spiral that would shroud the future in its cold spell. That their future had already disappeared.

They both looked up from their phones. Arna was wearing a handsome jacket, and Jonah complimented her on it.

"Thanks! Mariam helped me pick it out from this great little shop in Notting Hill. You would love her. Actually, I'm hoping she will come with me, you know, when I start. She's got this consulting thing based in London—I think I told you about how she was freaking out when going through the interviews. But they need her to do liaising with the offices in Frankfurt and Paris, and she speaks like seven languages or something, so I'm thinking we can coordinate some time to get away together. Plus, I feel like we would travel well together."

He picked up on the "get away," but it was taking him a moment to place the name. She had come up in their correspondence, but not as a main character; a friend she had gone to a karaoke night with, who was busy and ambitious and funny, spoke with a posh accent, and was involved with the

Oxford African and Caribbean Society. And possibly she had said something about a talk they had attended together on gender and queer studies?

"She sounds great. I hope I'll get to meet her one of these days."

"Me too. Look at these."

She showed him a sequence of pictures taken at a house party (lads, glitter, Smirnoff) where Arna and Mariam appeared always together amid others, whom she pointed out and named. Arna appeared happy and flushed. In one picture she was smooshed against her friend's face, the pair sticking their tongues out for the camera. Mariam was obviously fun and hot; she wore a stud in her nose, defiant punctuation on an almond-toned and -shaped face, South Asian, he guessed; more attractive than he had imagined.

"She's the best. I wish she didn't have to spend so much time at her job. I know she hates it. But we're both planning on doing these gigs for now to get started, you know, see where it takes us. Oh my god, look, I'm a mess in this one!"

"You guys look great together—like you're having so much fun."

Was she *with* Mariam? Arna wasn't exactly saying one way or the other. Possibly she hadn't decided, or maybe it wasn't a thing one did decide, or, at least, broadcast like the result of an election or a soccer match. It wasn't really any of his business. He wasn't hurt at all, except insofar as he felt he should have known, and thought she would have been more explicit with him about her feelings. But even as he thought this, he realized how stupid it was, how many good reasons she might have for not wanting to tell him everything about whom she was sleeping with.

The waiter came by to see about another round, but Arna, with the precise, almost sculptural language of gesture that Parisian women use, expressed her desire to pay for the drinks, explaining that she had to go see her parents while she was in town. Jonah thought about protesting but knew better than to insist. The entrance to the Métro was at the corner and they walked together to the steps. He went to kiss her on the cheek, but she pulled him to her intimately. She made him promise to keep writing to her. He promised he would. She looked at him, considering; she kissed him on the neck, once, just below the ear, then turned away and descended below ground.

Whatever he had known up until that point now strengthened his new resolve. In a sense, it was simple. He had wasted too much time already.

Jonah's mother accompanied him to the airport. On the train they slid past the familiar panorama of the banlieues, the peri-urban sprawl, feeder roads swooping under a Samsung Electronics billboard, container shipping facilities, grim little roundabouts, a dingy café de la gare. A Gypsy player with a young boy came into the car and started playing a ballad. The young boy sang and walked up and down the car with his cap out. No one gave him any coins. A mute woman came by and placed a key chain with a little note on top of one of Jonah's bags. He didn't touch it, and eventually she came by and picked it up again. His mother noticed that he was quiet and asked how he was, if he had everything he needed. He said he was fine. She asked if he was still friends with Arna. He said they were still close, that they were staying in touch. She told him a story about when he was a boy, one they both knew and that she always retold whenever they were about to part. Her eyes were very clear and light. There were deep wrinkles between her eyebrows. He could feel the exact length and depth of those ridges because he frowned in exactly the same place. Suddenly she had a coughing fit, and he frantically got a water bottle from his backpack. Her lungs weren't what they used to be. *She's growing old,* he thought. He couldn't sleep on his flight.

8

Laura Petrossian had not ruined Nathaniel Archimbald's life, but she had come close. She had overthrown his sense of himself, given of herself to him and taken from him in ways he had not recognized, and then vanished, leaving behind a gap like a vacant lot. He never entirely believed that her intentions were bad, though to the end they remained inscrutable. Still, he had to concede that even the pain she had caused had been a kind of good fortune. She had helped him to see what was worth saving in the world and forced him to think seriously about what he could do about it.

He had started thinking of Laura as Jonah described his relationship with Arna. Of their paradoxical combination of openness and elusiveness. Nathaniel thought of that openness now, of how happy it would have made Laura to know he had gotten this lost young man out of his fix. He thought of the face she would make if he told her the story. And it reminded him of her other face, the one she made when she was sleeping. The unvarying coolness of her voice when they were naked a long time in her bed. Of midafternoons in the little apartment on the rue des Cinq-Diamants.

Nathaniel leaned back in his chair, stretching out the red and green of his tracksuit with his albatross wingspan. He regarded Jonah intently now, appealing to the grown man in him.

"And you haven't spoken to this woman since?"

"We write to each other. She's always traveling. I get letters and postcards from the cities she's visiting on account of her government job, you know, collecting research about economic development, that kind of thing. We try to do mail the old-fashioned way, and it means that we have this slow-motion conversation over time. I think about her a lot, but then I'll save the thought and write it down, and then when I have some time it turns into something more, it grows into a letter, and then I send it."

"Now hold on, that's the word right there. This sending. Because I got to ask myself who sent you. See, I've been sitting here listening to you, and it's like this weird thing I've been running in my mind. The way I make sense of it is, maybe I saved you. Maybe something even worse was about to happen to you last night and we'll never know it. You don't realize how lucky you are. Only reason I was even downtown was to support a buddy of mine who is trying to get clean and has this meeting he goes to in Chinatown. I heard some stuff in the meeting that was so hard, I had to walk it off and ended up way over off East Broadway. I come round a corner, find you lying on the ground, down for the count and still acting all belligerent, and I seen the cops rolling up, and well, shit, I just acted on it. And I don't even know you. So why did I do that? Had to be a reason. And I been sitting here listening to you and I'm thinking I see what it was. I'll be damned if you aren't some kind of messenger. Universe trying to tell me something. You just might be a sign I got to revisit some shit I've been trying to put behind me for years."

"How do you mean?"

"Well, I'll bet you would never guess I was in a situation just like yours. *Long* time ago. My Paris days. Damn. You know, I haven't been back since. Don't plan to neither, to be honest. Feels like it was another life. It was another life, a whole other world. My first life was hoops. I guess you could say my second life was this love story that didn't pan out. I figure I'm in my third now. At least I'm happy where I'm at. I thought I put that whole Paris thing behind me; now you show up, and it brings it all back. Man, she had me *wide* open. Had me learning my words all over again, and in French. What a crazy time that was. Brings back memories, man, even after all these years."

"What was her name?"

"Laura."

Saying it aloud was like a conjuring. Nathaniel gave himself a few moments to recollect as he struggled to find the right words to describe her. There was the way she looked at a man. The defiantly brash eyeballing of a woman who had ceased to be a girl early in life. *Like so many sisters he had known coming up.* She had this toughness; she frowned more than she smiled, but when she did, she lit up the room.

"Tell me about her," Jonah said.

"I will. I'm thinking on it now. I have to get in rhythm when I'm storying. I'm not usually the talking type like you. But don't be thinking that means I ain't got a whole lot on my mind. Because I do," Nathaniel said.

There was a point in his life, Nathaniel said, when he noticed a shift happening around him. He could feel it happening, not just to him but to everyone. At first, he chalked it up to a frustration that he didn't have the championship rings he had always dreamed of winning. The hard facts of age and injury had dimmed that prospect, even as he battled the pains that became more frequent and that he refused to acknowledge. But it wasn't just his body. The game was changing. It was glossier, louder, bigger somehow. The splash of money was in your face, and it changed attitudes. On the court, in the locker room, but most of all in everyday life. Things that weren't done in his day were becoming common, some of them rumored, but a lot of them showing up in the newspaper and sometimes on the six o'clock news. He felt cut out, as if the segment of history to which he belonged had been dropped from the big board. He spent more and more of their games watching from the bench. He saw a shadow in his future, a time beyond the game that only recently had been unthinkable to him. How would he fill it? He thought about going back to school. He had always felt he had to hide his love of school. He never talked about it. But the truth was that he regretted how little he actually read in college. He had barely gone to class. If he had more time, and eventually he would, he could read whatever he wanted. He always had so many questions that lurked in the back of his mind. But the game was everything, his career, his future, how he put food on the table. He had pushed those questions out of bounds.

But he had always felt a deep desire to learn more about history. He knew his people were from the Carolinas. His grandfather had moved the family to New York in the migration. And he knew that his mother's side had roots in Haiti. At least that was what they always said. In fact, his mother had even sung some Creole lullabies to him as a child. The little bird, *ti zwazo*, going where he's not supposed to. When his mother sang it fired his imagination like the sun. It was all that kept him and his sister alive in those early years, the worst years, after his father left with no news until they learned he had been charged and locked up in another state.

Nathaniel had been hotheaded from the beginning. What his father called "a knucklehead." The Bronx streets never gave an inch. In the static there was no other way to be. He'd seen his first body when he was eleven. A Puerto Rican boy only a few years older than himself in Echo Park with a hole in him and no one coming to help. He had seen the pimps handling the streetwalkers, and the women lined up and fondled by the cops on Southern Boulevard. By the time he was fifteen he had scrambled in and out of hot rides, seen a kid lose one of his eyes to a brass knuckle, had a knife pulled on him by a man twice his age who pulled him into an alley and told him he was going to die that day. If it wasn't for his sister, Naia, who knew how to talk sense into him, he almost certainly would have ended up dead or behind the wall like his old man. It was really only by chance—and the fact that his high school coach took a liking to him—that he started playing ball. Discovered that he was unguardable off the dribble; could shoot the lights out when he wanted to. They let him know if he wanted to keep playing, he had to get his grades right. He was never happy with schoolwork, though. The desk chairs gave him cramps. In class, the way people snickered and put eyes on him when he spoke made him feel stupid. But he loved to read the paper, something he could remember seeing his father doing when he was a little boy. Especially the sports section, where alongside the gray columns and score boxes were pictures of the greats immortalized in their action. The Big Dipper rising for a layup, skywalking like a graceful astronaut.

He never had too many illusions about the business side of basketball. The trades, the scouts, the college reps, the coaches. He knew it all came down to the numbers: his stats, their cash flow, being docile, telling them what they wanted to hear, getting minutes. The only thing he cared about was getting a chance. He was good and he knew it. If he got the right opportunity, he could take over a game. They would see what he could really do and then it would be set. He would be able to provide for his mother. With his success he could give her the protection he had always dreamed of as a boy. He could move his mother out to Jersey. And not a day too soon. The block wasn't just bad. By then, it had become apocalyptic.

He got his break and pressed his advantage as best he could. The years in the league flew by in a blur of sweat, bright lights, adrenaline highs, and crushing blows. He would never have believed the rise and fall through the seasons could happen so fast. He could replay entire games, or parts of them, in his head. Feel the gruel of a walk to the locker room. Hear the ecstatic roar of big wins. He had played alongside and against heroes and legends, guys who had changed what the game could be. Dr. J in Philly, Magic on the Lakers, Earl the Pearl with the Knicks. He was proud just to have been there, to have been part of the generation that brought swagger and soul to the game. He had walked with giants. Fourteen seasons. All, in one way or another, good. Except the last one.

The last year, his mother's sickness meant, for the first time, she couldn't come to his games. Then, shortly after an away game in LA, she died of heart failure. She was sixty-three. He was devastated. For all that Nathaniel had accomplished, he felt he hadn't done enough to do right by her. To make good on the hardships of her life. Women never get the credit that's due them, Nathaniel said. How little they get recognized. And by folks that's closest to them, who really, truly know what it took to bring another generation through. The world is what it is. Women who make everything, who allow themselves to become life itself as it passes through to the future, have the harder road. And who could deny that more often than not, it's a road paved by a man without the slightest notion of where he is trying to go. Losing his mother was a nightmare, Nathaniel said. The dreams of basketball, even if he had won a championship, could not compensate, not even come close. Nothing else had ever anchored his life. She had held his hand for days, refused to leave his bedside when he had to have knee surgery. Now he would have to continue alone.

Staring into the future was like staring at a wall. He had made and saved enough money to not worry about bills. He could pay for the hospital, for the funeral. If need be, he could support Naia; she didn't need him, though—she had graduated from nursing school and was living with a court translator in Montclair.

He was thirty-six years old and in reasonable shape. Yes, he had started to feel his age when he played, but in his mind, in some ways he'd never felt younger. The passion for learning that he had buried for years returning like a tide, rising up to roll back feelings he had locked up in a single word: ignorant. Even the sound, the way some folk said it, made it seem like just a different word for that other one.

His mother would have wanted him to go back to school. Basketball had been his world; looked at one way, that might seem like a good deal, and it was, especially for a black boy from the Bronx. But basketball was also a self-enclosed sphere of existence that could be suffocating. Besides, he could see that the sport was beginning a new chapter, one that Michael Jordan was going to make his own. The pages had already turned. He was a figure from the past, he never had a sneaker deal, didn't know you could have one. Give it a few seasons and the kids would barely recognize him or his name. The machine was moving on, into an Olympic stratosphere of international celebrity and wealth he had never conceived. He still felt lucky. He'd had a good run. He had made the best of the gifts of his body. The question was: What could he do with the other thing? What about the *mind*?

When he and Naia had gone through their mother's things, they had found, besides a study Bible, only two books. One was *The Bluest Eye*. Naia wanted that one, and it seemed natural he should take the other. It was an anthology with a strange title that appealed to him. *The Negro Caravan*. Flipping through it he found only one marking, beside a poem by Langston Hughes, where his mother had penciled in the words *what I want to know* next to the lines

When love is gone, O,

What can a young gal do?

He had never thought of reading poetry, and he felt a flush of shame that he didn't know it was important to his mother. Shame that he had never heard of most of the names in the *Caravan*, who had written all kinds of books, not just poetry, but stories, essays, theater, history. He resolved to get his learning, if he could.

He found a night-school program at City College. At first, it was very hard. He hadn't been in a classroom in so long and hadn't liked it the first time around. He worried that he would stick out, possibly even be recognized and embarrassed by professors or the other students. But the students in the class and the professors at the chalkboard didn't know who he was. They all knew he hooped. But that was on account of his height, not from having watched his games.

History was captivating. Nathaniel learned in detail about slavery and the Civil War, events and epochs he'd only ever had the vaguest notions about. He discovered that there were black writers and thinkers who had studied these things. He was genuinely astonished, and angered, that he had never heard of them before. While he was preparing his final paper, he discovered a history book in the library called *The Black Jacobins*. Something about the image of the black general on the cover intrigued him. He quickly realized from the first few pages that there was too much he didn't know for him to properly understand this Haitian hero, this clue, he thought, to his mother's heritage. The void created by her passing still lived within him. He found himself up late at night, pacing his room. He would stop and stare at the color photograph of himself that he kept on the wall over the TV. In the image he was suspended in air, driving to the hoop, his clover-green jersey rippling, his knees and arms held almost as if in a flying prayer, small beads of sweat on his forehead, his face locked in an expectant grimace. He couldn't stand to look at it anymore. He wanted to change everything, to be someone new. The Haitians had taken the French ideas and the French language and set themselves free. They had thrown the slave masters out and set about making a new world. He wanted to understand that, he wanted to get to the source of things. His stack of books grew, and his learning deepened. He enrolled in an intensive French language course at NYU and read history books as he rode the express trains up and down the length of Manhattan.

He had always wanted a reason to get out of the Bronx and see how things looked from somewhere else. Why not go to Haiti? As it happened, the island was in the news and the news wasn't good. He followed the coverage but couldn't understand enough of the politics to make sense of why there was so much chaos. US soldiers were leaping out of choppers and running through Port-au-Prince like they were still in Vietnam. It wasn't a time to visit. From his language class he learned that, if he paid a fee, he could enroll for a semester as a foreign student at the Sorbonne, in Paris. Obviously, he had the money. And the destination was romantic, an old ideal. It was where the Negro Caravan stopped on its voyage through the desert wilderness. He knew James Baldwin had gone there, Richard Wright, and others. Why couldn't he?

His first days in France were unpleasant and lonely, Nathaniel said. Perhaps, in retrospect, the loneliest days of his life. His classes had not yet begun, and in that first month he mostly encountered American tourists as he made pilgrimage stops at the city's famous monuments and museums. The Parisians were apparently elsewhere. Maybe on one of the far-flung, turquoise-ringed possessions advertised in the Métro that promised all-inclusive packages and discount airfare. The Americans dressed like they were going to the mall. He noticed that waiters, bus drivers, ticket booth operators, and strangers assumed that he was African. They always changed their expression when they heard his accent. Their faces brightened and relaxed as if a stink was gone. Apparently, in Paris his blackness was an African problem. They weren't afraid he was a criminal; they were afraid he was colonial. Never in his life could he have imagined constantly meeting people who were relieved to discover that he was a nigger.

Nathaniel had taken up residence in a small but comfortable room in a three-star hotel on the rue de Rivoli. He wanted to live in style, to have a place that did justice to his vision, or, since he had never before really entertained fantasies of living in Europe, to what he thought his friends and family back home would imagine when they pictured him living abroad in Paris. The image relayed back home and the need to control and manage it was important to him, even if it was unpleasant to think of it that way.

Still, living detached left him prey to certain doubts that had never crept to the forefront of his mind before. He thought of his mother often. Some days he woke alone, consumed with the fear that he was becoming ill. It was a new experience. Although he had suffered injuries, even a serious injury to his hamstring that the doctors thought might keep him out of the game, he had almost always enjoyed optimal health. He took pride in his physical form, in those indomitable qualities that he deployed at will to shake his adversaries. He had always been strong. But ailment was not the same thing as injury.

The only remedy he knew was the rope. He had used the same jump rope since he was sixteen years old. He got it from the manager of a boxing club that no longer existed, a dank, funky old place near the ballpark that was always incensed with a combination of cigar smoke, Pakistani leather, and freshly spilled sweat. People said Joe Louis had practiced there, and Sugar

Ray too. There were two sounds that attracted young Nate as boy on the streets. The whap of gloves rapping on the bags, and the crisp, metallic snap of skipping rope. Before long, he and his rope were virtually inseparable, his nirvana instrumental. Once he got started, he could keep time like a Rolex.

He never would have guessed his training would come in handy in Paris, but it did, one memorable day in September. After his last class of the day, he had tried to take the RER B, which he understood to be like an express train, back to his apartment. But he had ended up taking it in the wrong direction. He didn't realize his mistake until the train was pulling out of the Port Royal station, outbound towards the periphery. A crew had boarded at Port Royal and immediately headed for the far end of the carriage where he was sitting. One was black, three others Arab, the last one possibly Arab or white, it was hard to tell. They were obviously riled up, perhaps not unusually rowdy, but deliberately imposing on the other passengers. Just as the train pulled out of the following station, one of the posse members said something to a young woman who was facing away from them. After a moment the crew burst out laughing, and the same guy got up and stood over her.

There was time for Nathaniel to evaluate the situation. He was outnumbered, but he was also older and stronger than any of them individually by the looks of it. And he was black. Now the same kid was shouting at the woman, obviously telling her to answer him while she sat frozen and looking straight ahead. Furious at her defiance, the kid raised his hand to her, not with much force—more like a humiliating pat on the cheek. He was laughing. Instantly, she threw her arm up and hit him back. Stunned, he came back across her face, hard enough this time that her head audibly cracked as it met the thick plexiglass window of the train.

Nathaniel jumped out of his seat. The other travelers gasped and turned, pretending to see the situation for the first time. He marched right up to the kid so that anyone in the crew would have to get through him to the girl. "You need to back off, now," he said in English, putting a deep *Don't fuck with me* into it. The English surprised the kid, and he seemed to take a second to reconfigure the scene in his mind. "You heard me, step off." The crew was reacting with a mix of incredulity and hilarity, but they were also signaling that they were ready to back their words. Nathaniel readied himself for a blow. In a flash, the kid spit in his face. Nathaniel was so startled that he was slow to react to the first punch. It was a weak one, but the action had signaled the game on, and they jumped over the seats and started pummeling. Nathaniel lashed out, landing confused blows, trying to keep his eyes open, looking out for a knife. He cracked the tallest one with an elbow to the nose. But they surrounded him, kicking him on all sides so he couldn't get to them. The train was slowing. They all started shouting at once. The kid who had accosted the girl did exactly what Nathaniel had feared. He pulled out a knife. Nathaniel tensed, backing against the doorway. The black dude was telling his friend to chill with it. Nathaniel could see the plan forming. They'd stick him just as they pulled into the station, then book it. But they didn't have him pinned down; his chances were still good. Maybe he'd only get grazed. The brakes were whining. The whole train was coming to a nauseatingly slow stop on an embanked curve. The kid was still holding the knife pointed at Nathaniel's midsection. All he needed was a good lunge.

"Je vais te niquer ta race," the kid shouted, laughing and waving the blade. Then suddenly before the doors could open, he reached over to the girl and thrust his left arm out, putting her in a stranglehold. He put the blade up to her face. Nathaniel had seen enough to know what was said by tone. The put-down that compensates for what the knife won't do—this time. "Vas-y, je te laisse cette fois, t'es belle, petite salope." The doors opened. He let the girl go, and the whole crew jumped out. Nathaniel looked at the girl, then bolted. His heart was pounding. He could see them at the far end of the tracks turning off into a corridor. He sprinted as fast as he could, cursing between clenched teeth. He turned at the corridor; it was a long underground passageway. He could hear their shouts echoing from the far end. It was a straight line, nobody in the way. He put the run on like Jesse Owens, ducking his head, pumping. He reached a staircase leading up to the turnstiles. At the top of the stairs directly in front of him were the swinging pneumatic doors. He burst through them, ready to let all hell break loose. As he came out panting, he noticed figures in blue sweeping in from his peripherals. Two men with gloves and clubs tackled him from behind and sent him smack against the floor. They immediately kneeled on his back, pinning his chest to the ground so that he could barely breathe. One of them started beating him, cracking the baton over his legs and arms. They held him on the ground and told him to shut up while one of them spoke into a crackling radio. Nathaniel could feel the blood from his mouth pooling the cheek pressed to the ground and spilling out onto the cold floor in front of him. Out of the corner of his eye he could see the sneakers of the other members of the posse. They were lying facedown, side by side, with their hands behind their necks. Some more cops showed up with dogs, muzzled German shepherds yanking on their leashes. Commuters walked by, glanced without slowing down. Still more cops arrived, and long discussions ensued; everything was conducted in a dispassionate, even subdued manner, as if each of them really wished they were somewhere else. Finally, it was decided that the posse would be cuffed and taken out in a van. Then they cuffed Nathaniel and walked him out of the station, ducked him with great difficulty into the back of their blue Renault and took off.

At the police station Nathaniel couldn't do anything right. At first, he was so furious at being taken in at all that he refused to even try to speak in French and cursed loudly in English, at which point they threw him in a holding pen and told him he could wait there indefinitely for a translator. After a few hours, since no translator materialized, they decided to try again, and this time, Nathaniel, using his broken French, gave them his basic information. This only seemed to make them even more suspicious, convinced that he was an African trying to pass himself off as an American to avoid having to confess his illegal immigration. He wasn't carrying his passport, but he did keep a New York driver's license in his wallet. The officers passed the little plastic card around, making faces. No one asked him about the events on the train. They asked him about drugs. Then they simply told him he was going to continue being detained until they cleared things up and he was sent back to his holding cell.

He put his head in his arms and tried to sleep. He couldn't. Never in his whole life had he gone to jail. The only time he had ever even seen the inside of a police station was when he was seventeen and had gone with his mother down to the Forty-Second Precinct on Washington Avenue to pick up his uncle, who had been taken in on a domestic abuse complaint. His mother had told him then and he had never forgotten it: "Boy, don't you ever do anything in this city that might land you anywhere near a police station. You can't afford it. People disappear in this system. Don't matter what you did or say you did. Once they have you, they can make you go away. We love you. But we won't be able to do nothing for you. Once you in their hands, you belong to 'em. Right and wrong ain't got nothing to do with it. That's just how it is."

But that was before he became a star. He found himself laughing uncontrollably. These bastards have no idea, he thought. They've arrested an innocent man, an innocent black American who also happens to be a famous basketball player. And they had busted him for trying to be a Good Samaritan! If only he had a Topps card. He was detained for three more hours until finally an officer came in and led him out to the reception area. The girl from the train was standing at the desk talking to one of the officers. When she saw Nathaniel come out, she was visibly moved. After hearing her story, the police captain said he was satisfied that the man they were holding was not a criminal, but that he still needed to clear up some issues about his identity and background. The young woman told them she refused to leave until he was released. She insisted he be let out from the holding cell, so they moved him to a bench in the hall. She sat down next to him. It was then he realized that she looked familiar.

"Thank you," she whispered in English. "I'm sorry about all this."

"It's okay."

"Do you recognize me, from the university?"

"Yes, it's you—I've seen you, well, I saw you outside the tabac, the Ravaillac."

"Ah yes, everyone goes there . . . except you. I guess you don't smoke."

"Hell no! I'm an athlete—or I was—I seem to be out of shape. A few years ago I would have caught those guys easy. Taught them how we get down in the Bronx. I used to play basketball."

"Of course."

"Of course?"

"You're so tall. You stand out in the amphitheater. I'm not the only one who noticed. All the girls talk about you."

"Is that a fact?"

"This is so terrible. I'm so sorry they are treating you so bad. Nothing like this has ever happened to me before," she added after a moment. "My name is Laura. Laura Petrossian."

"Nathaniel Archimbald," he replied. "You can call me Nate. Hey, you know, your English is really excellent," he added after a moment.

She burst out laughing.

"Your French is very bad!"

❧

The university courses took place in a grand amphitheater with a waxy fug. A professor would stand center stage and discharge the lecture in rolling waves of latinate complexity. Laura's attendance was irregular, so Nathaniel never knew if he would see her. He was learning about the history of France, and Napoleon's conquests were carefully and rather lovingly examined for their triumphs of grandeur, cunning diplomacy, and personal hubris. Inevitably, Haiti came up, though more as a footnote than a fatal and world-altering check on French dominion. Nate was primed for this and eager to intervene. But this was not allowed of him, nor of any of the other students around him, who dutifully took down their notes in the same bemused, impassive way they took down everything else. But just hearing about the treacherous and dishonorable treatment of Toussaint Louverture made Nathaniel's blood boil. Every day after class, he needed a couple of hours just to decompress. He found a corner of the Tuileries Gardens where he could stretch and skip rope in the evening. His shoulder blades flexing, his posture proud and linear like one of the Louvre's Egyptian statues, his feet tapping like a ballerina, Nathaniel would skip rope staring with a severe, disciplined intensity. He strengthened himself in rhythm, murmuring to himself the names of his mother's ancestors, the heroes and generals of the Haitian Revolution. François Mackandal. Georges Biassou. Cécile Fatiman. Capois-La-Mort, the Black Achilles.

It was after such a session, returning in the evening to his hotel suite, when Nathaniel first met Claude, the new desk clerk on the nightshift. At first, Claude's English was so good it had Nathaniel suspecting he must have an American parent or attended an international school. But Claude smiled and insisted he had only taken the usual classes in school. Everything else he learned by listening to hip-hop.

When Claude learned that Nathaniel was from New York City, he was ecstatic. His whole face, round as it was already, glowed with excitement and admiration. His questions were endless. Nathaniel couldn't make an inch through the lobby without a symposium on the state of hip-hop, the situation in New York, the possibilities for blacks in America. Did he have a position on West vs. East? Biggie vs. Tupac?

The night clerk's queries took Nathaniel back. All the way back to the distant memory of his father's voice, and the voices of his friends scrapping around the blocks of Morrisania and Melrose, the Hub off Willis and 149th Street, the dead buildings that scorched the neighborhood, barbecues and summer jams, block parties. Night games on basketball courts where every drive to the hole was also a shot at someone's character. The rattle of subways and the smell of peanut butter crunch and musty bodegas. The sound of a watermelon-red Buick guzzling up Third Avenue, and girls in high-tops sitting on stoops, laughing, calling out his name. Nathaniel spent more and more evenings hanging out in the lobby with Claude late into the night. Within a few weeks, Claude had convinced him to leave the expensive hotel and move in with him and his friends in Maisons-Alfort, a suburb to the south of the city.

Nathaniel knew what living in what they called the banlieue meant. It was basically the hood. But he wanted to be around skinfolk at least some of the time he was abroad, and that was where they were at. It would also mean spending a tiny fraction of what he was spending on hotel luxuriance and room service. It was time to see what the Other Paris was about.

Claude was renting an apartment with two other West African friends on the eighth floor of a housing block. Their unit was in the bottom half of an L on the far side of six identical buildings that made up the Cité Lamartine. The buildings were joined by a barren concrete esplanade, along which several rows of scooters were always parked, and where there had once been a low-rise frontage for shops (most boarded up and closed down) and a kind of gravel extension where kids played soccer. In fact, there was only one business still open—Faisal's, a kind of café or tea shop run by Ahmed, an Egyptian, that served as the informal meeting room for the men of Cité Lamartine.

It was at Faisal's over Moroccan tea that the new roommates all met for the first time. Claude introduced Nathaniel as his American friend, which drew large smiles. He was introduced to Ghislain, a young man from Cameroon who worked as a cook in a Senegalese restaurant in the Marais. Then to Apollinaire, a slightly older Senegalese man, nearer to Nate in age, who had arrived in Paris almost ten years before, and who had a job working as a sanitation worker for the city. And Claude explained finally that he was French, born in Sarcelles, but that his parents were from the French island of Martinique. They toasted to a new beginning.

The apartment was small but functional. Nate had his own room, as did Claude, while Apollinaire and Ghislain agreed to share a room and pay less for their share of the rent. Nate had a window that faced out onto the scrubby outskirts of Maisons-Alfort, which consisted mostly of a car-and-motorcycle dealership, more apartment complexes, and a low, flat, boxy building, which turned out to be their local Leader Price grocery store. Claude's window faced the inside esplanade of the Cité, and in front of it, he had set up his decks, his mixer, and a synthesizer he had hooked up to a PC. His bed was often covered in clothes that he would mix and match, crisp outfits that he kept meticulously ordered in his mirrored closet. The rest of the room was devoted to his records and to the neat rainbow rows of a nice sneaker collection.

With his new friends and warmer living arrangement, things were falling into place. At the university, Nathaniel's heart always jumped when he spotted Laura entering the amphitheater. She would come over to him and meet his cheek with a warmly perfumed *bise*. They often paused to chat before class in one of the grand stairwells, a flirtatious islet in the hubbub of students streaming in and out of the lecture halls.

He continued to struggle with his coursework. His French was still pretty bad, as she had pointed out, although he found he could understand a good deal more than he could speak. But the professors certainly didn't make it easy. They had a way of talking about an idea or an event without ever really saying what they thought about it, or what had happened.

The history of Iceland, one professor seemed to argue, was crucial to understanding the origins of the French Revolution. Nathaniel had never thought about Iceland in his life, nor the people that lived there, and it occurred to him that had he not taken this particular course he most likely would have gone to his grave without ever even once having considered them. The professor said that one of the great human tragedies of the modern era took place on this tiny North Atlantic island. A period known as the *Mist Hardships,* which followed the eruption of the volcano Laki on June 8, 1783. This massive eruption, the professor explained, produced the closest thing to nuclear winter that anyone had ever experienced until Hiroshima. In Iceland, anyone living at that time would have believed it was the end of the world. Clouds of poisonous sulfur and ash blotted out the sun. Rivers of fire and falling molten rock set fire to the villages. The clouds of death spread to Europe. In London the fog of noxious gases made navigation of the Thames impossible. Laki's pall of doom generated extreme weather that spread chaotic and toxic conditions around the globe. In the winter of 1784, as far away as North America, the Mississippi froze at New Orleans, with icebergs spotted by bewildered slave and sugar traders in the Gulf of Mexico. The extreme weather lasted until 1788, when disastrous hailstorms put the final nail in the coffin of Europe's peasant underclass, causing widespread famine, notably in France, where passions stoked by the Jacobin intelligentsia set the house of Europe on fire, igniting a revolution that forever changed the course of history. Geography. Meteorology. The seasons of the Earth are as much an actor in History as any other force, the professor claimed. Even the origins of the French Revolution could be traced and explained, at least in part, by a spell of bad weather. A change of climate issuing from a dismal and humiliated island in the North Atlantic that no one cared about. History, the professor concluded, is a deep ditch of diabolical misfortune, out of which Man has always struggled to climb by filling the cavity with the bodies of other men somehow unlike him and using them as a ladder, only to discover that the bodies and the ditch are one and the same thing, and that nothing is more like oneself than one's enemy.

⸎

Nathaniel had recounted his story with Laura to his roommates. They listened and they offered their advice. "The women here are not trustworthy," Ghislain said. "You have to be very careful. Don't get involved in something you can't control, or you'll have problems and the police will come and deport you if they can, and if they can't, they will harass you so much you'll want to leave anyway." Apollinaire said that he had never been with a white woman, that he wasn't interested in white women, that every time he had ever interacted with a white woman it had only further confirmed his feelings. Ghislain passed around a joint. Claude said women were not something you could

110

know about one way or the other. You had to accept that and flow with it day by day and not judge them because, in the end, you can only judge yourself.

One evening, Laura invited Nate to dinner at her new apartment, a fifth-floor walk-up in an old building on the rue des Cinq-Diamants. You could see most of the place from the entryway. It was more of an attic with a kitchenette and a shower. She had a little oval window with a view of rooftops and potted chimneys and a patch of sky. It reminded Nathaniel of a painting that he had seen at the Musée d'Orsay.

Laura made grape leaves stuffed with ground lamb and rice in a mint yogurt sauce. They drank a bottle of burgundy with the meal, and a second one kept them talking late into the night. After clearing the dishes, she went over to the window where he stood and put her hand on his back. As he turned, she raised herself on her toes, leaned forward, and kissed him. It was a good kiss. Nathaniel found himself surprised at how safe he felt. He had wondered if he would actually be capable of feeling at peace in her arms. But he did. He had also feared a certain intimidation on her part. But she was without hesitation, as if the pleasures she would give and receive would have always been self-evident. If anything, he was the one who was slightly intimidated by her feistiness. How she strapped herself around his torso, pressing her dark nipples to his chest, nipped him with puckish kisses, came with unassuageable ferocity.

When he woke up, Nathaniel felt a cold breeze running along his arm. Laura was asleep, curled under the blanket like a teardrop. He got up. It had rained, and there was a puddle forming along the wall and the baseboard. He closed the window and glanced around the apartment. He ran some water and did the dishes. Then he brought the wine bottles down and slotted them one by one, with shattering cries, into a giant municipal-recycling container. He spotted a bakery. Laura looked confused when she opened the door to let him back in. "I brought you some breakfast," he said. He took the warm pastries out of their paper pouch and set them on the table. They spread spoonfuls of confiture along the innards and talked.

They decided to go for a walk in the Parc Montsouris. Nathaniel was convinced that the people they passed were staring at them. He thought for a long time about how to put this to Laura and wondered whether she was seeing the same thing. But by the time he had put together the words to ask her, they had crossed all the way through the park and arrived at the station where he would have to take the train back out to the suburbs. The way she held him as they kissed made putting it off indefinitely desirable.

"No life is really meaningful without good food. Without eating well. Without fish and rice and mango and okra, the world would be a mistake," Ghislain said. "There is no greater food to be found anywhere than in Cameroon, a land, thank god, blessed with the best fish and the freshest fruits in all of Africa. I must teach you how to cook real dishes from Yaoundé, which, if you prepare them only once for your lover, she will never leave you. Like Roger Milla, you will score every time!"

"What Ghislain is saying is wise, leke mo bax," said Apollinaire, "but not entirely true. The greatest food in the world, it is well known, comes from Senegal, which makes the finest sauces and the most raffiné cuisine in all of Africa. And the real way to a woman's heart is to make yassa with fresh catch from the Casamance caught by the excellent fishermen of Ziguinchor. Or a chicken mafé with a spicy peanut sauce that they also love in Mali. Or a delicious lamb dibi if she is more of a city girl and you want to show off the savors of the capital. Basically, love in a marriage should resemble a long meal, pleasantly sauced and served with care. That is, grosso modo, all there is to the good life."

"Taking a woman out to dinner can be expensive," said Claude. "If you cook for her you will save money, but she will also love you more because good in the kitchen means good appetite, which means good sex and good health, and if you can have all those things in your life at once then you must be doing something right with your life, because God bestows his favors and blessings on the just."

Nathaniel and Laura spent many nights together. And many days too, days when they were supposed to be in lecture but remained marooned in her blankets pleasuring each other in the quiet part of the afternoon when folks were still at work, and the traffic was light, and they could hear the leaves outside whisking greenly. He would hold the curves of her belly. Smell her olive-black hair, pressing into the pillow beside him like his picture in the history book of an old Roman aqueduct.

One day, on a square near the Métro Jourdain, he came upon a large poster on the side of a building of a starving African child. The eyes were sunk deep in their cavities, and the skin around the mouth was so taut to the jawbone that the expression was fixed in a tawdry, heinous smile. The slogans asked passersby to give, to fight, to support, to end hunger. He froze for a moment before the black-and-white advertisement.

Why was it always like this? A nameless starving African. And people going to work averting their eyes, the message assimilated, quietly disposed of. How much had really changed? The agency behind the poster had probably hired a marketing team to produce their campaign. They had offices in London, Geneva, Paris, and New York, and employed wealthy and upper-middle-class whites who could afford to live in the great cities and chose to take up more attractive volunteer work. The life behind the starving face had no substance or will. A fly crawling over the mind of Europe.

Nathaniel felt a swelling rage. There was such a vast canvas of injustice, bigger than he had ever previously imagined, worse the more he learned. All the knowledge he had acquired since he had moved abroad was coiling together, glowing hot as his own sense of futility increased. It was like the time when he stood in that awesome hallway in the Louvre, nearly deafened by the massive paintings on all sides, furious at the hollering mobs of tourists knocking into him with flagrant fouls. He was surrounded on all sides by pinkish angels and Madonnas and bearded saints with their marks of holiness, their place in history. But nowhere, in the entire palace, could he find a celebration of the goodness, the power, the intelligence, the glory of anyone who looked like him. Not one instance in all the sacred imagery of the Occident of a black man crowned with power and holiness.

And yet he felt especially peculiar, perhaps more alien than ever, when he passed the groups of young black teenagers huddled together in the gray wastelands in the city center at Les Halles. Boys who looked so familiar to him, and yet who regarded him with a wary curiosity. And he couldn't deny that this was, at least in part, because they (like whoever had built the hideous shopping-mall complex where they copped their cheap Euroburgers and chased skirt) seemed astonishingly indifferent to the flying buttresses of Saint-Eustache. A building whose old stone arches and spires filled him with awe.

At the top of the rue du Transvaal, there was an esplanade from which one could see the whole city spread out below. It was lovelier than the Bronx. It had art and aspiration. But did it have *soul*? Did it have a place for *his* arts? *Would the mind of Europe ever be able to incorporate him?* Just then, as if to banish any further thoughts, an overwhelming need to urinate came over him and he marched furtively down into the sketchy park below. There, he found a suitable tree and released a torrent which, in an alternate universe, he would have made gargantuan enough to drown every embassy, every sleek arms-dealing bureau, every petroleum office tower, every pompous government office building in the city of light.

The questions nagged at him. Could he love the woman and not her city? Could she ever love him across the vast gulf of experience that separated two people like them? What was it in her that he couldn't reach? What filled her with the sadness that he had detected from the very start, but that she wouldn't reveal or hadn't yet? He had seen the traces of that sadness. They could show themselves in anything or nothing at all. In the way she said, "Toss me a cigarette, I think there's one in my raincoat." Or those odd moments, he noticed, when she stared absently at her own hands. Sometimes when they fucked, he would catch a glimpse of her mouth biting at the air, uttering words that he couldn't understand, that he supposed were

Armenian, or maybe not even words at all but a lost or alternative alphabet accessed only in those fleeting moments when sex makes language strange again, keeping a part of the world secret, sacred, free from the will of men.

One night as they left a café in the Latin Quarter, Laura pulled on Nathaniel's arm, and said she wanted to talk. They moved off the boulevards and took the narrower, older streets. They came to the fountain square at Saint-Sulpice. One of the bell towers of the church was covered in scaffolding, the clasped fingers of planks and girders covering its massive, ghostly presence in a loose skin that rippled and ballooned gently in the wind.

Laura said she was thinking a lot about her brother, Mehdi. Nathaniel felt as if a jab had caught him in the ribs. "I didn't know you had a brother," he interrupted, stopping in his tracks for emphasis. She had never mentioned him before.

Laura stared at the pavement as she fished through her bag. "I'm sorry, I thought you would be overwhelmed because Mehdi adds a layer of complication to my life. He's really only my half brother, and he's Muslim. He stayed in Lebanon with an uncle. I haven't seen him since we left Beirut. We were very close before my parents took us away. I get letters from him sometimes, very beautiful letters in Arabic. He's a great writer. So good." She paused to light a cigarette. "My parents won't talk to him. My father never got over his decision to stay in Beirut or his disdain of science. Mehdi embraced religion and totally rejected Paris and the studies that my father wanted him to pursue. He said he didn't need the French to understand his place in the world or the universe that Allah set in motion. Sometimes I think he was right to want to stay. When I read his letters, I think about how long it's been since I've seen an olive tree. Just sunlight and an olive tree in a garden. The smell of cypress and lavender and the wooded closeness of earthly things."

They walked slowly up the rue Férou. Laura continued. "I thought God was real when I was little. One summer, my parents took us on a trip to the Sinai. We stayed with Bedouin in a camp by the Red Sea. In the distance on the water there was a city we were forbidden to go to. At night, one of the old Bedouin men took us away from the campfires and up into the dunes. His blue shesh was wrapped under his chin and his hands were very bony and strong. We rested on one of the highest dunes overlooking the camp, with Mehdi on one side of the old man and myself on the other. 'Look up,' he said. We looked into the deep and all that was there were the stars. The old man said, 'Look close,' and he lifted a hand into the darkness above. 'Do you see it?' And Mehdi said yes, he did. And I asked, 'What are we looking for?' And the old Bedouin laughed and tousled my hair roughly and then took my hand and made an arc with it through the middle of the sky. And then I did see it. A trail, a phantom plume like fog on a windshield. 'What is it?' I asked. The Bedouin said that it was the fingerprint of God. And then he said something that I didn't understand, but that Mehdi nodded to in agreement. He told us that men's fates were written in the stars. And then he coughed loudly and spit in the sand. He told us not to live dangerously. That danger was always a sign your life was out of balance. He told us to love life and to love Allah, who gave us the chance to know Him. Then he put his bony hand on my thigh and held it very hard, which scared me. He said it was necessary to live very close to Allah. 'In the cities, a life in accordance with the will of Allah is impossible,' he said. 'Only the desert nomad knows his ways and does not stray from the righteous path.' It was one of the most frightening experiences of my life," Laura said. "But I think about it often. And when I do, I think of Mehdi."

Back in the apartment on the rue des Cinq-Diamants, Laura undressed in the bathroom. When she came out, Nathaniel was lying naked on his stomach. She slipped down next to him and kissed him gently between the shoulder blades. Their bodies wanted as immoderately as ever. But something was there that was also different. The distress of brittle sex that is not as it once was.

9

The central stairwells of the Cité Lamartine formed a vertical chorus. All through the day, the crying of children, the muffled shouts, the scurrying whoops and shrieks of schoolchildren, the racket of scooters coming in through broken windows, the laughter and ritual greetings saturated the life on the landings and even in the spaces between them. Sisters, mothers, neighbors from every corner of the former colonial world raised up a babel from their impromptu salons, chatting, gossiping, arguing as they braided, twisted, brushed, picked, locked, roped, pressed, and prodded.

Behind this polyphonic hubbub, Nathaniel recognized a recorded music that amplified as he rose toward the upper floors. It was coming from the apartment next door, and he knew from his time at Faisal's that it was the extraordinary voice of Umm Kulthum. She sounded to Nathaniel like a blues singer. When he asked his African friends about her they told him, only half-jokingly, that her voice was the only thing the Arabs agreed upon. An experience of transcendent beauty that some, in moments of weakness (and near blasphemy), said even rivaled the surahs of the Qur'an. If the windows were open, and he knew that on a day like this they probably were, her call to her lover, her habibi, would carry out over the balcony, a faint wail reaching the ears of the kids playing soccer in the concrete lot.

Ghislain was cooking, and throughout the apartment there was a heavy aroma of okra stewing in peanut sauce. Nathaniel dropped two grocery bags in the kitchen and exchanged greetings with the chef. When the food was ready the four men sat down and ate by hand from a large bowl set in the center of the table equidistant from each of them. At first, they all ate in silence. Then they discussed their plans for the evening. Each of the roommates desired to know how Nathaniel's affairs were progressing with Laura, and if he had yet considered marriage. Ghislain produced cups and boiling mint tea, which he poured from very high without losing a drop. For a time, they drank in silence as they listened to the faint voice of Kulthum through the wall. "Nathaniel," Claude asked suddenly, changing the subject, "do you think one day there will be a black president of America?" Nathaniel felt as if he should have anticipated the question, even though he had no prepared thought on the matter. He looked around at the other men. They met his gaze gravely in a way that suggested they expected him to take some time to answer.

Nathaniel closed his eyes. For a moment his father's voice wavered in his mind. The time he had talked about Malcolm. Nathaniel was twenty the year they shot King down in Memphis. And the poet Henry Dumas just a month later, right there in Harlem. He hadn't taken it as badly as others had, certainly not as badly as his father. But that was before. That was then. Now he had taken more time to learn, to think and reflect. When he thought on it hard what he saw in his mind was dishonor. Too many nameless dead. Ship holds. Coffles. The deaths he had seen in his own lifetime. At Orangeburg over a bowling lane. At the hands of the police. He thought of the years of lynching. The faces smiling under the charred flesh of Jesse Washington down in Texas. He thought of the Freedmen betrayed in the Reconstruction. The long centuries before then, all under the whip of the founding fathers, as they took in their immeasurable lucre, built their empire westward, fiddled in their private Monticellos. He thought of all the brothers behind bars. The acquittals of officers, as regular and predictable as tides. Nathaniel opened his eyes. It was shocking to realize how powerfully he missed home. How the catalog of infamy that he had wanted, consciously or unconsciously, to run away from for so much of his life, to somehow ignore or work around, was still not powerful enough to keep him on the run forever. How strange it was to be here in this other land, in so many ways a better one, where he was seeing and understanding more than at any other time in his life, and yet his experiences, his study of history, all of it was only solidifying an itch he had repressed: a need to get back, to return home.

"No," he said finally, looking over at Claude, "I don't think there will be a black president in my lifetime." He thought a moment and added, "But that won't keep us from trying."

Of the three friends from Cité Lamartine, Apollinaire was the one Nathaniel had gotten to know the least. Yet the week before it all came to an end, they had shared a most intimate moment together, one that Nathaniel could never forget. Apollinaire had insisted they go for a drive. Nate had to practically crouch to get himself in the little green Simca, but once they were packed in they peeled out marvelously, swerving out of the projects with a beastly guzzle, accelerating along the wide boulevards extérieurs, crossing the arm of the Seine at Bercy, switching lanes, the suspension yawing as they darted through traffic. A wooden cross on a string of colored beads jangled in a syncopated dance over the dash.

"Open the glove box!" Apollinaire ordered, as he imperiled their lives in an attempt to light a pungent cigarillo. Nathaniel popped the notch and instantly, an avalanche of papers began flying into the back seat. Nathaniel quickly shut it again, but not before having nabbed one of the pages as it whipped past. Compiled with a wobbly ballpoint pen was a list with the heading *The Plot Against Africa*:

Jacques Foccart / François de Grossouvre / Paul Barril / Bob Denard / Étienne Léandri / Charles Pasqua / Félix-Roland Moumié / Bolloré / Outel Bono / Eduardo Mondlane / Herbert Chitepo / Amílcar Cabral / Dulcie September / Steve Biko / Patrice Lumumba / Thomas Sankara / Aginter Press / Robert Sobukwe / Union Minière du Haut-Katanga /

"Don't worry about that," Apollinaire said. "Just some research of mine. Look in there for my OK Jazz." Nathaniel rummaged through the papers at his feet and pulled out a plastic cassette box. *Franco et le Tout Puissant OK Jazz Band, Paris 1984.* The tape was a mess, looping out in a crazed tangle. Nathaniel stuck his pinky in one of the eyes, felt the teeth pinch his fingertip, wound it back till it was tight again, then shoved it in the car deck between their knees.

The twang of African guitars and Lingala poured out of the car stereo. Electrified guitars clanging Franco bellowing out with his chorus chiming in behind—*LIBERTÉ*—the guitar ringing out *eh pa! OK Jazz en forme* Apollinaire agreeing slapping the gearbox through second and third and fourth up the boulevard Leclerc—*LIBERTÉ*—Franco insisting on it the guitar chimes spilling over with a shattering clarity like diamonds in a briefcase on a flight from Goma to Kisangani to Antwerp like earrings chilling a glass countertop at De Beers—*LIBERTÉ*—Apollinaire gliding the whip expertly round the Place de la Nation the tires of the Simca skittering over the neatly combed cobblestone the two friends leaning magically in time muziki na biso—*LIBERTÉ*—in their wake the frown of disbelieving Gauls bopped on the head by the swinging congas of the Simca this African parrot green and raucous and loud her chassis screeching in bittersweet spasm—sweet *LIBERTÉ!!!*

"Ah voilà, mon ami. Nous sommes arrivés." Apollinaire brought the car to a stop by the side of the road just off the roundabout at Porte Dorée.

"My friend, I wanted to bring you here to tell you a story, to illustrate to you so you might know my situation. You see that telephone booth over there. That one. I used to sleep in it. No money, no job, nowhere to go. It was a very bad time. That café over there, I would go in there when they were closing and offer to clean their toilet in return for some bread and a glass of wine to help me sleep. At first the waiters just said no. But I came back again, and the barman who was very nice, he said okay, but just a few times, a week maybe. Then I had to go elsewhere. I was very scared. It was a very hard time. And then, my friend, a miracle happened. I met a woman. Here, right here, where we are now. Her name was Florèse. You see over there that great building? That is the Tropical Aquarium of Paris. That was where she worked. One evening when she came out, she saw me, and she saw how I had nothing. How I was scared. My friend, I was so ashamed. That was the first day, the first day of my life, I really began to believe in God. Florèse took me home with her. She lived just around the corner in a tiny room on the rue de l'Alouette. You know, I had not washed and I smelled so bad. But she didn't say anything. She gave me soap. I thought I was in heaven. I was so happy. I was sleeping on her floor. And I would lie there and think, this is the greatest gift God has given me. Florèse gave me life again, and I began to fall a little bit in love with her. During the days I would look for work. I found some small jobs but always in the evening I would come back. And I asked, 'Florèse, what can I do for you?'

"She had pain to her back when she worked. So she'd take me some evenings into the aquarium, secretly, when it was closed and there was no one. And I helped with her job. I was doing cleaning, washing things so she could rest. It was water all around us. We were alone under the ocean. Florèse knew all the fish and she would name them to me, like a goddess: gourami fish, green and pink Malabar fish, Picasso fish, Blue Hamlet fish. We would walk together and talk this way. And little by little I came to see two things. That Florèse was very intelligent, like a scientist or a saint. And that she was a woman who loved women. She was always talking about her lover. And even so, I know it's crazy, but I found myself falling deeply in love. I hid my feelings, of course! What could I do? Besides, we became good friends. It was Florèse who introduced me to the music of Franco and the Orchestre Kinshasa. And it was Florèse who opened me to poetry. She was always writing on her days off, and sometimes, if I was helping her, she would write during her shift while I mopped. She encouraged me to make my own poems. She said it helped when you were hungry. She said that when you write you do not feel the time so much, and I discovered this is true.

"Florèse gave me books to read and she taught me many words. I was changing and becoming better in many ways that had escaped me in my past. But the burning inside of my love would not go away, and I did not know what to do. Florèse wrote poems in Lingala for her lover who lives in Saint-Denis and is married to a very religious man. She would read her poems to me and try to teach me words from her language. And it stung me more than you can imagine, because I wanted to learn everything from Florèse. I wanted anything that was drawing us nearer to each other. It was Florèse who introduced me to Rabearivelo. Jean-Joseph, *mon frère austral*, who changed everything in me, whose poems I drank *coup sec* like cups of coffee at six in the morning. I would be hauling trash or moving crates in a warehouse and my mind would drift to the palm beaches of Madagascar, to campeachy trees and willowy filao, to the bars and taverns of Antananarivo. Florèse would read to me from his journals. And I suffered with him the pain of wanting to get away, to get to Paris at all costs, and yet desiring the fragrance of home only the more with each passing day. Florèse told me that it was Rabearivelo who gave her the courage to continue writing in the face of everything. Florèse was a great poet too. But she was hopelessly in love with a married woman. I knew from the tone of her poems, even though I couldn't understand most of them, that I would never be able to reveal my feelings for her.

"Then one day, the immigration police came and arrested her, right in front of everyone, all of her colleagues at the aquarium. It was terrible. Of course, there was no way I could see her, or find out if she was alright. I had to think of my own problems. Through contacts I learned that they had deported her. She had been working with false papers. Some people said that she had gotten them through Papa Wemba. I don't know if it is true. What I do know is that she made it back to Kinshasa, because about a month later a person from the community found me at the café and gave me a letter from Florèse postmarked from the Congo. In the letter she asked me to act as a courier, to discreetly forward her poems to her lover in Paris.

I wrote her back and promised her that I would take this job. Soon letters began arriving regularly from Kinshasa. Nathaniel, would you believe, to this day they come in thick envelopes with many stamps. And every couple of months I meet a woman I know nothing about, only her first name, and we always meet at the same café. I wait at a little table with letters from the woman I love in my hands, and her lover comes in and joins me. We talk about the weather and such things. She leaves a coin for the coffee, takes her packet, and leaves. This is what I owe Florèse. I have to do this for her. She saved me, out of the goodness and the strength of her heart. This is how I live, my friend. It is hard, very hard to live away from the people and the places that you know and love. My heart is not broken, but it is heavy. It is far away in the Congo where I know the most wonderful woman in the whole world is writing poems and love letters, but not for me."

⚔

Life in Paris came abruptly to an end. But when it did, Nathaniel did not find himself entirely surprised. It was as if there had been an off-ramp he knew was coming, and perhaps had even somehow wished into being. Still, he was deeply hurt that Laura never came to say goodbye. It was a friend of hers who delivered the message one day after classes. She simply said she was charged with telling him that Laura would not be coming to classes anymore and handed him a letter written on a loose sheet of quadrille paper. He knew what that letter meant even before reading it. And he had resolved, even before hearing out its arguments, to leave the country.

It turned out she was not only leaving him. Laura said in her note that she was heading to South America, that she needed to get away, and it was a trip she had always wanted to make. He took no comfort in her faint apologies, but he couldn't bring himself to hold the decision against her. After all, he had felt the same urges and made his own moves when he had the chance. Coming to Paris, he had wanted to acquire knowledge that he felt he lacked. He had learned enough. The affair with Laura, the life at

123

Cité Lamartine, the stories of Apollinaire, all the recent past took on the force of wisdom, the last of it dashed with pain. The whole freewheeling world be damned. He knew where he belonged. He wasn't going to hit the hardwood again. He was too old for that. But he could take the young boys from his neighborhood and teach them to play ball. He could live in the streets of New York with his people and hear those voices again and share those burdens and make something out of the places that made him. Mixed with the hurt that she didn't have the courage or the desire to confront him in person was an ironic sense of relief. He had lived the dream of a black man abroad in Paris. Now he had to complete the other half of that curious pilgrimage: return to the native land.

10

Under the high ceilings of a Tremont Avenue duplex, the young teacher and the retired hooper examined each other closely. Both had listened; both had talked. They enjoyed sharing memories. Across space and time they were connected by so many experiences that connected at odd angles, like crooked street corners. Nathaniel had let the floodgates open within. Talking brought relief and even a little thrill from realizing how crisp his recollection of those days remained.

They had indulged their inward feelings and most private remembrances in the manner of people who believe they will never meet again. Now there was a hesitant energy of expectation between them.

"I'm supposed to go down to South America soon," Jonah said suddenly. Nathaniel squinted, as he gauged this new knowledge.

"You serious?"

"Next week. Flying down to Rio with a friend."

"You mean for the summer?"

"I don't really know. I didn't buy a return ticket. I think what I want right now is just to get away from it all, just sort of be invisible . . ."

But he stopped because Nathaniel was chuckling to himself.

"You want to take off somewhere for a bit. Okay, and then what? It's chess out here, you gotta have at least one or two more moves than that!"

Jonah rubbed his temples.

"I mean, truthfully, I don't know that I'm cut out for this teaching thing. And there's all these places I never been before. I feel like if I don't get to them now, I never will. I'll get stuck in something, maybe something I don't even really like but that I feel like I *have* to do."

"I hear you. That's what *you* want. But just remember, at some point it's not going to be *about* you. At some point you're gonna have to make it about something bigger than that."

"Why?"

"*Why?*"

"Yeah, I mean no disrespect, but like, *why?*"

Something in the tone of this set Nathaniel on a different track. It wasn't that he didn't have enormous sympathy; in a way he'd been just the same even if their life chances had nothing to do with each other. But he couldn't shake the feeling rising in him now that this brother was off course.

"I'll tell you why. Because there's a city right here that needs help. There are children born in this city everyday who are being thrown to the lion's mouth. No education. No opportunities. Damn near half the kids who grew up on my block either dead or in jail, and everybody's lives scarred. You don't really know nothing about that, do you? You don't know what it feels like to look out every day on the same broken streets and know that if you can't play ball or rap, you never going nowhere. What you know about that?"

"I ain't arguing that though."

"You ain't arguing but you ain't saying nothing neither. And I'm calling you on your bullshit, pardon my French. You've had this amazing life. You've had this perspective. You have it all—the sheer *possibility* to do and be anything you want. Now you telling me all you can do is go hide somewhere with your Ellison blues? You gotta own up to some things. You a grown-ass man. It's time to take a look around and take this thing seriously, figure out the reality of the moment. I know that ain't easy. Trust me, I get it. It took me coming back here, back home, to see how privileged I was, and how much trouble my people, our people, are in. And it's deep. I know you're smart enough to *see* that. But do you *know* that?

"Well, I totally get where you're coming from, but see I feel like—"

"Excuse me, brother—but you educated. Not just educated, but worldly in ways most of our people will never get to be. Don't you see how important it is that you share that knowledge with a younger generation?"

"But that's the thing, why does it have to be *me*? You got the media, the corporations, the politicians—what the hell can I do? Nothing's gonna make a difference, so why not just get the hell out, at least go see something else before it all goes to shit, before like everyone in this fucked-up country, I lose my goddamn mind!"

"What I say about that cussing in my house?"

"My bad."

"That's okay, it's a fair point. You just wrongheaded about it is all. Are people's heads all messed up? Yeah. But that's exactly why you got to speak the truth. Why you gotta give it to 'em raw, uncut, straight to the gut—no bullshit. You got to call out the folks you know is wrong when they wrong, and do it right where you are, right *here* in the community, where it matters, where it *can* make a difference. It's like how I teach when I'm coaching. Talking to the kids about how you got to keep your head straight out here, think for yourself, respect yourself and your community. You don't think it matters that they see someone around them who has that message?"

"But they can't hear that message though."

"Nah, *you* the one not hearing the message. The truth always comes out on top. The best players can go cold, but they don't lose their shot. If you have it, soon enough it will manifest, and when it does, it's a wrap. These phony rappers out here today, flashing they cash and don't have no talent—they can't win the battle for these young minds forever. Not if you show them what else is possible."

"Yeah, but they got money and in this world that's all that counts."

"In the short run, yes. In the long run, no. Ask folks around here, they all want money. But there are lots of other things they want too. Lot of folks want to see they family together again. People want to feel respected and useful. Lot of folks want to see a world where children can be children and never worry about nothing bad happening to them. People want a place to honor their dead. Or make something beautiful that will last beyond their own life. There's all kinds of things."

"Then why does it all feel so hopeless?"

"I don't know, Teach, you tell me! All I know is that nothing good happens when you have no sense of history. No independent sense of values. When you caught up in the propaganda. Don't be fooled when they sell you on that 'We can do anything now' line. We can have all types of achievement. We always have. But it still don't shake out *for the people*. What that tells you is they got us in a funhouse. That tells me, if we're not careful, *we're going to lose our form. Because it can be lost. You feel me? I'm talking 'bout the things that give us shape, substance, form.* You know what I see when I look around? I see black jelly. All this rawness, all this raw energy that's beautiful but got no *direction*. Smuckers, motherfuckers. And you know what I think? I think that's exactly what the Man wants. He don't want you *thinking*. He don't want you knowing too much. Getting your bearings and deciding, on another level, how to *live*. No. He wants the formless energy of our blackness, seedless, no substance. Without form, without agency, without *power*."

"Black power—right, and how we supposed to get that? We've already seen how the Panther picture show ends."

"Well, the first thing is to stop abusing each other. The first thing would be committing ourselves to the point where we are incapable of taking each other's lives—because we *need* each other and *love* each other more than any differences that have come between us. We gotta quit playing ourselves. We gotta come together block by block and city by city to to work this thing out. We all agree that doing whatever it takes to change the basic situation is what needs to be done. And that's where *you* come in. That is exactly where you have a role to play."

"Wait, wait. But why *me?*"

"You a teacher, a natural. I've listened to how you talk. You have the ability to reach these kids. I can *see* it."

"They didn't hire me for my ability, they hired me 'cause no one else wants to do the job! They hired me because it looked good on an Excel table in an email someone had to forward to someone with the power to fire them. And, look, man, I don't even know that I'm *good* at it!"

"But you are *doing the right thing!* Instructing our young men and women. Giving them the understanding they need to get themselves up out of the mess they living in right now, the damn lies and confusion, all the media hype and the garbage that's being thrown at them and they don't even have a chance to form their own damn minds! Only reason I'm here is I was lucky enough to have talent. A rare gift, and then lucky to have all the breaks work in my favor. You have gifts too, and you have this great chance to make a way for others. Who's gonna do it if not you?"

"I don't know."

"*I don't know* . . . You scared. That it?"

"Nah, it ain't that. Like I said I just want to get out. I want out. Isn't that what you did?"

"It is what I did. But I also came back."

They both paused over this last point, which held different meanings for both of them.

"Listen," Nathaniel continued, "why don't you work *with me?* You can help me *right here* in the Bronx. I've got a nice program going. We coordinate with the schools, get the kids out playing ball in the sunshine, keep them away from the dope, the gangs, and the guns, all that shit. I could use a young guy like you, smart, fresh, ready to make a difference, to help out a little bit around here, you know."

"All that's fine, Nate. It really is. I really admire your program and what you're doing, and I do think it's important and all . . . but really . . . why does it have to be me? Why do I have to be the one to do it?"

"Simple. You have to take responsibility for your blackness."

"But . . ."

"You have to take responsibility for *our* people! If the ones like you that have it all won't do it, then no one will. Can't you see that?"

"But I don't want to! I don't want to do any of that! I don't want to be responsible, I just want to live my life!"

Nathaniel let this go without reply and an uncomfortable silence settled over them. In spite of what he was saying, Jonah thought of his students. He thought of B. and her dreams of getting into a fashion school and all the others who would have to continue without him, who would once again feel rejected and abandoned by the people they were told to trust. There was no way to say it, but he knew Nathaniel was right. He *was* scared. He just didn't know what he was scared of or why.

Nathaniel hadn't meant to get so worked up. "Hey, listen, Jonah. We not gonna solve the world's problems in a day. And nobody's saying it's *all* on you. Shit, I didn't mean to make it sound like you the Messiah, cause you damn sure ain't that!"

"I know, I'm sorry, I feel confused is all. I want to do what's right, it's just that . . ."

"Look, man, life will take its course. You're gonna do what you think is best for you, and that's okay. I'm just trying to give you some perspective from where I'm coming from. To remind you that at the end of the day we all gonna have to answer for our choices, what we done, and what we didn't choose to do. I'm just reminding you that you have the choice, the privilege and the choice, to do a lot of good, and if you don't know, well, now you know. All right?"

"All right."

"But yo—don't let me catch your faded ass downtown no more. I find out your black ass is still knockin' back drinks when you supposed to be teaching kids, it won't be no cops. I will come down and give you an ass-whoopin' myself! Fair?"

"Fair. I really do appreciate it, man. Getting me out of there."

"Ain't no thing, I know how to handle that type of situation. It's always nice to play the famous-ballplayer card on some city cops."

Jonah said that he should probably get going. Nathaniel didn't answer him immediately. He got up with a sigh and moved to the window. He stared out at the sky. It was a marvelous deep blue. The planes were shifting east over Queens; others were coming out of Newark flying up the West Side. So many planes, even now, he thought. Grains of light were prickling the dusk over the five boroughs, and the forked tongue of the Cross Bronx Expressway flickered more brightly. The Harlem River quivered. A line about the riverside from one of the hymns his mother loved came to him. *Old ship of Zion.* Old songs. Why did they always sound like history calling?

Nathaniel went into his office and pulled out a small paper envelope. It had lain there in a corner of his desk drawer for a long time. For a long time, he did not know what do with it, or why he had even composed it in the first place. But maybe it was for a moment just like this. He brought the unsealed envelope to Jonah and placed it carefully in his hands.

"Here, take this with you," he ordered. "You going anyway, so do me a favor and take it. If you find Laura somewhere down there, you'll give it to her. Most likely of course, you won't. And in that case, you can bring it back to me. That way I know I'll get to see you again. And you'll remember that you always have a reason to come back."

Jonah didn't refuse. He was moved by the gesture, by the great dignity in this man who had rescued him. It was an intimate gift, and even though it was awkward, he felt that he understood it in light of the stories and conversation they had exchanged on this extraordinary day. He understood that Nathaniel wanted to mark the occasion with some material token of its significance. It was a gesture of nobility and hope, and he felt unworthy of its aspirations.

"I'll hold on to it," he said simply.

They shook on it, and Nate gave him a bottle of water and an extra Advil for the long ride back to Brooklyn.

When he was alone again, Nathaniel would stare out at the city once more. He would think of what Laura would make of all this if she knew—how this kid had brought back to his mind with such force what they had shared, how close it all still felt, after all these years. But it was getting late. He still had phone calls to make and a late dinner to prepare. He had a group of kids to shepherd and tend to in the morning. The encounter with the lost Jonah would leave him feeling both young and old. Why this pull of remembrance? Why now, when he was past the time of life when it is possible to sincerely believe in new beginnings? But all beginnings are uncertain and hard to see. The coming of the night is not.

Back in the borough of Kings, Jonah pressed his key into the lock and stumbled wearily into the apartment. He knew before he had turned the corner into the living room that Isaac was around. He could hear the soft scratch of a record playing, something mid-century and bluesy. The mournful whine of a trumpet. Isaac was deep in the chair by the window, his chunky Dell laptop casting an eerie moonlit glow on his face.

"Hey man, I don't mean to get all on you and shit, but rent is due *to-morrow*."

"You're right. My bad, I'll get on it."

"Oh, and before I forget, you got another letter from that French girl— excuse me, *pardonnez-moi*, from your *mademoiselle*."

"Oh, yeah."

"Yeah, I put it on the desk in your room. You musta put something special on her, boy—she's really feelin' it, you got her jonesing for you long-distance. I mean, how many times she gotta write you before you go over there and do something about it?"

"Nah, man, it ain't even like that."

"Oh yeah, what's it like then?"

"Man, I don't know. If I did, I would tell you . . . Hey, is this Miles?"

"Nah, this Booker Little. My uncle Darren played trumpet for a while, knew all about the music. Always told me Booker was his favorite. No one knows how great he was, or how great he might have been 'cause he died so young. 'Bout our age, come to think of it. Cut some beautiful records before he left, though. Contributed his one little piece to the edifice, to the tradition. Played his part. See, I knew you would like this one."

"Oh yeah, how's that?"

"It's all about *you*, chief. It's called 'Man of Words.' And that's you, brother; just listen to that *there* . . . Now that's a blues for ya. A blues for the man of words."

PART TWO

Era bom
Aquele tempo em que eu vivia junto de você
Aquele tempo que se foi
—ELZA SOARES

I'm writing to you from the Hotel Rubens in Antwerp. Mariam came to visit me here last weekend. She wanted to party, so I took her out clubbing and we took ecstasy together. I'm still trying to process the whole experience. At one point we were dancing, touching each other's faces and laughing hysterically in a kind of feverish game. The music was shit but it didn't matter because I felt lucid and uncomplicated and happy. I didn't want it to stop. At first, I wasn't sure if Mariam wanted to go as far as I did. Only that we kept having this magnetic sense of wonder at each other's bodies. It was so hot and there were too many creeps trying to hit on us, so we left and walked back to my room. I never felt so beautiful. It wasn't just the sex, it was this energy ringing inside of me, this need to tell Mariam things I've never said before. I think I may have frightened her a bit. We didn't sleep at all, just stayed up in our bathrobes talking for hours. When it was light out, we went looking for breakfast pastries and ended up walking together through Nachtegalen Park in a cool leafy blur. I had this overwhelming desire to tell Mariam that I loved her. It's so hard to know what it would mean to be worthy of that word. I wondered whether our experience was honest, or if rolling together had created an artificial paradise that would evaporate as soon as she got back to London. I still have this unshakable worry that I'm not on Mariam's level. She always knows exactly what she wants. It's what makes her so hot. But she is so confident that it's hard for me sometimes to assert myself. I can tell she thinks she has to educate me. It angers me because I can show her things too. It's just that I'm too much in my head, always composing instead of playing. I'm under no illusion that Mariam couldn't get any lover she wants. But I don't want to be settled for. I don't want to be the one she's with just because I'm smarter than her other girlfriends—because I read books and they just watch television. I want her to want me because I'm desirable in every way. But should I have to prove it? If that's what it takes, I need time. But that's the problem.

I don't know if I have enough time before she loses patience or interest in me. And then I'll lose her. If things don't work out, it will be my fault. Do you think I'm afraid of letting myself truly have what I want? Am I sabotaging and dodging the very thing I seem to be pursuing? I ask you because I know you will answer me in your own sweet way by talking about something else. It's funny how the two of us are alike and also so different in our muddles. No one knows you like I do. I hope it's okay for me to say it like that. I feel like you will understand. You and I have this ability to talk across the world to each other, across everything that makes us so distant. I will always value that. But I also know there are some things that are only mine to discover, and some that are only yours. I need to find out what I really believe. I've got to find out about living for myself. I want to know how much of this world can be mine. I want to live all that I can. And if you still love me, you'll understand this, and you will know how to think of me no matter what.

—A

11

Closing your eyes when a jolt of turbulence rocks the cabin makes it worse. When the sucking feeling in his chest came, the temptation was to go dark, but he refused. Below the belly of the plane was the black Atlantic. According to the in-flight map, the little islands of Cape Verde and the tip of Africa at Dakar were somewhere out his window. They were crossing the great slave-shipping lanes now, cruising swiftly over the swollen past, the vast stretch of black-and-blue veins that sealed the fortunes of the Americas. In the greatest empire the world had ever seen, he had paid two hundred dollars for a tourist visa at the Brazilian Consulate on Forty-Second Street.

Jonah put down his book. At his side, Octavio was snoring peacefully, his eyes covered with an airline-issued sleeping mask. A paisley tie was flicked back over his shoulder and splashes of a lasagna dinner bloodied his shirt; on his lap, a weathered copy of the war diaries of José Martí was propped up on its pages like a general's tent.

Jonah had paid for the airfare with money from Uncle Vernon's will, but how long would the rest last on the ground?

A stewardess came up the aisle. There was another jolt, stronger this time, and Jonah flinched. His eyes were squeezed shut. He prayed, in the most secular way, for time to pass. Into his unpeaceful mind came a vision. At first, he thought it was the spirits of the holds, of the drowned, rocking the plane. But this struck him as an absurd, primitive fear. The spirit level, if it existed, wouldn't stand a chance against the computer-assisted engineering of Boeing. So why then, of all things, was he moaning? Why did his moaning seem not his own as it swelled? He felt a cold heat starting in the pit of the stomach and rising up through his chest. Let it be. A surrender of the body, the pure flame giving up. For a moment it was the peace of weightlessness. And then, against every conviction, he felt them as they passed through, rushing onward in a shimmering grotesque and clanging with languages he had no tongue for. They passed eastward into the night leaving behind a cavernous emptiness. Their fading cries, sending for him, sounded like warnings. Against what? The unavoidable, for it was too late. She was already upon him, moving out of the roiling depths, a giant shadow living within the shadows. Her great rim closed in overhead and the ocean gave way to a living hold. A home within the darkwater.

He came to in a fright. The plane was still. He was safe. Around him rows of bodies were slumped in their cushioned seats, absently focused on pale screens. There was a soft ping. Seatbelt lights.

On the ground, Rio de Janeiro was a new world. Verdant pockets of lush floral beauty smashed into the concrete of mid-century bank towers, which in turn towered over baroque colonial ruins. The street life was teeming, overflowing, hot; a bouillon concentrated in the countless outdoor bars, cafés, and hole-in-the-wall eateries where raucous Cariocas gathered around glasses of beer served bem gelada from tall garrafas sweating in their cold sleeves. Jonah noticed the abdundance of popcorn carts, little trolleys in the zany intersections attended by sad-faced men. The sound of Portuguese was almost unbearably sweet, like a caramelized French. Jonah scrambled to jot down lists of words as they came up—pipoca, "popcorn"—but the new language poured easily through Octavio. He churned it right back out, a bit choppy, but alive to its unique rhythms and intonations.

Octavio had directions for how to get to the apartment where Barthes was staying, but they were clearly wrong. Someone had cherry-picked the intelligence. A thrashing rain started coming down and it was getting dark, so they ducked into a bar to wait out the worst of it and give Octavio some time to try and formulate a better plan. Plump men idled at the counter, scanning the street front or watching the mounted television in the corner. Jonah watched the flickering box, inferring content from the images. Commentators were shouting hysterically over soccer replays. Then a news segment came on about an upsurge of violence. A "pacification" operation was in effect across the city and state in support of the Pan American Games. The toll was apparently high, several police injuries and many deaths among the traficantes, drug dealers. Octavio had figured out how to get a telephone card and ducked out to use one of the Skittle-colored booths to call Barthes. He came back with a confident swagger, proud that he had gotten them back on track.

The new orders involved a long walk, at one point taking them along a highway, which cut underneath a mountain covered in shantytown constructions that Octavio pointed out to him were the "favelas." They followed a narrow walkway caught in the violent tangerine glare of oncoming traffic. By the time they emerged the rain had finally passed, and you could see the stars again, pinholes in the tropical night.

They came to yet another beach, long and brightly lit like a bracelet studded with empty café tables facing the ocean. There was a faint smell of rotting fish in the air. On one of the beachfront terraces, Jonah watched a middle-aged American couple as they struggled to order their drinks. Splotches of rose branded their arms and calves. It was the first time, he realized, that he was somewhere nobody would find his complexion remarkable. Now *they* were the minority, pinkish flotsam in a sea of honey, brown, and black.

Dark-skinned women in heels walked distractedly back and forth in front of the hotels. Street vendors hawked anything on which they could print a Brazilian flag. A group of younger men came up from the beach laughing loudly and jabbing at each other. Hotel staffers in drab uniforms wandered in and out of their establishments, verifying things, making rounds, and scanning the beachfront expectantly. Begging children came asking for money and food. A shirtless boy in ragged shorts asked Jonah for a cigarette. He hesitated, then gave him one.

Barthes had a room in a condominium tower on the rua Gustavo Sampaio in what appeared to be, from what they had seen, one of the ugliest parts of the city. When they rang her bell, she cracked open the door and then, seeing it was them, threw her arms around Octavio, greeting them both in the familiar, bubbly Esperanto of American collegiate irony.

Jonah recognized Barthes immediately, right down to the way she swept her sandy blond hair under a bandanna. She had worn one around campus, as he recalled, a sign of alternativeness balanced out by pastel monochromes from American Apparel. Her place in Rio was really a studio, which meant the guests would sleep in a corner that Barthes had padded with some blankets and sleeping bags. Octavio noted that her minimal adornments to her pad reminded him of the tribal-patterned accent pillows and throws she had used to disguise the institutional prefab of her dorm room. Barthes said something sharp in Portuguese that Jonah didn't understand. Somewhere along the line, she had acquired a confidence that Octavio hadn't counted on, one that could not be reconciled with the geeky moniker he had pinned on her.

Back home, she was Maggie Reynolds from Newton, Massachusetts. But in Rio de Janeiro, she went by her middle name, Grace, converted locally to Gracia. She seemed not entirely displeased to have Octavio and Jonah visit. Aside from the ex-boyfriend situation. The history with Octavio—or what remained of that history—was likely to prove "complicated." Already, they were reprising a familiar game with each other, their banter sandpapery, with quips and ripostes over small talk that were clearly arbitrating much else besides.

The studio room only had one window and it faced the favela of Chapéu Mangueira. During the day, music and the sound of construction work on a little botequim, a bodega that sold dry goods and fresh tropical fruit, came up from the bottom of the hill. The first time Jonah heard gunfire he almost convinced himself it was a firecracker. But the report was too acute, and it happened too regularly, rhythmically even, so that eventually you could even decode warning shots: a sharp pop with a loud echo shattering the night, then one shot in reply, then silence.

Barthes was always up at dawn and heading out to far-flung corners of the city for her work. Octavio and Jonah would wake closer to noon, and usually began the day by roaming in search of a place to eat. At first it was difficult to get around, on account of the complexity of the bus system and the perilous street traffic. But once they learned how to give and receive the thumbs-up, a gesture of subtle significance and usage, everything else about the city became strangely logical. In Laranjeiras they spent an afternoon going down the menu of one of the thousands of juice bars, many of which offered fruits they had never heard of before.

Barthes only worked three days a week, so on her days off she showed the boys around the city. Octavio refused categorically to be taken anywhere "touristic," nixing the Sugarloaf, the *Christ Redeemer*, and the grand beach at Copacabana. This was agreeable to Barthes, and she walked them instead through random commercial shopping centers, and through the dense streets and public squares behind the old theater in the city center. They were a trio now—a bande à part, Jonah thought—living beyond the reach of family, of internships and institutions, beyond responsibility. That was how he wanted to see it.

One day they took a commuter bus out across a long causeway to Niterói, a neighborhood on the eastern shore of Guanabara Bay. Octavio and Barthes sat next to each other, arguing; really Octavio was arguing while Barthes looked away furtively in despair. Jonah sat behind them gazing out over the traffic and the fast-food chains and the ocean. He was keenly aware that things were not as simple as Octavio had claimed they would be. Like all ex-lovers, these two were united in an unhappy need to pluck at the strings of the other's desire. Octavio was constantly teasing, but Barthes parried handily. It looked like no matter which way things went, Jonah was going to be left holding the candlestick, as the French liked to say, a result he had dimly predicted without ever resolving what to do when it came up.

The beach at Niterói faced back toward the city, so you could make out all the different neighborhoods with their cream-colored high-rises tucked between the green mountains, and the reddish bric-a-brac of the favelas atop the green. Octavio spread himself facedown in the sand while Barthes installed herself on a beach towel and opened a tome on microcredit financing in the developing world. Jonah had with him a pocket-size volume of poems in Portuguese by João Cabral de Melo Neto that he had picked up in a bookstore in Centro.

He was fairly sure that the poem that had caught his eye when he was browsing, and that he now turned to again, was about the world coming to an end. Melo Neto said the world would end in a melancholy of indifferent men reading newspapers. One line was clear to him: "the final poem nobody would write." But what was the final poem? Was it the melancholy world itself? Was it the words in the newspapers read by indifferent men? Was it some other poem entirely, one written for whatever people were left, who didn't read newspapers but still wanted to get the news from poetry? Perhaps the world ended within the poem and the reader was one of the melancholy men waiting for something that has already happened?

When his eyes tired of the page he watched the ocean. A Petrobras supertanker showed its stenciled letters against a block of orange rust. Octavio ran down to the water and dove in, his body splitting the blue like a porpoise. Barthes applied sunscreen. After a moment, she looked over and pointed the bottle in Jonah's direction.

"No thanks, I'm good for now."

"No, dummy, on me. Get my back."

She presented herself to his touch and pulled down her straps. As he was finishing, a group of European-looking young women set up their towels and beach chairs nearby. Reclining on his side, ostensibly keeping his eyes on the book lying on the towel, Jonah tried to identify what language they were speaking, but their voices were carried downwind and he couldn't make it out. He tried to read more poetry. The poet was like an engineer, said Melo Neto, or the poem itself should be neat and clearly delineated like a tennis court, or perhaps it was precisely these things that poetry was not.

Octavio was rejuvenating himself in the sea. The salt on his shoulders flashed in the sun as he thrust himself through the waves. A Brazilian man had joined the European women near their spot. He laughed with them while he took off his shirt. He was wearing a black Brazilian-style Speedo that ended at mid-thigh, and, around his neck, a thin gold chain. He stood watching over the women with his arms crossed and his feet planted beneath his shoulders, like a lifeguard. Jonah had never seen such a perfect man, not in the sense necessarily of absolute beauty, but of masculine ideal. He was chiseled, his hair cropped and trim, his skin dark—darker than Jonah's and with a glowing vermelho in it. Handsome in the inimitable, charismatic way of black men. Barthes was looking at him too, over the spine of her textbook. Jonah glanced at her breasts. They were small, not flat really, but diminutive. She still had an adolescent figure. Just then Octavio came crashing into view, dripping all over Barthes's books and tearing towels away to dry himself. Barthes looked up from her reading.

"How was the water?"

"Spectacular," said Octavio. "You need to stop all this reading, it's unhealthy, we're in Rio, try and act the—"

"The water is filthy," Barthes cut in. "They drop raw sewage in there for miles up the coast, so do me a favor and don't touch me." Instead of following her orders, Octavio came after her. Barthes refused to scream as Octavio wrestled and tussled with her in the sand and Jonah remained neutral until they kicked up sand in his face. He noticed the Brazilian man looking over. He didn't seem bothered at all, just indifferent, as if he expected the foreigners to be exactly what they were.

On the bus on the way back Jonah felt sick. The couple sat in front of him bickering. Or at least Jonah thought they were bickering. But then after a while, to his astonishment, Barthes's head was resting on Octavio's shoulder, and he had placed an arm around her and was whispering something, or really kissing her softly, his face buried in her hair. To feel alone in the company of quarreling lovers is not the worst kind of solitude, Jonah thought. But few things are more grating to the demands of ego than to be alone in the presence of their reconciliation.

12

About a week after their arrival, Barthes invited them to a beach picnic her NGO had organized for her students. When Jonah and Octavio arrived, they found the young woman everyone called Gracia surrounded by a circle of kids and assistants handing out pieces of fruit, small sandwiches, and potato chips. Barthes was radiant. The sun was shimmering in her hair; she seemed less pale and twiggy, full of a raw vitality she hadn't yet fully displayed in their presence. She was wearing bangles and colored bracelets and she laughed easily with the kids as she played with them, chasing them around in the sand. Jonah and Octavio joined them and ate hungrily like little boys, and then Octavio got a game of soccer going.

The three friends played against five younger and more skilled kids who threw themselves across the sand diving and dribbling while the Americans tried to keep up. Octavio scored just enough to keep them in the game. After one goal Jonah saw him looking at Barthes and thought he saw a glimmer of relief, a look that said—*Why haven't you always been this way?*—and—*I knew you were like this all along*—and—*This is how I like you*—and for the first time it was clear to him that their abrasion against each other had also polished them like lenses. This in no way assured they would always be together, or even that they would always be there for each other in times of need; but it had fostered in them an inconvenient conviction that no other person would ever understand them so well, that all other relationships, even happier ones, must suffer a little for their comparative misalignment.

It was getting dark, and Barthes announced that she would be accompanying two of her students, Taìs and Angelica, back to their homes in the favelas. Octavio quickly insisted on joining them, which meant that Jonah would have to go as well. They all caught a van on Avenida Atlântica and headed north in rapid bursts, swerving over as the fare handler threw open the door, crying out a string of destinations, and hustling more rides. Along the way, Taìs and Angelica quizzed the young men on their sightseeing accomplishments and were tickled that they had been in Rio for weeks without visiting the *Christ Redeemer*, or the famous Lapa steps where Snoop Dogg and Pharrell filmed the music video for "Beautiful."

By the time they reached their stop night had fallen. In the increasingly narrow lanes where they were walking, the streetlights either hadn't come on yet or someone had disabled them so that they never would. Barthes was walking ahead with Octavio and Taìs, who had taken him by the hand, while Angelica walked quietly at Jonah's side. A moped driven by a young man, carrying an older woman with some grocery bags behind him, squirreled past noisily. Octavio was becoming quieter as Barthes, ever sure-footed, marched them up to what they could see was the beginning of the favela. They climbed a long flight of stairs in near darkness. At the top Jonah looked back and saw the twinkling lights of the city strung out below in undulating waves. They had passed the first low brick constructions when he heard the click. Two boys came out of the shadows with long guns dangling casually at their sides. Their faces were sullen. Barthes was pointing at the Americans, signaling they were her friends. One of the boys lifted his weapon at Octavio's head. Then he swiveled and pointed the muzzle into Jonah's face. He stared at the mouth of the gun. A half inch squeeze of a finger the only thing it needed. Here it was, Jonah thought. The end of the world, and it would be their own names in the newspapers being read by indifferent men. Jonah couldn't understand the gun boy's words, but he understood what he was saying perfectly. *You shouldn't be here.* Then Octavio spoke up. Instantly the barrel swiveled upon him.

It seemed something bad might happen then; even Barthes began to lose her composure, her voice breaking into a panicked plea. But the boys, excited by the presence of Americans, were tripping on Hollywood now, calling Octavio "Taxi Driver," toying with the muzzles as they cackled to an improvised version of De Niro's lines. Perhaps Angelica felt how stricken Jonah was with fear, or perhaps she simply felt momentarily more mature than the clearly floundering adults around her. She must have passed through checkpoints every day of her life, and here these Americans couldn't even do it once. She grabbed Jonah's hand, gripped it tight, and spoke to the gun boys in a tiny voice. When he heard her name, the boy with the gun shouted in surprise and lowered the Kalashnikov enough to signal a détente. Angelica talked with the boys for a minute. They were asking about her family. After a moment, they shrugged, gave a thumbs-up, and waved them all through, laughing.

Jonah's legs felt heavy; his jaw clenched. His hands were trembling, but he focused on his pace, on keeping it even and rigid. Tripping over a stone, making any false movement, anything unpredictable or unexplained might set off a nervous trigger finger attached to a boy who was high and hearing things. It was worse with the boys behind them now. The feeling of a gun possibly aimed at the back of one's head.

They moved deeper into the favela, rising along narrow streets that were lit in spots and where there was more life and the sounds of children and babies crying and hundreds of families preparing dinners. They dropped Taís off first, and then made their way to Angelica's home.

Angelica's mother, who addressed Barthes as though she was part of the family, insisted they all stay for dinner. An aunt was helping to cook some chicken and rice. In the far corner Angelica's older brother was sitting on a wooden stool watching a soap opera about drug lords and their love lives on Globo, apparently the only television station in Brazil. Angelica helped her mother and her aunt and brought them soft drinks. The older women spoke with Barthes as though she were saintly. Not a spiritual saint, not a figure of salvation, but *saintly* in her ability to do no harm, to say nothing wrong, to bring only good. Did Barthes feel that way? Sometimes it seemed to Jonah as if she was driven by a tremendous guilt that she had recast in an armor of irreproachability.

While the visitors ate, Angelica looked up from time to time and asked the Americans to teach her new words for the things they were eating. Octavio talked animatedly with Angelica's mother, showing off his Portuguese and trying to make a good impression. Despite the terror of the ascent, there was a spectacular peacefulness in Angelica's home. It looked out over a ziggurat of corrugated roofing and down to the bright lights of the city below. A balmy breeze lilted inland from the ocean.

After dinner, Angelica and her mother thanked the visitors profusely for coming to visit and made them promise to come back. When they stepped back into the alleyways, Jonah noticed that his eyes had adjusted to the darkness. The favela cascaded down below like a river winking with isolated lamps. Somewhere farther above in the honeycomb, the distinctive propellant of American rap sent down snapping echoes of growling bass and syncopated voices interlocking call and response.

They followed Barthes back down a different path that took them into a gully and then across a narrow walkway made of wooden planks and back up a new set of stairs as they made their way along the side of the neighboring hill. They came up to a small roundabout with streetcar tracks. Largo das Neves. The Square of Snows. A strange name for a roundabout in these parts, Jonah thought. The night, with its sudden brushes with death and pockets of eerie tranquility, had turned surreal. His mind jumped from Nas rapping from the point of view of the gun to Villon's *mais où sont les neiges d'antan?* Criminal lingo for those in the know. Bold steel shoved in your face runs the blood hot; the mind ice-cold. Enough of this, Jonah thought, and Rio would get to feeling like Paris in January.

They were ambling gingerly now through streets marked by snaking entranceways to baroque and once ornate villas that were now caving in on themselves and smothered in knotted arboreal growth. They passed a disquieting mauve facade. Barthes said it used to be a dance hall where people came for the Samba de Gafieira and stayed late into the night. There were plans to reopen it, she said, as a hookah lounge.

Eventually they arrived in the neighborhood of Catumbi, where Barthes's friend Teresa lived. Barthes had met her at the Universidade Federal, where she took her language classes, and Teresa had more or less become Barthes's best friend in Rio. Teresa's house was set back from the road and covered with a fragrant mousse of flowers. Laundry was hanging from the fruit trees on her porch. Inside, an older man with a wizened head of dreads pulled back tightly in rows was rolling a joint on a mouse pad. Teresa introduced him as her boyfriend Lazaro. He was studying sociology at the State University, trying to document the living conditions of street kids. He smiled quickly and easily and talked in measured tones, often lingering on phrases in English, which he spoke quite well, as he worked the green buds between his thumb and forefinger.

The friends made a small circle on the floor, and Lazaro slid in a CD on his computer and lit up the joint as the samba of Cartola filled the room. Octavio asked Lazaro if he could recommend any Brazilian writers for them to read. Lazaro went into his bedroom and came out with a novel by Clarice Lispector for Octavio and one by Machado de Assis, which he handed to Jonah. *Memórias póstumas de Brás Cubas.* Lazaro explained that Machado was one of the greatest Brazilian writers. A black man. Jonah looked up, met the other man's fixed gaze, and nodded with grave approval.

This ceremonious moment led Lazaro to initiate a long conversation about Brazil and the way it had become a lagoon within the ocean of world literature. He was also deeply versed in candomblé and explained that he had written a paper about Nina Rodrigues's anthropological studies on the religious practices of the Africans in Bahia, but so far had been unable to publish it. Given his paltry understanding of the deities whose exotic names Lazaro invoked, Jonah could barely make out what he was saying. But Octavio was deeply enraptured and kept pressing Lazaro for more, occasionally exclaiming in Spanish as he recognized the equivalent of a certain figure or ritual he knew by a Cuban alias.

Teresa held the joint precariously and learnedly, tilting her neck way back, as she steered their talk back in a direction Jonah could more readily follow: the Brazilian cinema of the sixties and seventies, the brilliant madness of Glauber Rocha. The Americans listened intently, and Lazaro nimbly set about preparing more smoke. By the second round, the conversation had gotten predictably hazy and garbled. Teresa, Lazaro, and Barthes were slipping more and more back into Portuguese. Octavio seemed annoyed at his inability to keep up. He started tugging at Barthes's sleeve and when she pushed him away, they got into a playfully sloppy tussle. Teresa started hooting and yelling at them to get a room already. Everyone was high.

A long report of gunshots crackled through the house. There was a second of silence. Then more gunfire, louder, traveling in bursting echoes. Lazaro shoved the Americans to the ground. There were two loud bangs, then the sound of cries and the helter-skelter of human feet as a new hail of machine-gun fire sweltered the air with deafening metallic impact. People were screaming. Single shots ricocheted, loud enough to come through distinctly above the fray. Jonah looked over at Octavio. He was holding Barthes against him, covering her head with his hands. He looked over at Lazaro, who said something, but the gunfire came again even louder, and he couldn't make it out. There were more screams, some close and some distant, disconnected, lost to each other, coming from indeterminate corners of the night. Then it got quiet. Lazaro looked over. "Catumbi," he said, without lifting his head.

A tinny voice barked through a loudspeaker. It was coming from the top of an armored vehicle, climbing like a beetle up through the favela. They could hear crying now. Above all, they heard the voices of women screaming, calling names. The armored car was close, and they could hear the heavy diesel motor changing gears. The samba was still playing, and Cartola continued his song:

. . . Mas o pranto em Mangueira
É tão diferente
É um pranto sem lenço
Que alegra agente . . .

Jonah thought of Angelica hiding on the floor clasped in her mother's arms. Of her being shot, or, more likely, it occurred to him, her brother being shot. Was this the cleanup operation for the Pan American Games? There was an astonishing quiet for a time, with only sporadic, isolated shouts. But as the machinery of the military police receded again, someone somewhere in Catumbi turned the rap back up.

Barthes, who hadn't quite lost her composure, said calmly that they should go home. The acrid smell of the firefight was in the air, and there was an ambient tension all around them. Men shouted at each other in the darkness, and the sudden beam of search-patrol lights and gleaming muzzles clasped by paramilitary forces in balaclavas seemed to emerge from the darkness swift as roaches. Jonah and Octavio walked directly behind Barthes single file, at her own recommendation, as she was least likely to trigger a nervous shot. She had dealt with patrols before and she had a set pattern of phrases in both Portuguese and English to signal that they were American tourists. The soldiers barked at them and instructed them to proceed in the direction they were already heading. The sound of children crying came from the maze of shadows.

It was dawn by the time they got back to the rua Gustavo Sampaio. Coconut vendors were setting up their stands and adjusting their displays. Joggers headed out for their morning runs on Copacabana Beach.

13

wo days later, Teresa invited the three friends on an outing to an area
south of Rio that was renowned for its beaches and popular with the
locals, who preferred to avoid the iconic waterfronts like Ipanema.
Everyone agreed it would be good to get out of the city.

They piled into Teresa's blue Volkswagen Beetle and headed south on
the highway, rounding the favela of Rocinha, then jetting past unfinished
condominiums, the New York City Center on the Avenida das Américas,
and the guarded entrances of gated communities built on the landfill of a
newly dredged lagoon. The road broke away into higher altitudes as they
followed the coastline, and the massive relief of the land came sharply into
view. The green counterforts and protrusions guided them along, thumbing
grandly into the glittering sheen of the ocean. The magnificent voice of Elza
Soares and her *bossa negra* poured out of the car stereo hooked up to Teresa's
new iPod. Barthes's spangled hair kept flicking past the headrest. The sun
rushed the windows. Below them the ocean spread to the horizon, and they
descended gradually toward it.

When they arrived at the far end of a mostly unoccupied beachfront,
Lazaro went down to the water with Octavio and Barthes, leaving Teresa
and Jonah to set up the picnic. As they were waiting on the blanket with the

spread, she suddenly turned to him and asked in her broken English, "So, what you think of Brazil?"

He had sensed a question like that coming but didn't have a good answer worked out.

"I love it," he said after a moment.

"You love it."

"I mean, I love the atmosphere, I guess. The people, the life."

"The shooting, you love it too?"

"No. It's true, that was pretty bad."

"For us, it's like this . . . from forever. We are more used to it than you. I saw you were very afraid. Yes, you were very afraid. It was a lot of shooting for you, I think."

They had finished setting up the spread and Teresa was sitting in lotus position now at one edge of their checkered blanket, rolling trees.

"It was a lot; I'm not going to lie. I was scared—weren't you?"

"Mmm, yes . . . but, how you say . . . I'm coming from here, so it's my home. I know the favela . . . I know what can happen, but I am always walking in my beliefs. Like God, he is watching for me . . . Look, you see how it says?"

She was pointing now to a tattoo done in an italic script running along the inside arch of her foot.

"In faith."

"Faith? Yes, I am walking always in faith . . . I have it here with me. And I am not afraid for this. But *for you*, I think, I am afraid."

At this she laughed, and he felt the playful warmth of it rousing him.

"Are you believing?" she asked, grave again, but looking past him toward the shrieking and laughter coming over the waves. "Are you walking with God too?"

This brought him up sharply, and he considered whether to take the time to ask himself and then tell her what he genuinely believed, or to tell her what he thought she would want to hear, except that he realized he couldn't entirely know what that was, or indeed if she would care to the degree that it would be worth maximizing or minimizing the accuracy of his response. Fortunately, Teresa was just then preoccupied with lighting up, tilting back, taking in the sun and the fragrant smoke with her eyes closed to the world. When she opened them, she was looking straight at him. With a soft smile, she reached out to pass him the joint. The hot smoke rushed in, its peppery fumes watering his eyes. Teresa watched him struggling with his composure and laughed.

"It's strong," he said. "I don't know . . . I might have to go easy on this one."

"Yes, it's strong. Here, I will take some more, but . . . you still haven't asked me my question."

"Asked your question?"

"Are you believing in God?"

"Ah . . . well, I guess I believe in the universe, you know, everything all around us, I feel like I believe in that . . . but I don't really go for, like, a church thing. But I would like to think that I walk with faith . . . I just think for me it's more of a personal thing, you know?"

Teresa was smoking pensively and examining him. Her attitude suggested that his answer had not impressed her, and he wished that he had formulated a better reply, something perhaps closer to a useful lie.

"You don't believe—you are like my old boyfriend. You want things to be easy, you have answer for everything, but . . . when it is the bad times, when it is not so good for you, when an evil comes. Then you are scared. You say everything to make everyone happy. You say this to me now because you are wanting to make me happy. You want to get what you want . . . but you don't want to trust. That you cannot do, you could not go that far, not for God, not for me. So you believe in everything . . . but that way you can get nothing. Can you be happy with nothing?"

Jonah guessed that the tone of her last question was harder than she probably intended, but he wasn't sure.

"I know I don't have a good answer. But I don't think it's nothing—at least I hope it's not nothing. I try to be in the moment, to believe in that. Like right now, here with you, in this beautiful place, I feel like I can believe in the importance of this, even if I can't say for sure that it means what God means for other people."

"But how you can love this place? You don't know Brazil. You don't know even Rio. You don't know me. There are tourism where I live. With guides they come up into the favela to look at us. Like we are animals. But what do they know? They want to enjoy Brazil, like you. They want to have their photo and see Copacabana and see football and maybe sleep with Brazilian girls. What makes you different from this tourist?"

He didn't know what to say to this. She had caught him in a crosshair he couldn't dodge.

"Maybe you too . . . you want to sleep with Brazilian girls?"

He didn't answer.

"Don't be sad," she said, cocking her head. "I am making you feel sad?"

"No, no . . ."

"Don't worry, Jonah! I am liking you very much . . . Don't be sad!"

She repeated this last point again in her own language. The tone in her voice had stung him, but to his astonishment and relief there was also more than a hint of a smile in her face. It was a mocking smile, but it wasn't cruel. It left him no room for escape—but whether instinctively or in accord with her beliefs, it also afforded grace. What saved him, however, was the raucous return of the others traipsing up the beach, their shoulders glistening with salt water.

They ate sandwiches and drank beer that Lazaro had brought for the occasion. There was no talk of the police raid, other than a passing reference by Barthes to the fact that she still hadn't heard from some people that she wanted to check in on. The others had tired themselves in the ocean, and after eating there was a certain cozying up between the two couples, and Jonah felt increasingly awkward in the arrangement. He let them know he was heading out for a swim.

The water was colder than he had expected, but the waves were not rough, and he easily made his way through the breakers to a place deep enough to tread fully immersed. He enjoyed swimming alone, the solitude and sense of space. He relaxed his body upward in the water so he could stare into the brightness of the sky.

Teresa's body was magnificent, her color, everything. Her voice, the words she had said expressly for him: *eu sou muito apaixonada pra você*. He wished Isaac were with them, that he could talk to him about Teresa. He would have to write to him, describe all the crazy things that he had lived through since arriving. It was as if the place had intoxicated him with equal measures of nightmare and fantasy. Visions of being randomly shot and dying in the street, but also of a life far away from America, with a woman exactly like Teresa, living in one of the little houses in Santa behind a wreath of tropical flowers. Teresa reclining with her back against a shutter, reaching for a joint resting on the little yellow serving dish, taking a hit and waving off a spiral of smoke before stretching out her dark legs in the sunshine as she listened to the sound of the tram going by on its way to the Largo das Neves. Its lilting grumble showered in the cries of schoolchildren jumping on and off the sides, chasing it down the street. *Eu sou muito apaixonada pra você . . . você sabe isso . . .* The weight of her breasts, the heat of them chest to chest. The blue Fusca parked outside under a palm tree. A world of cold beer and trips down to the ocean on any given day, the breath of solar splendor and the beauty everywhere of colored bodies like his own; the sweat of lovemaking in the afternoon.

Barthes was shouting his name down the beach. The crew was ready to head back. He stumbled out of the water and Barthes came to him with a smile and a towel.

"How was it?"

"It was great. The water is fantastic."

"You looked like you were having a good time out there. I was watching you."

She gave him a look, and then they were interrupted by Octavio shouting about wanting to avoid traffic. Barthes was already heading back. Jonah dried and toweled in a dopey run up to the car that Lazaro already had revving and ready to go.

Teresa was in the driver's seat, beaming as usual, adjusting her headwrap and setting her playlist. She eyed Jonah in the back through the mirror.

"Someone has been smoking too much today, even when he's gone swimming, that one still looks like he's stoned! Octavio, your friend, our marijuana is too strong for him I think."

"Nah, he's all right, we do more than this in New York on a long night—*caballero, mi socio*, how you doing, man? I swear he's getting skinnier though! Man, you need to eat more—I need to get you back to the city for some churrasco or something."

"Truthfully, I feel good, man. I feel good, don't mind me. I'm just taking it all in. The sand, the water, the sun. It's just beautiful to be here."

The colors in the sky over Rio were beautiful, and everyone was somewhat fatigued. Lazaro and Teresa sang along with each other to the sambas. The Americans each basked alone in their thoughts.

The next morning they learned that Taìs was in the hospital. From what they could gather, she had been hit in the head with the butt of a heavy rifle. It was unclear whether the gun belonged to a police officer or a drug-gang commando. By the time her mother had gotten her to help it was too late. There was heavy hemorrhaging and she had slipped into a coma.

Barthes was furiously making phone calls all through the morning to people who worked for her NGO. She set up a meeting with Angelica so they could go to the hospital together. Octavio and Jonah asked Barthes if she wanted them to go with her. But she simply packed an overnight bag and left without an answer.

There was nothing to do but wait and pray. To the universe, if that was what might rescue her, although Jonah felt keenly how much better it would be to walk, as Teresa did, with a deity one believed would deliver. He could remember only sparsely what he had read of the Bible. Now, involuntarily, he thought of an image that had bothered him when he first read it in the Book of Job. It was the line about the human body being crushed like a moth. He had been a boy when he first heard that passage and had seen himself trapped under a boot, his slim chest crumpling like a chocolate wafer. He was so seized by the image that he looked it up online when they went to check their emails. He had basically remembered it correctly, but it was the lines that followed that now struck him viscerally, with an almost unbearable realism. *They are destroyed from morning to evening: they perish for ever without any regarding it.* Jonah thought of the students he had left behind in Brooklyn. He tried to think of something else.

The weather was gorgeous, the city humming with life. Octavio and Jonah wandered, saying little, trapped in a daze. Eventually they ended up in a café in Copacabana watching a telenovela called *Paraíso Tropical.* That night Barthes didn't come home. She left them a message saying she would be at the hospital and that she didn't know when she would be back. The next night there was no word from her, and they assumed she was staying on at the hospital. Octavio got in touch with Lazaro, and he invited them to come watch a soccer game. Jonah hoped Teresa would be there.

The night was warm and the doormen of the edificios they passed were sitting on the edge of their swivel chairs, their shirts opened a button or two even more than usual, their heavy gaze not sunk into the surveillance monitors but riveted on the Japanese handheld radios broadcasting the Flamengo vs. Vasco da Gama match. You could follow its progress as you moved from building to building, bar to bar, corner to corner; it blurted out from passing taxis, from the corner grocers, seeping out of the living fabric of the city itself. Team flags and pennants appeared in windows; every other person in the street was wearing the anarchist colors of Flamengo.

At the bar they found Lazaro drinking with a group of friends and cheering on the squad. Flamengo had already opened with a scorching, if opportunistic, golazo by Renato setting the Maracanã Stadium on fire.

Octavio was in his element, and immediately fell in with the group, yelling about the qualities of the various players, annotating the progression of the play with his sweeping gestures, entering into passionate dispute with anyone and everyone, singing the heroics of Ronaldinho and the young Argentine Lionel Messi, poised to bring glory to Barcelona. Teresa wasn't there.

Jonah pretended to be involved, but he couldn't match Octavio's fluency, and in its presence he had a creeping sense of isolation. In the dance halls, when the sambas came on, the dividedness only deepened. On the one hand, the rhythms connected; a wall of sound, the battery of drums crashing with a relentless, implacable sweep. The whole thing was suffused with African synchronicity. But the vocals were another matter. It was as if each and every song were a national anthem, and every person in the crowd lifted their voice on cue. Everyone knew the words, everyone loved the same songs and sang them with the same passion, the same understandings. To be surrounded by this ecstatic chorus, and be left unsinging, was an insurmountable indicator that you were a gringo. Without the words to the sambas, without a soccer team, without becoming one with the spirit of the people, there was no way to truly be a part of the city, to be whatever it meant to be Brazilian. *Eu vou torcer.* He had asked Octavio to translate the words from Jorge Ben's song for him. They meant, he explained, *to cheer for,* the way you cheer for a team, but more than that—because in Brazil a team is more than just a team, and soccer is more than just a game. One cheers not just for the team, but for the hope of goodwill, for peace and comprehension among men, for the beauty of women, for the garden that is the city, for the seasons and celestial science, for the green beauty of the sea, for the haven of the human heart. Jonah felt the soulfulness of this. He was in awe of its expression. But he was not of it. He could not make it his own.

14

The burning sensation of cachaça coated the back of Jonah's throat and his head was pounding when he woke to the sound of Octavio and Barthes arguing. He was too groggy to care about the details, but her tone conveyed displeasure. He heard Octavio leaving the apartment. There was quiet for a time, and then a long strip of light along the floor coming from the bathroom. Barthes was in the shower. The room was dark. Someone had closed the shutters and the apartment was still cool, but he could see through the small slats that it was bright outside. He half dozed that way for a time, listening to the ceiling fan overhead and the shower spraying with a lulling flush.

When he opened his eyes again, he saw Barthes, or rather Barthes's wet feet and ankles. She was wrapped in a beige towel and her hair was dripping. The air was pungent with the aroma of her soaps, and he could smell her body. The towel fell. Before he could make sense of it, she was down beside him. Running her fingers over his legs. The tips of her wet hair stringing along his chest. She whispered and he nodded. She took him in her mouth, and when he was ready, she sprang up and went to the bathroom and returned with a condom. She kissed his shoulder as he rolled it on. Her body was frailer and bonier than he had imagined. The sex was uneven, and because it was going that way it was not easy. He felt as though he had to prove something to her, perhaps something he would have wanted to prove, but not just then. And he was too conscious of wanting to be away, anywhere else, and with anyone else. He was also disconcerted by not knowing the sincerity of her desire for him, or her motivations, which in that moment seemed the same thing. To satisfy a curiosity, to attack her lover, or simply because she felt like it—these were not the reasons he wanted her to have, but not reason enough for him not to go along with it. Since it was happening, if it was to go that far, what he now wanted was to make Barthes come. To see something, anything, through. But her moans remained deeply ambiguous, the tow of her pleasure rising and falling away again, her breath vacillating so that he wondered if the either of them would make it. And in the very moment of wondering he felt an iron tenseness in her arms that was not pleasure but panic, or rather instinctive fear, as they heard Octavio's voice rising in the hallway.

The first blow came in the ribs. Barthes was screaming. Two more blows came to the shoulder, the jaw. Octavio was kicking, trying to stomp the shit out of Jonah and hold off Barthes at the same time. He managed to roll away and get up. Barthes was screaming at both of them. With the towel in one hand, Jonah was trying to reason with Octavio, insisting that they take it outside. But now Octavio had turned on Barthes and was all in her face. When she refused to answer him, he tried to slap her, but she anticipated it and blocked the blow. That got Jonah back in the melee, the two struggling in a wrestling hold. Barthes joined in, kicking at them as she screamed in the center of her tiny flat, "GET OUT! The both of you! Just get out of my LIFE!"

They gave up the struggle, exhausted, and looked up dazed at Barthes, who was still trembling with rage.

"The two of you. Spoiled brats, two pathetic kids so full of themselves you don't even see what's going on around you. You're an egomaniac, Octavio. And Jonah, Jesus, you're a loser—all you do is follow him around. What are you even doing, like, with your life, other than being mopey, acting cool and shit? You're insane. Both of you. Why did you even come here? I never asked you to come. I never asked you to visit. I never called for you to come down here and just take over my life. I've been making a life, my own life down here! I've been trying to accomplish something. Which is more than either of you ever could imagine doing for anyone!"

There was a pause. Barthes pushed her way between them and threw Octavio's arm violently away when he reached for her as she passed. She had moved to the window, and she threw it open. The sounds of light traffic, birds chirping, and children playing flooded in with the fresh air. Her tears started to flow, which they could see made her angrier. She wiped them away before turning back to face the two still standing motionless and mute, as though waiting for her further scolding. She steadied herself.

"Do you know I made a website for the kids in my classroom so they can share their art with the world? Do you? Do either of you have any idea what it is I even do? Do you even care? Christ, you could at least have pretended to care! I learned Portuguese. I made friends, and guess what? I've had plenty of lovers. All of them better-mannered, better in bed, better than either of you. God. Get over yourselves. You hear me? Get over yourselves; in fact, get out of my apartment!"

At this last, Barthes crumpled down in a corner, heaving. Octavio, ignoring her command, kneeled down beside her, trying to give her his hand. She pushed him away.

"No . . . it's over. I'm sorry, but it's over. I'm leaving," she said. "I'm leaving you and I'm leaving Rio."

"Pero no me puedes dejar así. Mi amor. No seas así," Octavio was saying.

"No . . . no, no. I can't. I don't want to do this anymore. I don't want to do this. Anymore. I'm leaving."

"But I love you," Octavio said, now in English.

"I don't," she said. "I'm sorry. I'm so sorry. I did, I did at one point, actually, at several points . . . but I don't anymore. I don't know when it happened, please don't ask when . . . or why . . . I don't think . . . I don't think that would be a productive conversation."

Barthes got up and went over to her laptop. She opened a few windows on the screen and then began typing. Jonah looked at Octavio who had rolled over onto the floor with his back against the wall, his hair falling over his reddened eyes. His face was pathetic. He could not compose himself. There was a menacing sense of cruelty in the air.

"You know, I was just considering not even telling you, but you might as well know. Taìs died last night," Barthes said, without turning away from her screen. "I watched her vital signs go flat. Her whole family was there, watching. There wasn't a damn thing anyone could do. I've never heard . . . I never heard anyone scream like that. She was eleven. The NGO people think it was a drug soldier who did it . . . possibly unintentionally. Either way, it doesn't matter now. They're probably gonna torch the guy they think did it in a pile of tires up in the favela. That's what I've been dealing with. That's how things work around here."

There was nothing to say. The little ball of life from the soccer game, from their walk up through the crooked streets, who was an entire world of joy in the present and full of promise for the future, was going to be buried before her twelfth birthday while they lived on. Felled for no reason, for no purpose or motive other than the fact of exposure. The misfortune of having being born in a time and place where the risks to her life were infinitely and unfairly grave, even compared to that of some other girl living in a doorman building within spitting distance from the favela Taìs had called home, who might at that very moment be watching a popular movie about the elite squads fighting the drug wars or playing with friends in her private pool.

They had no standing to give Barthes comfort, certainly not to attend the funeral. They were strangers passing through, and they had outworn their welcome. Suddenly, Barthes was banging on the hard plastic of her keyboard.

"I have to get out of here . . . goddammit, I have to get out of here . . . Shit. Shit. Shit. I'm leaving. Don't you get it? I hate you, both of you! You bastards! I'm leaving."

Two days later everything was settled. Maggie Reynolds's parents eagerly paid for her ticket back to Boston. The month's rent on her sublet was paid for in advance but Barthes insisted on leaving extra money to have the place cleaned up. The elderly lady she was renting from came by to wish her well and when they embraced Barthes began to apologize and then burst into tears, and then apologized for her embarrassing display. The old woman hugged her, patted her back, and told her not to worry.

Octavio wanted to take Barthes to the airport, but she refused. They helped her pack her things and carried her luggage down to the taxi waiting on the rua Gustavo Sampaio.

When the taxi was out of sight, the hapless Americans walked to the Avenida Princesa Isabel and stood with their bags on the corner. They were homeless, they had nowhere to go. Octavio peeled a banana. Jonah felt in his pocket for a lighter and lit a cigarette. To their left the beach stretched out to meet the waves. The crowds were coming out for the afternoon, and most of the people heading up the Copacabana strip were giving themselves to the sun. A light breeze rustled the awnings of the coconut-vendor stands. To their right the wide avenue of commercial banks and hotels on Princesa Isabel led to the ugly yellow mouth of a tunnel.

"What do you want to do?" Jonah asked.

"We follow the plan. We'll go south."

"What plan? South where?"

"Florianópolis. Porto Alegre. I'm not going to let this define me. I have come too far, and I intend to go farther."

"Don't you think we should go back? What's the point of going on now?"

"You can go your own way if you want. I don't need you."

"I'm sorry, Octavio."

"Cállate! I refuse to talk to you about that. Do you understand? In other circumstances I would have you tried like Che did the counterrevolutionaries at La Cabaña. But now is not the time for tribunals. Now is the hour for decisive action. We must go like Martí to the Battle of Dos Ríos. To meet our fate."

"You mean we're going to die?"

"No. I mean we still have a reason to live."

"What—"

"Too many questions! We'll need to conserve our resources. Or find a way to make some quick easy money. I'm running low on funds. An intolerable situation, especially in our precarious position, which you put us in!"

"Well, I can loan you some money if—"

"Excellent. Buy my bus ticket and we'll call it even. For now."

PART THREE

*Nous avons goûté, aux heures de miracle,
une certaine qualité des relations humaines:
là est pour nous la vérité.*

—ANTOINE DE SAINT-EXUPÉRY

I'm in Berlin, writing to you from my favorite café on Weichselstraße near the canal. My work meetings are dull and endless, of course; but as soon as they end, I become an enchanted wanderer in this city. I sail down the hushed boulevards of Kreuzberg. I stand in awe before the Gates of Ishtar, visit with Tiye and Nefertiti. Even the bone-headed students from all over Europe spending their Erasmus money on cheap beer and techno have a cheerful innocence about them. Everyone clicks along in a timely fashion like the yellow cars of the U-Bahn on their viaducts. And yet nobody ever seems rushed to get anywhere or do anything. There's a kind of parallel time here, a gritty but lovable heart murmur that everyone agrees not to notice, like an underworld in daylight. A realm of libertine nights. I've been wanting to tell you about how I slept with another girl. Does it surprise you? I mean, my acting this way? I don't even know her name. I met her at a new club they've set up in the old gasworks. We were both smashed. She had this wonderful deep voice, and she was saying all this stuff to me in German, which I was too out of it to really understand. She was cool with leaving together. We walked, I swear it felt like miles, and at one point we ran into some friends of hers. I thought they were her friends but then it seemed like she was going to get into a fight, and I realized it was because they were making fun of me. We stopped at this sausage place and I needed to pee, but they wouldn't let me in, and she started yelling at them and we ended up getting thrown out and peeing between some cars. When we finally got back to her place it turned out to be gorgeous, full of plants and mirrors, and these big atelier windows that she nudged open, letting in the plush summer daybreak. I was thinking we would pass out, but she lit a cigarette and watched me and waited. Right away it was more intense and very different from what I've known with Mariam. In my mind it went on for hours—who knows how long it really was—but eventually I blacked out. When I finally came around, I knew I was going to be sick. Ran to what I thought was the bathroom but was actually the kitchen and heaved all over her sink. It was bad! I was shivering, trying to get it together, and all I could think about was Mariam. Trying to compose a text message to her in my head to send later. But for a split second I didn't know at all who I was. I did know, but it also felt like I didn't. And I stumbled around this apartment getting my things together, and there's this stunning girl lying naked in her bed. I'm looking at her and I hate myself because I know I'm hurting Mariam even if she never knows. And I'm walking out on this girl I just met. Would you blame me? Did I screw up? I swear I'm ready to be in love. I used to think I didn't want it to happen, I mean the confusion and neediness of it. But I'm feeling more and more that it would be better than the confusion that I feel without it. What I'm afraid of is letting myself make it that serious, of taking it there with Mariam, especially if she won't feel the same way. I worry she won't. I worry that she sees me as a fun thing, not a life partner. But how can anyone know? I'm ready for a change, I just don't want to ruin what's good about my life already. What do you think I should do? If you were here, I know we would walk through the city and talk it out. I would show you the trams rolling past Zionskirchplatz, and the little bridge in Neukölln where the swans come to sleep at night. The green water in the canals. They remind me of my Indre. If I could, I would bring you there one day and show you the bridge outside the town that my grandfather lined with dynamite in the summer of '44. My Indre, moving so slow you can follow a leaf on foot. As I send you this letter, I think of its waters as a poem, a hymn to the globe between us. My sweet Jonah, you are always so far away. I imagine you bounding across the great southern night like Saint-Ex in his aeroplane. But I can always recognize the lonely boy that I know, the little prince who is still probably madly in love with me despite everything. Look at the two of us, in love with our idle, fickle wanderings. Sometimes I wish I could do or be one thing sincerely. Have my motion fixed in space. Like the Indre, which goes only in one direction and takes its time and knows its place and is loved for some reasons that we can say, and some that we can't.

—A

15

Thick rolling forests of palms, large patches of them charred and covered in chalky stumps of ash, yielded to flatland, then badland, horizon-spanning swatches of rust-red earth stretching out to mountains that must have formed when the ocean shoved the continents apart and the land bid farewell to Angola, home of the human cargo who would journey back across the waters in chains. The wheezing bus advanced, road conditions worsening as it plunged farther south, the monotony of travel hours bleeding out.

When Jonah woke it was raining. Curtains of water swept across the windows of the bus as it sloshed through murky streets. They had arrived overnight in another distant city. He clenched his teeth and stared out the dark window. Beside him, still curdled with Barthes's contempt, was Octavio, his body wracked by spasms of inconclusive origin.

They were in Porto Alegre, the capital of a federal state called Rio Grande do Sul. The Great Southern River. They had traveled to a city they did not know, with no plan for where to go, without a friend to call, or a reason to stay. In the fetid air of the crowded bus station they studied a cheap and poorly printed tourist map they'd bought from a black boy in a Yankees baseball cap. Octavio decided they should aim for the Albergue Rialto, located close enough to what appeared to be the city center.

At the Rialto the rates were cheap, made even more so by the favorable exchange rate, and they took a room with two cots, a sink with a mirror, and a small table desk. Most important and improbable of all, there was a "business center" in the hallway with an old desktop that provided internet for guests. The room had a window that opened onto a courtyard with some trash cans, an old wall covered in growing vines, and the hanging laundries of an adjacent apartment block.

Octavio was feverish, and for the first time during their trip Jonah began to worry about him. Even though the weather was temperate, the man was pale and sweating and refused to eat. Jonah went in search of soup and juices and when he returned some hours later, he found that Octavio had gone down the street and procured his own medicine of choice: yerba maté, or chimarrão, as they called it locally. He had bought the necessary gourd and was imbibing the stuff like a hydrating sports beverage. Having commandeered the desk, he spent hours hunched over it like a scrivener, muttering phrases that sounded like incantations in Spanish, Portuguese, and French, followed by a nasty suction upon the gourd's metallic straw as his sallow cheeks puckered, the bitter green flowed, and his addiction grew. Octavio's physical state, to say nothing of his mental condition, made further planning impossible, and they agreed to stay put at least until the end of the week to see if his condition improved. Jonah was concerned for him, but no matter how much he wanted to help, Octavio was verging on unbearable. He moaned and talked to himself in different languages through the night; worse still, he was constantly rising with sharp cries of pain and stumbling in the dark to urinate with loud splashy relief.

Between the two of them they had already amassed a small library of Brazilian poetry, though most of it remained unread. Jonah had hoped to practice occasional translation to acquaint himself with the words, but Octavio was becoming obsessive in his feverish way. He would lie in bed all through the morning reading slim, often incredibly rare volumes that Lazaro had recommended to him. Lazaro knew book dealers and handlers who operated from their homes, and against Jonah's advice to remain in bed and rest, Octavio insisted on going out into the city alone to make specific purchases, as though dealing in highly sensitive contraband. He seemed to have gotten it into his head that he should have an edge on Jonah, and he made cryptic maté-fueled warnings to the effect that the books were his personal property, and he hoarded them accordingly, stuffing them under his shirts at the bottom of his travel bag. In just a few days Octavio had snagged a rare printing by the black poet João da Cruz e Sousa, one of Lazaro's recommendations, an obscure Symbolist of the late nineteenth century who died of consumption in poverty and neglect. The next day he was obsessed with a volume of tropical haikus by Paulo Leminski, who wrote a biography of Trotsky and translated Bashō before drinking himself into oblivion. But his most revered discovery was a rare collection by Ana Cristina César, who threw herself out of a window in 1983 in the nineteenth year of the dictatorship. The same year and month, Octavio noted, that he had been born at Saint Vincent's Hospital in Manhattan.

Jonah decided to do his best to steer clear. He spent late evenings online in the "business center," writing emails to Arna and Isaac and reading up on news from home.

It was uniformly depressing. The war in Iraq was going badly. Even the stalwart bureaucrats and blabbering policy wonks grinning their way through the morning shows were starting to admit that they were wrong. They had miscalculated. They had lied from the beginning through Colin Powell, who had done the state some service. His loyalty was exploited and he was being forced to take the tarnish as the story fell apart. This was the news—avarice and hubris smothering the future like burning oil wells. In New Orleans the black neighborhoods drowned by Katrina were still in ruins, most folks still displaced across neighboring states, some still in shelters, the stench of needless death extended by a spiking murder rate. The bumbling president was still insisting the government had done everything it could to help. The number of controversial police shootings was growing. Another kid had gone berserk and shot up a college campus, leaving scores of dead bodies in classrooms and hallways. It was said to be the worst shooting of its kind in American history. Talking heads warned there would be more to come as "copycats" stocked up their weaponry.

Arna was in Poland, according to her typically brief email update. Reading between the lines, it sounded like the first hairline fractures of disillusionment with her job had started to appear. The email didn't suggest she was unhappy, but possibly that she had a better sense of the difference between what she had expected the job would be and what it actually was. He would have to wait until he could read one of her real letters to find out more. Isaac's email was characteristically laconic. His take on the media frenzy over the massive school shooting: "Nothing new under the sun, chief—just another day in America."

Jonah was often up late clicking aimlessly through screens that loaded with a sluggishness that made the experience brutally hypnotic, so he tended to wake up late, sometimes around noon when Octavio was already gone. He left behind the traces of his ongoing mania. A mound of reeking maté filled the trash can. Greenish-yellow dribbles keyed the sink. Normally, Octavio stashed his writings away with his books in his personal affairs, but one morning Jonah woke to find Octavio's journal still resting on the little desk. Checking the hall to make sure he wasn't around, Jonah returned and rifled through some pages. With a sense of curiosity and some alarm, he skipped back to the first one, squinting hard to decipher the dense Vesalian microscript.

Perhaps it is my turn. The hour of my madness. Santa Yemanja! She has brought me to this—to this!! *Te acalma, minha loucura*, I hear you, Ana Cristina. But is it even my fault? From my Asturian forefathers who came for the money. Who came feverish for cruzeiros. Didn't I inherit? A case of King George's disease? Across the world for money. *Oro y plata* for a Habsburg plate. Silver and gold for a Habsburg jaw. O yes! Cienfuegos men and women. My people in the centrifuge of history. Navel of Las Américas. Immortal Martí standing at the waters of the Contramaestre, the blood of the soldiers Quintín Bandera and Antonio Maceo, son of Mariana, mother and warrior, Paulina Pedroso "madre negra" de Martí, patriots of 1895, of the Grito de Baire, forged in Santiago, raised out of the generations that came in chains in the galleons and brought the African gods of the slaves Xangô and Ochún and Obá into the green hills of Guantanamera where the flowers of the virgin Guadalupe come into the songs of the people and inspire the feast days of San Juan, the tumbadoras calling forth the dancers into the square . . . *ay, que linda la mélodia*, sweetness of the rumba flaring like the heat of a wound in the open sea, *el mar, el mar . . . elle est retrouvé . . . moi . . . l'éternité* . . . for what was I a century ago? what am I today? *Vagamundo*. I only understand revolt, my voice planted in its wild survivors, the whole island entire, planted like Virgilio Piñera says, *los pueblos y sus historias en boca de todo el pueblo* . . . so what do I care if I come from an inferior race? A race blasted by science, a race the technocrats will always want to do away with, just as even now, someone, somewhere, is scheming to rid the world of blacks. To rid the world of all tropical tribes, to do away with once and for all those who refuse to be regulated, who refuse to work, who refuse to behave, who refuse the orders of the police, refuse the orders of the Big Men. Barthes could know nothing of this, she could never understand . . . I lost my mind for her anyway. And yet how she stays! *O cheiro inebriante dos cabelos* . . . O Ana Cristina, she has destroyed me so wonderfully, so exquisitely . . . I call on Cruz e Sousa, *coração, tristíssimo palhaço* . . . the heart a sad clown. But I go to Martí again . . . as one must . . . *para aquel que ha logrado imprimir su pensamiento en la mente de los hombres, la muerte no existe, la muerte es un galardón*—for he who has imprinted his thinking on the minds of other men, death does not exist, death is a wreath of honor. Will I go too far one day? I will go too far. Then they will come for me. Power always does. I will tell them what they cannot hear. I am the wild one. The Savage. The Poet. The Last of the Last. What could I do? Was it not the madness, the malady of kings, of my—

"Pinche pendejo!"

Octavio had opened the door before Jonah had time to put the journal away.

"What's this shit about, Octavio?" he said, brazenly.

"What's it about? You steal my girl, now you spy on my work! You're so jealous of my success that you can't help yourself? You can't even mind your own business?"

"I'm traveling with you. You are my business. Look, man, I'm getting a bit worried about you."

"You should be worried about yourself. I should beat you then leave you by the side of the road!"

Octavio snatched his journal back and glared at Jonah like he would hit him. If it was going to come to blows, Octavio would have the upper hand.

"Calm down. Look, man, you're unwell, I don't just mean with a flu or whatever it is—you're a mess, I mean look at you. Your skin is practically the color of that shit you're drinking. C'mon, man, let's get out of here and go see some sights along the river. That's what we're here to do, isn't it? Maybe there's a bookstore where you can re-up on some poets. I'll *buy* you a poetry book. Whatever you want as long as it's not more Rimbaud or any other tragic poet who died young. Just, let's go, yeah?"

Octavio looked at Jonah and then back at his journal. He flipped through a few pages, then tossed it on the desk.

"All right then, a truce, but don't think I'm not gonna remember this, Jonah. Don't think you can just slip out of this shit, *cabrón* . . ."

In Porto Alegre the jacaranda trees were in bloom and puddles of purple blossoms rounded the dark trunks all along the quiet streets of Bom Fim. Jonah and Octavio strolled around a park and examined the area around the university before turning and making their way back to the city center. There, close to the banks of the Guaíba River, they came across the semi-enclosed terrace of a grand former waterfront hotel—the Majestic. The building was an art-deco palazzo painted pink, spruced up and converted into a cultural center named for the poet Mário Quintana, with a café, a cinema, a bookshop, and a multivalent space for contemporary artists. Jonah examined the movie-house marquee. They were showing a film by one of the old French New Wave directors who was still alive and working, a nostalgic black-and-white remembrance of Parisian youth and revolutionary aspiration in the heady days of May 1968. Jonah was pleased to see that it was being projected on thirty-five-millimeter film. They paid forty-five reais each and went in.

The theater was empty. They decided to sit three rows from the screen, dead center. As the dark and grainy images swept over them, Jonah felt the languor of Paris. A jump cut between worlds. The lead actress, who played a young sculptress more in love with her art than with politics, had a mischievous intensity that reminded him of Arna. Octavio was entirely entranced by the actor who played her love interest, a morose *poète maudit* whose death was the inevitable and symbolic price to be paid for the tattered dreams of a failed revolution. When the lights came back on, they made their way up the aisle past the only other person in the theater, a young woman who must have entered late and taken up a seat in the very last row. They exchanged glances, but she remained seated, her eyes returning to the rolling credits.

They were sharing a cigarette outside the theater when she emerged. From the way she dressed, Jonah figured she was an art student. She spoke to them in Portuguese and Octavio answered "Pois não," and handed her a smoke. She said something back to Octavio in Portuguese, which erupted into a discussion that Jonah struggled to follow. Then Octavio gestured at Jonah and himself. "New York," he said.

The woman started sputtering scattershot words in English that had the lovely and strange coloring of her Latin cognates. It was obvious that her English was as poor as Jonah's Portuguese. She smiled gallantly. She said something to Jonah in Portuguese, but Octavio beat him to a reply. "I told her you don't speak Portuguese very well," he said. Jonah attempted to rebut this claim with some imitations of the native tongue. Her smile turned into a concentrated frown. Octavio again came to his rescue and translated for Jonah as they attempted to discuss the film they had just seen. It wasn't until Octavio told the woman that Jonah had also lived in Paris that they found a common tongue. *"Tu parles français, alors,"* he said.

"Oui . . . mmm, un peu," she said. At that, they both burst out laughing.

The three of them entered into a conversation where everything had to be translated to someone, and eventually the person least translated to was Jonah.

The woman was slightly older, he guessed; it was hard to say because her features were youthful, but something around the eyes and about the way she carried herself suggested her age. She was dark-haired and rocked gently on her feet when she talked. He could see Octavio picking up on the same things. In fact, he seemed enthralled, if somewhat subdued. Octavio was trying to summarize what they were doing in Porto Alegre, and he was struggling because she seemed only increasingly puzzled, if also amused, by these wayward Americans.

"Tourism, tourism." She kept nodding and pointing at them.

And Octavio, in a panic, kept trying to nuance the label. "Traveling," he said. *Viagem.*

She didn't seem to buy it, but she didn't mind either. She turned to Jonah directly and surprised him with an entirely different question: Did he like Beyoncé? She was a huge fan of American music. Jonah wearied of being the ambassador for black America, but he was happy to indulge her.

"She's our queen," he said with a smile. "Tell her," he relayed to Octavio, "that to paraphrase the great Keith Murray, when we see her shine we feel like we're all the most beautifullest person in this world."

Octavio gave him a look and was coming up with a deflection that would bring things back to him, but she looked straight at Jonah with a smile and simply said, "I understood you are saying . . . I think so too." This placed the momentum back with Jonah, who now took a different line but one he hoped would make clear something about where they were coming from.

"Tell her," he said to Octavio, "that when you are coming from the United States, being in South America can feel like visiting the scene of a crime."

Octavio was game, and she absorbed this even more intently, her attention now fixed on Jonah.

"Tell her there is no place in Latin America where it can feel good to be a gringo," he said. This led to an awkward pause between the three of them.

Then she spoke, but too quickly for Jonah to make it out. "What did she say?" he asked Octavio.

"She said Americans are imperialists who have a lot of blood on their hands. But a lot of that blood is at home and not just abroad. She respects the black people of America because they have been so strong in the face of everything. She says they are an example for the world, and that is why she, like everyone, turns to them and loves their culture."

"Tell her I appreciate that," Jonah said. He did appreciate it; he also noticed that she was still looking at Octavio in a way that was different, that meant something more, and he decided to make the diplomatic move and excuse himself. "I'll catch you back at the Rialto," he told Octavio. To the woman he gave a simple *salut*, but she insisted on pulling him toward her and kissing him on the cheeks and, as he leaned in, his nose got caught up in the fragrant mass of her dark curls.

It was late when Octavio returned, and Jonah was now the one reading poems in bed. Octavio unpacked his washing kit and prepared to shave. Since leaving Rio, Octavio had let his beard grow, and now he seemed to take pleasure blading it off in front of their small mirror.

"You have a good time?" Jonah asked casually.

"With Francesca? Yeah."

"Francesca, got it. What did you all get into?"

"We had coffee in the café at the cultural center. She was over the moon when I told her I had been reading Clarice Lispector, her favorite writer. She even bought me a copy of one of her books right there at the store."

From a bag, Octavio pulled out a green book with the illustration of an undersea coral on the front and handed it to Jonah. He opened it up to the title page, where he noticed that Francesca had written her full name, Francesca Meireles, followed by her digits. He flipped to the first page and read aloud the Portuguese: "É com uma alegria tão profunda. É uma tal aleluia."

Octavio's face had regained its color, and now he even seemed to be glowing. *"It's with such profound happiness. Such a hallelujah,"* he translated proudly.

"Sounds amazing," said Jonah, a little more flatly than he intended.

"Francesca?"

"Yeah."

"She's more than that! She's . . . well, you know what, man, you can find out for yourself. Because she's invited us, both of us, to a gallery reception at the Pinacoteca tomorrow."

The next evening, they met Francesca on the second floor of a beautiful open-plan art gallery. Octavio and Jonah both wore ties, but the effect didn't come off as classy as they had hoped. Their accessories had been hopelessly creased in their luggage, Octavio's shirts were lightly stained, and neither of them had jackets. Francesca didn't seem to mind. She spoke in Portuguese, with a sprinkling of French art terms, as she walked them around the room, pointing out prints, acrylic paintings, installations that merited attention. Her own work was on display in one corner. She had cut out speech bubbles from local comic strips and used a magnifier to blow them up to canvas size before filling them with a collage of images of politicians, pop and movie stars (there was Beyoncé), newspaper clippings, old maps, sea charts, fashion icons, parts of wild animals, and zigzagging lines of pastel coloring that connected or bisected the fragments so that the whole thing had a kind of televised talismanic quality. She was proud of her work, and when she explained it to Octavio, their glances would invariably latch onto each other and she would turn away hurriedly and show them another piece. The place was crowded, and eventually they all ended up separating so that Francesca could greet people while Jonah and Octavio wandered on their own.

The show presented artists from all across the Southern Cone. An Argentinian had cut up a map of Buenos Aires so that only the cemeteries were left visible; a Chilean had created a wall of faces out of thousands of passport photos of the desaparecidos. There were international stars present as well. A famous white South African artist had a video installation that took you on a parallel voyage to the moon, an affectionate pastiche of Méliès, full of silvered light, scratchy Victrola piano, and a rocket fueled by unrequited love. Francesca found Octavio and Jonah there, loitering on the lunar surface. She suggested that the two of them join her on a cigarette break. Octavio agreed, and Jonah, sensing that his friend wanted to have her alone, declined.

"You sure?" said Octavio.

"Yeah, I'll catch up with you later."

Jonah watched the two of them gliding down the stairs of the Pinacoteca together. He felt happy for his friend, and envious too. Maybe he'd have the same luck too if he stuck around the opening. But with everyone speaking in Portuguese he just felt lost. On the other hand, he had nothing better to do, so he upgraded from white wine to a glass of champagne and made another tour of the show, trying to take an interest in the labels. But his glass was very soon empty. No one had come over to take an interest in him, and there was no sign of Octavio and Francesca. He looked around for somewhere to leave his plastic flute, smiled at an elderly gentleman he didn't know, and completed his desultory retreat from the gallery.

Ravines of gray and pink high-rises dominated the scuzzy streets around the Pinacoteca, but the older street-level shops, many of which were closing, spackled their bases with a dusky warmth. He walked back toward the Rialto with the discomforting feeling he was being watched, even though he knew it was really the opposite—he was insignificant to everyone he passed. At a corner, by the large roadway that marked the transition out of the historical city center, he passed a McDonald's. He hadn't eaten anything substantial all day. He looked around. What were the odds Octavio or Francesca would see him if he slipped in?

Everything was the same: the smell, the cold lighting, the demographic combination of working-class families and friends at recreation, and under-class drifters or loners camped out at the formica tables. The girl behind the terminal was dark-skinned with a lively, trained smile. He pointed to the image of the chicken tenders above her and she laughed and helped him through his order. He considered a seat by the large plateglass window overlooking the thoroughfare but opted instead for a booth closer to the condiment dispensary. Maybe it was only fair given the whole situation with Barthes. He hadn't wanted that, of course; if only Teresa had been available it would all have been different. Was this what it all came down to? There was a tap on his shoulder. The girl from the register was holding a soda out for him. He had forgotten to take it off the counter with his order. Embarrassed, he blurted out an awkward obrigado, which made her quiver with laughter. Her lip gloss sparkled as she said something he didn't understand beyond its sisterly compassion. She sauntered back to her station. He hadn't finished his meal, but he was so flustered by the interaction that he wrapped the remaining chicken to go and took off.

When he got back to the room, Octavio was there, his maté gourd in hand, bouncing off the walls with frenetic energy.

"Hey, I figured since I didn't see you guys come back for a while that maybe you had, you know, gone somewhere, so I . . ."

"What a woman! Jonah—I'm telling you—this is tremendous, she's devastated me, there is nothing else to say, no other way to put it!"

"Okay, chill . . . What happened? What did you get up to?"

They had talked about Francesca's life in Porto Alegre, about her family. Her parents were involved in city politics but had separated when she was still a teenager and only saw each other when necessary. He also learned that she was a mother. Divorced from the father now and raising the child on her own. A little girl named Paolina. They lived with Francesca's grandmother, who watched the girl when she went out. She wasn't from the city originally but from the mountains to the north. Her father was from the nearby city of Alvorada. Apparently, they were both invited to a family dinner at her grandmother's home that Sunday. Octavio had already said yes, that they would go. He described how as they walked back down toward the gallery she stopped and demanded that Octavio tell her if he had intentions. He said that he did. She demanded that he kiss her so that she could decide if he was worth it. She had approved. The next thing he knew they were back in the champagne chatter of the gallery looking for Jonah.

"When we realized you had gone, Francesca was very upset, actually. I told her it was fine, that you wouldn't mind at all, but she was all bent out of shape about it. She really likes you. But I'm warning you—don't get any ideas. Don't even think about it. This is not a game. I won't tolerate any more acts of treason."

16

The following Sunday in the waning afternoon, they made their way to see Francesca Meireles at her grandparent's apartment on the Travessa da Paz, a tiny street just off the city's largest park, the Parque Farroupilha. Octavio and Jonah were pleased with themselves for managing to arrive on time, bottles of wine in hand.

Francesca's grandfather answered the door. He was tall and ushered the Americans in with a small grin and a tilt of the head. He had great Ellington pouches under his eyes, and his hands trembled when he held them up. He coughed and laughed a little as he gave the guests warm hugs. His eyes were sea-greenish like his granddaughter's and what was left of his hair frayed outward at the sides like the head of a well-worn toothbrush.

Then they saw the girl, a little bundle with a Tintin cowlick, curled up against Francesca's grandmother, Antônia, a small woman with graying hair in a chignon. They were watching television on a brown couch in the living room. Antônia smiled and pointed at them as she nudged the girl in their direction.

"Paolina, diga olá para nossos convidados."

Octavio was transfixed, and Jonah responded for both of them, putting forward his best Portuguese. Paolina looked at them wonderingly and half waved before returning her attention to *Procurando Nemo*, the adventures of the pixelated fish who was blubbering on the screen in dubbed Portuguese.

Francesca was in the kitchen preparing a bottle for her daughter. They all embraced and set about working on trimmings for the roast beef and drinks. They were expecting her father, Euclides (her mother couldn't come because of a political engagement), and her younger brothers, Carlo and Theo, both still in school and, Francesca noted proudly, avid salsa dancers. So eight people in all, plus Paolina, who would nibble from her mother's plate. Octavio got to entertaining her grandparents in the living room with tales of their travels, with an emphasis on the marvels (and an elision of the perils) of Rio de Janeiro.

Euclides arrived next. He was a bald-headed bull of a man who clearly had downed more than a few drinks before arriving. Her father gave each of the guests a bear hug—in Octavio's case, one that looked a little too intense to be comfortable. But when Euclides learned that he was Cuban, he was immediately bellowing and roaring with approval, demanding to know why Francesca hadn't told him so in the first place. Now the drinking began in earnest, and even Francesca's grandmother had a full glass of wine. Around eight o'clock, as everything was nearing completion, the brothers arrived. Carlo and Theo came in together in mud-streaked soccer jerseys, declaring themselves victorious and tramping about the apartment singing their club's fight songs. They barely noticed the Americans as they swept up their grandparents in their arms, dancing around the living room, tossing Paolina in the air, and romping all over the furniture. Euclides barked at them to get in the shower. Francesca shouted from the kitchen that they smelled. And without any further prompting, like a passing cyclone, they disappeared to get changed.

When everyone finally sat down to the family meal, Octavio was seated between Francesca and her father, while Jonah was placed in a corner seat next to Antônia. They all took each other's hands around the table to say grace. Francesca's grandfather intoned the benediction in a soft near-whisper. Jonah closed his eyes. Antônia's hand was buttery smooth like a leaf of chard.

The dinner could begin. Euclides carved with pomp as he quizzed Theo and Carlo on the details of their match. When everyone had been served, they all began eating and there was a general silence until from across the table, Francesca's grandfather addressed the guests in a quaint English:

"So, my boys, what are you doing in Brazil?"

Theo and Carlo chuckled to themselves. Octavio decided to take it on.

"We are traveling. We came to visit a friend, but some of our plans had to change, and we realized it was a chance to see more of this beautiful country, and to delay going back to the United States."

"Are you with some kind of an exchange program?" her grandfather pursued.

"No, not exactly. My friend Jonah is a great teacher, and I am . . . a poet . . . and I am on a mission, an expedition, I have come to understand, to learn, to discover the true materials I need for my poetry."

Theo and Carlo burst out laughing at this point and would have continued unrestrained if it not for Euclides's admonishing glare.

"They come all this way to see us, isn't it wonderful, and what do we have to show them—a country bankrupted by violence and corruption, our whole society a charade for these rotten politicians to plunder at will . . . a carnival, yes, a carnival of greed, and with the Party as—"

Francesca, who had been spooning rice for her daughter, jumped in with tender exasperation.

"Papa, please!"

At this her grandmother advised Francesca not to raise her voice, and then asked the table at large if maybe a discussion of politics could be left for another more appropriate occasion. Everyone fell into a cumbersome silence. The brothers suddenly declared that they had to go, the weekend had landed, they explained, and they were going out dancing. They cleared their own plates and gave a hasty salute as they bolted for the door. After they had gone, Euclides struck up a conversation with Jonah about politics, but kept his voice down.

Octavio asked Francesca if he could give Paolina a present, a book he had bought on Jonah's recommendation. He wanted to inscribe it, and Francesca helped him write a note.

When he showed Paolina the book, she pried it open cautiously and mussed a few pages before looking up.

"What is it?" she asked.

"It's *The Little Prince*," he said. "A book for you."

The girl looked down again, this time at the cover, which showed a French boy with hair the color of stars, wearing a bowtie and a flared pistachio jumpsuit, standing on a lonely planet. "But he's not a little prince," she said decisively. "He's a big king!" Octavio knew better than to argue with that.

Euclides insisted that if his guests had come this far to see the real Brazil, they must see his mountain cabin before they left. He explained that he would have business in Alvorada for the next few days, but that he could pick them up the following Friday and drive them to the Serra. Francesca urged them to come. They enthusiastically agreed.

Jonah saw less and less of his roommate that week, and spent more and more time wandering alone around the city or drifting through slow-motion cyberspace at the hostel. With nothing in particular to do, he felt a new kind of freedom, and as his Portuguese improved, he was getting better at navigating the small necessities of everyday life. It was pleasant to be untethered to, and unencumbered by, Octavio; he even enjoyed his best-friend role as he got daily news of increasingly romantic and intimate encounters. Best of all, it gave him time to write to Arna, and he spent more than one late night writing up his impressions of the new city, telling her about Octavio's manic episodes and his maté binging, the strange but oddly beautiful poetry of his journal, and their new adventures in the art world.

He told Arna about the things Octavio was relating to him about Francesca. How they would meet in the little barzhinos in Cidade Baixa with Francesca's small band of rowdy friends and go out to tightly packed spots where they danced to the slinky languor of forró. How late into the night, they would follow the other couples spilling out of the clubs and drift down toward the love motels in Menino Deus. How returning to the Rialto at dawn, he passed teams of black boys collecting trash by hand and filling carts pulled by donkeys on their morning rounds.

On the appointed Friday, Euclides appeared at the Rialto to pick them up. Octavio and Jonah clambered in the front of an aging Ford truck. Inside it smelled like old tennis balls, and the engine roared and groaned as he handled the staff of the gearshift.

Their first stop was a discount grocery store where Euclides ordered the boys out to get supplies. The truck loaded, they drove out of the city, north and slightly west. When they turned off the highway half an hour later, they passed over a drainage ditch filled with garbage and then onto an unpaved road that led through an extensive network of dilapidated and unfinished housing. The place was teeming with life. Francesca's father pulled over to talk to a young man who was kicking a soccer ball around with a little boy. An older woman came out of her home, shouted greetings, and went back inside. They continued farther into the settlement. "Where are we?" Octavio finally asked.

"This is Alvorada," Euclides said. "My hometown, my baby, my district, my jewel . . . It's a good place, good people. Some problems like everywhere, but good people, you know. Everyone you meet here, I know them. Everybody is who I work for. They know, I am the one."

He insisted on taking them to see some of the things that he was responsible for. The first was the site of a five-story housing project unit. The building, a gray affair that sternly blockaded the horizon, was obviously in disrepair. He explained how he had fought off the speculators and owners who had tried to have the building razed so they could sell the land. How he had organized resistance groups that infiltrated and sabotaged the wrecking crews that came to do their bidding. The second site was a vague patch of land with a partly caved-in warehouse. Some gravel, dripping puddles of mortar, and loose bricks had been poured on the ground. The better part of it was covered in sprouting weeds.

era when Internacional crushed Grêmio, their bourgeois Porto Alegre rivals. But, Euclides moaned, those days were past. Now the Gremistas were in a seemingly unstoppable ascendancy, a shift that could not be dissociated from the virulently bourgeois ideology of the present epoch, the grave malaise of the social situation; and one would have to mention the increasingly clear sense that even though the PT had come to power—and perhaps even for that very reason—the tide of class warfare had markedly turned in favor of the bourgeoisie. How could it be! When the Left came to power, they implemented the program of the Right. Madness. Under Lula the specula-tors in São Paolo had seen their fortunes inflate. The poor, of course, were being pushed down, shoved under the rug to make way for upscale shopping complexes, ostracized from the same cities they had built, cast out to the periphery, to places like Alvorada.

In the back seat, Francesca and Jonah had Paolina tucked in between them. Mostly she asked her mother about Jonah. Was he from Africa? He said no, that he was from America—*North* America. Paolina told Jonah that he should look out for the lions and zebras. Francesca was embarrassed and told her that she was confusing America and Africa. Paolina looked at Jonah and insisted on her cautionary note anyway.

"Does she know about dinosaurs?" he asked Francesca.

"A little bit, we haven't learned their names, but she knows about them."

"Tell Paolina we don't have lions and zebras in America, at least not anymore. But a long time ago, Africa and America were actually all one big piece of land stuck together, and back then we had some of the biggest animals that there ever were: the dinosaurs. They were ferocious but they all died when the Earth got hit by a large rock from space."

This took Francesca a while to relate but it seemed to leave a strong impression on the child, and she remained quiet for a long time. Her doughy legs were draped over his thigh and her wondering head rested on Frances-ca's hip.

They were climbing through green mountains. They passed a small white church and a long wooden-slatted hall, and then turned up a smaller dirt path that led up to a large sort of bungalow and, beside it, a stable. "We're here," Euclides announced with magisterial authority. "In the arms of the Serra do Mar."

Euclides had built the house himself. He showed them where he got the wooden beams for the frame from a grove of faveira trees. He had used a large trunk that fell in a storm to build a support for his veranda. The whole house had more or less the shape of a wide boot, with a roof patched together from different materials that sloped upward, culminating in the kitchen in the back and its stove-pipe chimney. In the entranceway there was a vestibule stocked with riding gear: saddles, harnesses, heavy wool wraps, stirrups and packs, leather boots and spurs, and embroidered Paraguayan blankets. At the other end of the room there was a shrine for Euclides's patron saints: Jesus, Che Guevara, and Lenin. Euclides had a small bookshelf as well, upon which were mounted several distinguished volumes, including books by Eduardo Galeano, the poems of Langston Hughes, *The Count of Monte Cristo*, and an elegant clothbound edition of *Memórias póstumas de Brás Cubas*. The Americans made a point of showing their familiarity with the great Machado de Assis.

"One of the great black writers of all time," Euclides mused, gazing lovingly at the tattered spine. "But," and now he turned, with special attention to Jonah, "not a great writer of blackness. No . . . not a writer of blackness at all. The greatest Brazilian novelist—a black man born half a century before the abolition of slavery in his own land . . . and what does he write about? The flings and pangs of aristocrats . . . the little underwear affairs of the empire! Yes, I'm afraid it's true! Nothing on the enslavement of his forefathers! A man of magnificent, innovative genius . . . maybe the only thinking man to emerge from that slumbering sick empire in exile . . . and he could not even talk . . . about himself. What he might have done with Palmares! What a *Monte Cristo* we could have had if he had looked to Zumbi for a hero! If he had the courage . . . to imagine the free slave societies of the Quilombos! I tell you, my friends . . . I have thought on these things a long time. A hero must have his labyrinth . . . a true hero struggles through one alone. But I have come to the conclusion that the labyrinth of the black hero has no exit."

Before preparing dinner Euclides took them out to the stable to see his horse. As they approached, the animal became very agitated. But Euclides cooed and sweet-talked his way inside. It was dim in the stable and the only thing you could see was a giant watery eye staring out of the darkness. It belonged to a dapper chestnut criollo named Garibaldi. They stood and watched as Euclides brushed down Garibaldi's neck, soothing him until only a little wreath of steam periodically appeared from his gray nostrils.

"I have always believed that a man is made complete by a horse," Euclides confessed. "I can't help it. In my blood, in my spirit, I am a gaucho. Sometimes I feel that I am even a horse myself," he said laughing.

They heard a shout and turned to see an old black man walking up the path toward the house carrying an enormous bundle of branches. He was wearing a tattered poncho and walking steadily in dust-colored sandals. As he neared, they could see that the bundle he was carrying was lashed together with rope that rose almost four feet above his head and extended behind and over his back so that he looked almost like a snail in its shell.

"*Oi*, Orígenes!"

The two men engaged each other in a hearty greeting. Francesca looked on attentively. Jonah looked at Octavio, who looked back to confirm that he could not understand a word the old black man was saying. His words slurred into each other in a way that made his speech impossible to follow. After a moment it was clear that Orígenes wanted to ask Octavio something. But Octavio didn't understand, and so he smiled, and the two became stuck in each other's perplexity. Euclides explained that Orígenes wanted to know if he and Jonah were brothers.

Octavio looked at Jonah. "No. No, we're not brothers. We're friends. We're visiting Francesca. We have been traveling through the country."

Orígenes looked incredulous. He started to laugh and wheeze as the branches creaked over his back. Euclides invited the old man to join them for a beer, but Orígenes declined, saying that he had more work to do, that a drink was a bad idea for him, that he had stopped drinking, more or less. More or less? Euclides prodded. Mostly chimarrão now, Orígenes clarified. Euclides nodded approvingly. And with that Orígenes moved off into the dusk, climbing up the hill behind the house along a line of cashew trees.

That night they cooked together, raising a hot ruckus in the kitchen. They were making a feijoada. First off, the sausage bits. Euclides cut the slices roundly, their faces mottled and rouged. Francesca cut up morsels of beef and oxtail, peeling away translucent strips of fat. Octavio worked on chopping onions, peppers, and garlic, and Jonah peeled carrots and potatoes. Paolina sat on the counter and, in her own manner, exhorted the workers to greater productivity. When the stew was ready, a small dune of farofa was added to each plate and served hot.

After dinner Euclides produced a bottle of clear cachaça and held forth on his two favorite subjects, politics and the past. He described his efforts to promote land reform laws that would eventually allow Orígenes to own a portion of the land that he had worked his whole life. But he explained that there were complications in the contracts of land ownership and inheritance that he had so far not been able to overcome. A second story was about his father, whom he referred to as Francesca's grandfather. The old man had been an important figure in the movement, and fairly radical. The military chief in charge of her grandfather's region had leftist sympathies. He arranged for sentences to be lightened or commuted. He wanted order, but he wanted his orders executed cleanly, without blood. So, at first, her grandfather was placed under house arrest.

"I could tell you a thousand stories about that time," Euclides said proudly. "The greatest stories are all from those days. How he fooled the guards to attend secret meetings using coded language on the telephone, signals and messages passed in toothpaste . . . It became almost like a game. But eventually the leadership changed and sometime around '78 they decided a heavier hand was necessary. A new station chief was brought in from Brasília. They started to torture people. He would never talk about it, but I know from people who went in with him, the ones who came out . . . They strapped him to a bed frame in a basement of the police station. They brought in a little generator and a voltmeter. Then they taped electrodes to his testicles. My father was tortured like this. You have to understand, when you go through something like that . . . you never forget."

Euclides was a man who took great pride in telling tales the way they should be told, at length and with notable digression, with recurring motifs and luminous surprises. But women always had the best stories, he said. Best because they were all true. They were the only ones who ever knew the truth, and who could still remember the stories of their mothers and hand them down in ways that allowed their truth to pass on—just enough truth, passed down through the generations so that the crookedness of men would never completely triumph.

After she had put Paolina to bed, Francesca joined Jonah for a cigarette on the veranda. Octavio was exhausted and had decided to turn in; he agreed to keep an eye on Paolina, who was still whimpering a little.

They sat smoking under the moths gathered along the sides of the house and over the screen door. The view on a clear night up in the Serra do Mar was sublime. Francesca moved away from the lights of the house and Jonah followed her. The grass was cool and dry underfoot. When they were far away enough, she motioned for him to sit down with her. Orion was lifting a leg over the ridgeline. Cool air passed over their bodies, and in the dark, he felt her hand feeling its way to his and then up to his arm. But she wasn't pulling him to her. It was more, he realized, that she was holding onto him, almost for support. She spoke very slowly. "I am thinking . . . he will go away again . . . you too . . . and . . . I will be in pain when he goes . . . I'm afraid for this."

Jonah thought on this carefully. "Yeah, I gotta go sooner or later—

probably sooner—but Octavio, I don't know . . . I can't speak for him." He watched her face, gazing out into the inky darkness of the valley below them.

"I have already had some man leaving me. I want to be happy . . . and Paolina . . . I don't want her to see always men coming and going." She dropped her head for a moment, but she raised it again. He couldn't tell if she was crying.

"I think it would be better if I left Porto Alegre," Jonah said.

She seemed to think on this gravely. And then said, "But then he will go with you . . . you will leave me both alone."

"No, it doesn't have to be that way," he insisted. "I just think it's probably best for me to give you space to be together, if that's what you want."

There was no reply to this, and they stayed that way a long time staring into the starry night, until with a start she leaned over, kissed him softly on the cheek, brushed his face with her hand, and walked back to the house without waiting for him to follow.

17

When Jonah awoke, he could hear Octavio singing Spanish in the shower. He found Francesca and Paolina in the kitchen making breakfast together and talking. They had been out that morning in the orchards and they had gathered a bowl of black marbles that turned out to be jaboticaba berries. There was a glowing force that radiated in Francesca when she was caring for her daughter. He was struck by her fearlessness, if that's what it was—some deeply humane folly. Parenting was the most common activity in the entire world, happening all the time, and yet he couldn't fathom how or where a human got the courage and the mental resiliency to keep track of all the possible risks, monitor and arrange for every contingency and danger, know how to do what Francesca did every day.

Jonah thought of his own mother and father. They hadn't spoken since he had left New York. He knew his email inbox was full of pleading emails from his mother, and threatening emails from his father, demanding to know his whereabouts. But he never responded. He simply read them and kept going. Eventually they sent fewer missives. He still regularly received junk mail, mindless top-ten lists, scam promotions, links to humorous headlines and videos. His father forwarded or copied him on increasingly bizarre and angry letters to gallery owners, accountants, and tax attorneys, or on salacious jokes between old buddies who had washed up like him and were angry at the whole world. He couldn't help but feel that the voiceless emails and the forwarded flotsam actually made them feel more distant. The concerns of their world, the one that he was really from, sounded trivial and more annoying than ever. The tone of things was increasingly ferocious and tinny, the content derisory and manic. His folks had their faults and contradictions, but they had also come up with these huge revolutionary clashes to fight over and take sides on, and rightly or wrongly they had lived under the sway of a historical dynamic that seemed to matter, that you could understand and take a position on. He had grown up knowing only different things, and they stayed apart, fragmented.

Everyone he knew was like this—busy trying to figure out some way through the web, barely taking the time to know each other. But the real time, the clock of the world, ticked off the hours indifferent to their confusion. Life was what it was, no longer or shorter or richer or sweeter here or anywhere else but made up only of what you had really touched, known, believed, sweated your tiny cup of being into. Francesca and Paolina were each other's world, and had to be, at least for now. But what a rich life they had. Francesca refused to let mothering stand in the way of her enjoyment of whatever she wanted in her life, whether it was her friends, her art (even if it wasn't likely to lead to a career), seeking out men and sleeping with them if she pleased. It was impossible to be indifferent to this prowess, her ability to burn with a soft, ribbonlike flame. To find the path that took in more with less.

The next day Euclides took Garibaldi out riding and left a note saying that he would return by nightfall. The day was open to them, and they decided to go for a walk in the mountains. They started up the hill behind the house, passing under the cashew trees and winding up a little mountain pass. In places the climb was steep and rocky, and Francesca carried Paolina on her shoulders. She picked her way around loose rocks, hiking uphill with her daughter's little hands wrapped around her forehead. She moved with serene confidence, talking to her daughter the whole time, pointing out flowers and beetles and bees as they went along. They passed over a ridge. On the far side sugarcane fields extended on a long descending slope as far as the eye could see. The green stalks sashayed under the breeze, rustling like water.

Francesca guided them down along the side of the field. Ahead, they could hear the *tack-tack* of a machete and the hiss of falling cane leaves. It was Orígenes. They stopped to say hello. Jonah and Octavio still couldn't understand him when he spoke. Francesca explained that Orígenes was saying again that the two Americans were brothers. Octavio said that perhaps because they had been traveling together for some time, they had acquired that kind of knowing way about each other that siblings have. Orígenes considered this and then spoke.

Francesca said that Orígenes understood this, but that all the same he could see they were brothers. What were the chances, he said, of the two of them being here, and all of them meeting on the mountain, in the scheme of the world made under God's vast heavens?

Octavio nodded in solemn agreement.

Orígenes continued after a moment, and, for a while, Francesca went on translating haltingly. Jonah tried to follow as best he could. Orígenes was talking about souls, the soul having clothes, or not having them . . . or souls needing clothes when they got too far from the heat of the creator . . . souls putting on bodies the way people put on different coats in the winter . . . going from one body to another . . . to animals too . . . everything going back to where it came from. And then Orígenes stopped and looked at them expectantly.

"What was that last thing?" Octavio asked.

Francesca thought for a moment as she translated in her head. "Orígenes says that even the most wayward souls come from God and so even the most wayward souls have to go back to Him, and so there is a confusion—or, how do you say—contradiction, in the idea of Hell . . . because God is all-powerfulness and infinite love, and so it must be that *all* souls go back to Him. All souls are eventually saved, he says, even the Devil's. All souls are brothers, you two and all of us here together share of the same soul. And all of it will be saved, he says, at the end of time."

Paolina wanted her mother to let her down, but Francesca felt they should move on. Octavio wanted to try cutting a sugarcane stalk. Orígenes showed him how to cut the end of the stalk and chew out the juice.

With that, they thanked Orígenes and he shouted farewells as they moved on deeper into the valley. As they marched Octavio sang in Spanish for Paolina. She squealed with delight when he sang, and as soon as he ran out of steam she demanded more, clapping her hands wildly as Francesca tried to concentrate on walking.

They came to a field of tall grass. Francesca put Paolina down and let her chase Jonah around in a game of tag while she and Octavio held each other and kissed. Suddenly Paolina was wailing. Jonah crouched beside her, awkwardly patting her back. She had a small cut on her forehead, a streak over her eye. It was a fine, superficial cut. Francesca licked the blood away, laughed, and soothed her. Paolina soon calmed, looking into space for a while, a little stunned.

Jonah was mortified. "I've hurt her," he kept saying. He was overreacting. Octavio knew why and he tried to reassure him. They were thinking of Taís. They had talked about her only once since leaving Rio de Janeiro. They never would again.

Octavio gave Paolina some sugarcane to chew on. Francesca disapproved but didn't say anything. They stopped on the way home to pull up wild garlic for dinner. Paolina demanded more and more sugarcane to suck on, and Octavio shaved off more pieces and obliged sheepishly. By the time they got back and started cooking, Paolina not only sang but also banged on everything, shrieking repeatedly in her mother's face even when she was told not to. Francesca seemed exhausted. Jonah struggled to keep Paolina distracted and out of the way. Euclides had not returned. Francesca told them that it was normal, and that they shouldn't worry. Sometimes he decided to camp out on his own on the mountainside. Sometimes he went to find one of his women. He would be back sooner or later.

After dinner Francesca tried to put Paolina to bed, but it was useless. The girl would start bawling and wouldn't stop unless her mother came and stayed by her side until she fell asleep. When she finally could get away, it was late and chilly outside. She joined Octavio and Jonah on the veranda, and for a time they huddled and chatted together like old friends. It was hard not look up at the stars, so clear at this elevation. To think of the world, and the sky, all those colorful spinning tops Jonah knew from the Hubble foldouts in *National Geographic*. He had read that the spiral arm of the Milky Way would one day reach the bend of Andromeda, and the two great puddles of stars would commingle a while, before returning into a void with no boundary at all, only an infinite thicket, like a wild jaboticaba tree climbing the visible realm, its billions of candescent branches fanning out through space and time. Perhaps Orígenes was right. On the other hand, he was still a black man laboring in a sugarcane field, most likely as he had been his entire life. As though even in all the immensity and beauty of the universe his world had no exit, no line of flight.

They heard Paolina whimper through the wall. Jonah decided to give the lovers some space and went inside to check on her. Later, when he overheard the muffled sounds of their lovemaking, he realized, to his surprise, that he didn't mind. He was happy for them. What kept him awake was not the grating loneliness of hearing others consumed in pleasure, but the deepening shadow of self-doubt. He thought of Nathaniel's words, and Isaac's, and he knew he had no better answers to any of the points they had made. And he knew moreover that he would have to leave his present situation, and soon. That he was not really *doing* anything, despite the fact that everything in the world was seemingly free for him to choose or take, most of all the freedom itself, which was in the scheme of history both an incredible accident and a miracle, but which he had, to his mind, so little to show for.

When they got back to the city, Jonah told Octavio that he was leaving Porto Alegre, that he wanted to see Montevideo and Buenos Aires, that there was no reason for him to stay any longer. He asked Octavio whether he wanted to join him or stay and explore his budding relationship with Francesca. Octavio asked for the night to think it over.

Jonah was packing and nervous about missing his overnight bus to Uruguay the next day when Octavio showed up.

"I'm staying," said Octavio. "Actually, I'm going to stay with Euclides for a while in Alvorada, and then we're heading back up into the mountains with Francesca and Paolina, possibly for a week or more. You're invited, of course, if you want to postpone that bus ticket."

"I'm good," replied Jonah. "You go have fun. Where's Francesca?"

"She's still packing. I came to get my stuff."

"I left you my portion for the Rialto," said Jonah.

"Cool, you'll keep in touch? Maybe if I can swing it, Francesca and I will come find you later on."

"Yeah, I'm sure we haven't seen the last of each other."

"I'm sure we haven't," said Octavio. "*Sin duda*. You take care of yourself."

"I will, compañero, I will. And listen, man. Whatever the case, be good to Francesca. Do right by her, if you can."

On this unexpected and yet vaguely anticipated comment, Octavio reflected solemnly but gave no immediate response. "We'll go with you to the bus station when you're ready."

At the bus terminal where they had disembarked, it now seemed, so long ago, the two friends embraced. Francesca was more emotional than Jonah had expected, and he felt almost immediately regretful that he was leaving. Francesca explained that she had a gift for him and extracted from her bag a little blue journal and a book of poems by Mário Quintana. Inside she had inscribed three words to him: *Sul. Sorte. Saudade.* "If never I see you again," she said, carefully, as she handed it to him. He thought she misspoke and meant to say, "I hope to see you again." But she shook her head and said it again in her own language using the word he knew meant what it did, but not what it would always mean to her. And when she tried again very softly, almost without sound, it was: "If I hope then never I will see you again." He knew that it was true. She put her arms out and they embraced. Then he stepped up into the idling bus, giving a faint wave through the bubble of glass as he found his way to an empty seat. He held close the gifts he had received as the rumbling behemoth lurched forward and pulled away.

PART FOUR

I run, but time's
Abreast with me
—COUNTEE CULLEN

A letter to you from home. I'm resting for a few days. Came down with one of these flu things. Got it on the plane, I think. The delightful side of this is that now I have an excuse to lie around in bed catching up on my reading and writing to you! I suppose the first thing to tell you is that Mariam and I are now officially "on a break." We're still texting, but I know inside that it's probably over. I'm unhappy with myself for not handling it better. The fact that she's in London right now is probably for the best. But I miss her terribly. What if I've screwed up a relationship with the one person who could make me happy? How do you ever know for sure if a relationship is the one? I think I wanted so much to fall in love, to be in love, that I panicked when it felt like it might really be happening. The smallest things seem to make all the difference, the slightest alteration of a day's plan and entire stories we might have lived just evaporate or materialize out of the void. For at least a week, I had this notion in my head that we would get married. We could go to Amsterdam, or Brussels, where it's legal, and be part of this beautiful new era that's opening before us. I sometimes have to stop and think about how extraordinary it is, what a time to be alive. All these new freedoms for love and acceptance expanding the picture of what a life could look like, what my life could be. The chance to be part of a historic moment. But I'm clearly not ready yet. Isn't it strange? It's like everything is possible now, there's never been a better time, there's never been so much hope, it's never been so easy to communicate and travel, to have fun and meet people from everywhere. And yet, I still feel somehow trapped. More unsure and frustrated than ever, more afraid that things aren't adding up toward something that will last. I secretly worry whether what I'm doing will be worthy of everything my parents and their parents did for me. Maybe there will never be an answer. It does feel good to be able to write to you about all this, though, because I know you'll read this and smile when you think of me, so serious and philosophical-like, laid up in my bed with all these balls of tissue and my endless cups of tisane, writing feverishly to you while the dreary rain taps on my window. I suppose if all else fails, the one thing I can say is at least I have you. In our own way, at least we've had each other.

—A

18

Jonah stared out at the trucks passing by on the broiling highway. Little dust tornados swirled over the copper-colored land. Then, abruptly, grayish-green fields of corn or maize sprouted out of the baked earth. Occasionally they passed low gray factory complexes with corporate names stenciled on windowless facades. They slowed to a stop next to a truck-servicing station. From his window, Jonah watched sex workers in nylon shorts take languid steps back from the asphalt as the bus passed them by. The driver loudly announced "Trinta minutos" and stepped off. In the convenience area, there were various food stalls and aisles of packaged snacks, all with unfamiliar designs and names. Jonah picked up a bag of Yokitos and stared at the alligator apparently wearing a ball cap made from a leg of ham. The thought of ham-flavored potato chips made him slightly nauseous. He felt homesick. For New York. For Paris. For familiarity of any kind. His heart rose when the cashier told him where to find a computer with internet. He quickly checked his email. Arna had not written him back, and he wondered if something he said in his last email had put her off. He wrote a short note to Nathaniel Archimbald.

> Dear Nate,
> I know this will seem kind of random, but I'm writing you from a service area not far from the Brazilian/Uruguayan border. Rio was crazy, amazing, dangerous. My friend Octavio

who was traveling with me fell in love in Porto Alegre, a city in the South, and now I'm continuing solo toward Montevideo, a bit of a relief as I have a stronger grasp of Spanish than Portuguese. Listen, man, I still have your letter to Laura, but I don't know what to do with it. You and I both know the chances of me finding Laura are as likely as finding a lost penny on the beach. I don't even know what she looks like, you know? Anyway, this next phase of my travels could be pretty unpredictable, and I don't want anything to happen to the letter, so if you remind me of your address, I'd be happy to send it back.

Un abrazo from a lost brother,

Jonah

Back on the bus, Jonah's window was now dark with night. He tried once again to sleep, and this time he succeeded. He dreamt that he was in Paris, in the projection booth. Yellowed movie posters floated in the darkness. The actors and actresses with their beautiful teeth no longer stared at each other full of rapture; they were staring at him, like a circle of mute lawyers. The Kinoton and its black snake whirred to life. A stock of silvery, crackling light wobbled against the screen, patiently clearing into the shape of Phineas sitting with his legs crossed, smoking a cigarette.

"Where am I going?" Jonah asked him.

Phineas took a drag but did not respond.

"What happened to you? Why did it all go south?"

Phineas looked out to a point in the near distance.

"It's all in the way it bends," he said. "It bends toward the heart, *always*."

"But how do I *know* . . . how do I find it?"

"The ear bends to the heart, brother, when you play everything *rightly*."

"Just play it right?"

"Play *all the notes* . . . Don't skip none now . . . You gotta let each one know

210

they *already there* . . . show they was ready to begin with . . . the thing is . . . if I messed up it wasn't cause I didn't love the music . . . my spirit was always right with the music . . . whatever I got to answer for . . . please let them know brother . . . that every note I played . . . I did my best to play it rightly."

Jonah awoke with a start. He was in another country.

✺

The trees were snowing in Montevideo. A dandruff of silky pollen came off the branches along the avenues, along all the hushed boulevards running down to the ocean. Jonah advanced in a daze, happy just to be off the bus. A bright pan of sunlight rinsed over the squat buildings that lined the boulevards, its warmth cut by the icy quills of the Southern Ocean. He leaned into the wind and the tumbling tufts of pollen flew in his eyes.

To Jonah the trees felt oddly familiar, their arrangement and disposition, the personality of their crowns. They looked just like French plane trees, and in fact the whole city seemed carved out of some idea of Paris in the late nineteenth century, as though a fragment had set sail and washed ashore at the mouth of the Río de la Plata. Like the French, the Uruguayans were fond of their cafés and bookstores, tons of them it seemed, especially for a country that was probably by population about the size of Queens. Inside a *librería* in the Ciudad Vieja he quickly discovered they were proud of their poets too. Perhaps the trees were a token of gratitude on the part of the French, in exchange for all the morose and maleficent Uruguayan exiles and dandies who pollinated their poetry—Lautréamont, Supervielle, Laforgue—who tasted the ozone of these austral latitudes.

Not far from the Rambla he entered an empty tavern where the bartenders looked like toughs from a Jean-Pierre Melville flick. The local whiskey seemed to be the thing. It went down fiery and marine. When he eventually stumbled out again, he was filled with hunger. In his sullen march for food and lodging he passed through the Parque Rodó.

The grounds of the park were impeccably kept and desolate. Making his way under the tall green palms, Jonah arrived before a huge obelisk done in Eurofascist thirties-style concrete. It was dedicated to Uruguayan writers and artists, and to the youth of Latin America. Dusk was enclosing the greenery around him in a canopy of chittering twilight. He turned from the monument in a mummified stupor. He was trying to gauge the quickest path back to the street, but he couldn't make it out. He felt like a feral spirit stranded on an island in someone else's world. And for a flickering moment, he was certain some oppressive force would try to keep him there, holding him in a state of wild captivity, solitary and enslaved, a native hypnotized into submission by a colonial magician. But the queasiness passed, and he eventually made his way down along a lake lined with eucalyptus trees, before finding his way out onto yet another avenue that abutted the park. A few streets farther on, he turned and came upon a catacombic alley illuminated by a single bulb of light. Jonah followed it like a beacon and came to a small pensión where the words EL VASCO had been lettered in green and red on the window. Without so much as a glance at the menu, he walked in.

Behind a lectern stood a man dressed in a frumpy tan jacket and drooping bowtie, his hair slicked back, his thin moustache regularly agitated by a twitch in one eye. The impression was of a slightly shabby and possibly shifty variation on the standard model.

"Hola," said Jonah. "Por favor, quiero una mesa para cena y una cama para la noche. Es posible?"

The man did not reply but instead looked around the room then up the stairs behind him. The tiny restaurant only had four tables. They were all empty. Four keys hung from hooks untaken by guests. He turned back to Jonah with a strained look, as if he were trying to dislodge a crumb scratching in his throat.

"All our tables and rooms are booked this evening," he said in unmoved Oxfordian English.

"Okay, so . . ." Jonah switched to English while steadying himself against

"This," Euclides announced, sweeping his hand over the spilled gravel like a wand, "will soon be Alvorada's first youth sporting complex . . . my dream—and I've had to fight for it, but you know, we have to do something for the youth. Look around you . . . who else will do it? The politicians? You know what they are: pickpockets, my friends; thieves! They line their pockets and then put their smiling face on a billboard over the highway . . . ha! I spit in their eyes. Always watch the generals, I tell you. In this part of the world, it's always the generals . . . Nothing that way has changed, nothing."

When they arrived at his home, Euclides pulled up to the curb and honked the horn with two fierce jabs. Children were coming in and out of the house and chasing one another through the front lawn and down the street.

"I'll stay in the car," Euclides said. "You go in and get Francesca and help bring out her things."

Jonah heard Francesca shout somewhere deep inside the house. From the doorway, he could hear through the living room to the kitchen, where someone was chopping vegetables. Paolina looked up at him from the floor by the television and continued ironing the rug vigorously with her wooden toy plane. It was a red airplane about the length of a pencil, and it had a slender white propeller. Just then Octavio stepped in the doorway. Paolina's gaze fixed and widened, and the airplane stopped mid-flight.

Francesca came swooping into the room, taking the girl up in her arms, balancing travel bags and packs in her free hand.

"I'm glad you came," she said, kissing Octavio on the cheek. "Paolina. Say hello, give the boys a kiss."

The girl was reluctant, but her mother coaxed her. Jonah got a kiss first. Octavio got one too, and for the first time, Jonah saw him blush.

The truck climbed steadily and gruffly into the mountains. They were long off the highway now, climbing narrow switchbacks on a path of ochre-red dirt. Octavio sat in the front with Euclides, discussing soccer. The patriarch was recounting the glory days of the Colorados: the forties, a golden the implication he was beginning to recognize. "Well, look, can I at least eat? I can be quick if the reservations aren't until later. Or . . . is there a problem here?"

The maître d' shook his head, expressionless. "The chef has not yet started to cook. By the time he begins, the guests with reserved tables will have arrived." He raised his hands in a slight shrug. "I'm afraid you will have to find somewhere else to eat."

The maître d' was now staring at him coldly, as if he were trying to glare him out the door. Jonah was trying to make up his mind on how far to take it. He was hungry, and now he was pissed too. On the other hand, he was a stranger in a strange land a million miles from home, and it was probably not the best time to test out the response time of the local cops.

From the kitchen came a sudden and loud clatter of pots and pans along with a shout of "Maldita!" The kitchen doors opened and a man with a chef's hat emerged, the cap ill-suited to his rather enormous head. The maître d' rushed over to him, initiating a ping-ponging of excited Spanish between them. Then the chef looked over at Jonah. His countenance changed from one of annoyance to glee.

"Miguel!" he said, slapping the maître d' on the chest. "No me dijiste que teníamos un invitado!"

Jonah couldn't understand what the chef was so happy about, but he sensed that his luck was about to turn.

"Muchacho! Estas aquí para cenar?"

"Sí."

"Sí, cómo no!"

The chef shook his head at the maître d' and they exchanged a few more agitated words that Jonah couldn't make out, but he gathered by the chef's hand gestures toward the upstairs and back to the restaurant tables that he was arguing for Jonah to remain as a guest. Finally, the chef approached him, flashing a grin.

"Perdónanos. El restaurante no está abierto aún para la cena. Pero Miguel lo llevará a una habitación en la planta superior donde puede ducharse y cambiarse sus camisas. Alguna comida y bebida le estarán esperando cuando baja."

Jonah was lost in the chef's flurry of Spanish.

"Lo siento, pero mi español es muy pobre."

The chef slightly raised his eyebrows. "Qué idioma hablas? Your language?"

"English or French."

"Ah, bueno. Where you from?" the chef asked.

"New York."

"New York? New York! *Newww Yawk Citayyyy! Qué suerte!* Do you remember when we went to New York, Miguel? And now, New York, she has come to us! Welcome to Montevideo, Yankee! My name is Oscar, and this is my pareja, Miguel. I was saying to you that we are not yet open for the evening. But it's okay. Miguel will take you to a room while I begin preparations for the dinner. After you shower and change your clothes, you will come back here, and there will be a table with food and drink waiting for you."

"*Que bueno.* Gracias, Oscar."

Oscar disappeared into the kitchen; with a lethargic flick of the wrist, Miguel gestured for Jonah to follow him upstairs.

Oscar's partner had not entirely warmed to Jonah, but he was more welcoming after Jonah spruced himself up. They had laid out for him a platter of meats, cheeses, and bread, along with a glass of wine. Miguel left Jonah alone to eat, but he was prompt in suggesting and pouring more red. There was only one other diner in the room: a woman, who sat facing away from him. She and Miguel periodically exchanged chitchat, laughing under their breath. Only when Oscar himself came to check on Jonah's satisfaction with the food did the woman turn to look at him. From her glance, he was able to discern that she was she was a little older than him, with features that lent her an enigmatic, foreign flair. From the kitchen doorway, Oscar appeared, and with a loud exclamation, greeted the woman, kissing both cheeks and exchanging pleasantries. Oscar asked if Jonah wanted anything further, but Jonah, apologetically declined, citing his exhaustion.

"Then tomorrow, we shall have a bigger meal. Something special for our Yankee friend."

Jonah slept fitfully. He seemed to be the only guest and sat alone with a breakfast of toast, jam, and coffee, served by Miguel, who said that Oscar had departed early to get to the seafood markets. Jonah observed Miguel at his lectern, seemingly waiting for guests that showed no signs of coming. Other than the maître d's distaste for colored folks, he wondered what it was about this particular pensión that caused people to avoid it. Certainly, in a city as generally pale-faced as Montevideo, his attitude wouldn't be the problem. Besides, the place wasn't without its old-timey charms. Jonah's eyes settled on the photographs that littered the wall, pictures of fútbol players and local celebrities from bygone eras. He noticed a newspaper photograph of what appeared to be Fidel Castro wearing a blue suit and being served food at an expensive restaurant. He thought he recognized the waiter, and, giving him a closer look, realized it was none other than Miguel. When he came to clear Jonah's plate, he asked about it.

"Oh yes, that really was something. I was chosen to be part of the wait-staff for the state dinner to honor Castro when he visited Montevideo in '95. Naturally, I more or less detested the Castro regime, but some of my dear friends still tease me and call me a Communist because I once served El Caballo. What do you want? It was a job."

Miguel gave a shrug much like the one he had given Jonah the night before. He seemed to be a man who kept his true opinions and those he shared in casual conversation in separately marked boxes. Jonah didn't push him and instead inquired whether Miguel knew of any independent theaters in Montevideo.

"Independent. What do you mean?"

"A theater where I could watch local Uruguayan movies or art films."

"I don't know, but maybe Cinemateca Pocitos. At least, that's the most famous one."

Following Miguel's rudimentary directions, Jonah walked all the way down to the waterfront. Cinemateca Pocitos was only a few blocks up from there. A film festival was under way, and people were congregating. He looked closely at what was being screened and was shocked to find *him*. Phineas stared back from a poster box. It was as if the places and cultures Jonah was from, that he had made all the effort he could to escape, were actually being reproduced everywhere he arrived. To move away from the center was to drag the center to the periphery. He had made efforts in that direction and what did he have to show for it? All too soon, he reflected, these circles would converge and there would be no outside, no elsewhere. No need for a future version of himself to travel at all. By then his failures would become like Phineas himself. Bowdlerized for passive consumption; languishing in the vast lot of the unfinished and unlamented. One more entry in the encyclopedia of black failure to achieve the greatness that black hope demands.

Spooked, he considered buying a ticket, but finally did not. Instead, in a kind of disoriented panic he picked a film called *Tango Amoroso, the* poster for which was peppered with award medallions. He settled down in his seat, wanting something to distract him from a creeping sense of anxiety, a dread that he was being followed, not by a sinister force or a surveilling state, but by the swirling accumulation of his own evasions coming to account. He could understand almost none of the dialogue, but that hardly mattered. The film was a documentary about tango dancers, about bodies in their color interlocking in the swiveling pattern that sailors and dockworkers, the sons and daughters of Africa and Italy and Spain, had invented on the shores of European outposts in America. But much of the film wasn't explanatory. It was simply a recording of human bodies expressing desire with extraordinary beauty. The smile of one dancer to another in motion. It summed up everything, it said it all. The pleasures of human dance swept over him. Everything about it effortlessly repulsed the very notion of cerebral tics, malaise, disgust with life. It was like a vision of all that he felt he was not. He found himself on the verge of tears and unable to move. He didn't want the movie to end. He wanted to hide, and when the last of the colorful bodies had dipped and the fade to black surrendered them to the theater's soft lights, he had to gather all his force to move on.

Outside, the city's nocturnal rhythms were beginning to take hold. Pockets of laughter and conversation reverberated under the pale evening sky. The thought of ambulating alone any longer, any farther, brought a leaky lightness to his bones. He leaned against a patch of wall between two posters for coming attractions and pretended to himself that he was merely catching his breath.

What was in reach? Across the way, directly in his line of sight, glowed the neon trimming of the cinema's Hollywood-themed bar. Before he knew it, Jonah had downed two, then three whiskeys, the slender bartender dispensing each shot and slinking off to the far end to continue conversing with a pair of older gentlemen with portly bellies and stylish glasses. From where he was sitting, he could watch folks exiting the theater. A porter opened the door and walked in with a broom. A few people staggered out, couples, students. Behind a small group, a woman in a dark coat emerged and moved swiftly past him toward the exit, and he had the fluttering sensation that it was the woman from the previous night at El Vasco, but he wasn't sure. He thought he should follow her, but he hadn't paid his bill, and in his excitement, it took him even longer than usual to get it settled. By the time he emerged on the pavement she was long gone.

In a state of anxious bewilderment, compounded by drink, he thought he must find an internet café and write to Arna and to Isaac to tell them about this lonely stretch of a trip that had taken him to a city in which he had never imagined setting foot. And then, if he was sober enough, he would find out about the most reasonable flights back to New York. He marched himself up to the more heavily trafficked city center and entered the first place that he found. When he opened his inbox, he saw a short note from Isaac telling him that he'd received a raise at his school and was happy about it, but not sure if it would be enough to keep him around for more than another year or two. But there was another bold line in his inbox that grabbed Jonah's attention. Nathaniel had written him back.

Dear Jonah,

It sounds like it's complicated out there, but look, man, don't think I don't envy your travels, it's a great chance that most of us never get. I am glad to hear you are okay. About the letter, it would mean much to me if you could hang on to it, at least while you are in Montevideo. I know you will make the most of your time, and even the thought of both of you being somewhere down there makes me feel hopeful somehow. I'm attaching a scan of one of the only photos I have of her—of us, actually. Paris, 1994. She was a beauty, man, and now I can see that I was looking pretty damn good then too. I wonder if she saw me now if it would even go the same, but you know, we'll always have Paris, like the movie says. And that's okay. I'm feeling more myself these days than ever, other than getting old and the fact that my jump shot ain't right, I'm what you might call a satisfied man. You can't imagine how great it is when one of my kids graduates, and I get to hug everyone in the family. Truth be told, I never had so much fun hooping as I've had coaching, even though our record isn't exactly pretty. Every time I see those eyes light up when I rap to them about this crazy world we're living in, well, it just makes me feel good, man. I mean sometimes we get to conversating *and* I can see it's connecting, how it's about the bigger picture, how the world is really theirs if they are willing to make it. But now you got me carrying on about myself again. Listen, be well out there, young brother, and remember to come back—that's why I gave you the letter too, because you can always come home again. We all got peoples who need us. We all got to find our own way to do good. So do your thing, man. Enjoy that life. I hope to hear from you again somewhere down the road.

Peace,

Nate

Jonah clicked on the photograph. Nathaniel did look terribly happy and handsome in the image. They looked very much like a couple in love. And Laura. Could it be her? The woman he had seen at the theater? The woman he had seen at El Vasco? She would be older now, so there was room for some difference, but the face was so strikingly similar; it felt uncannily cosmic, as though the universe were walking him to a crossroads. It seemed unlikely that she would return to the same restaurant two nights in a row. But Oscar and Miguel seemed to know her.

Jonah anticipated the evening playing out much like the one before it, with Miguel paying him little to no attention. But when he arrived for a table, he noticed that Oscar and especially Miguel were in noticeably good spirits. Miguel tapped his fingers to the music playing from a little Toshiba stereo, his hostility all but evaporated.

"Ah, muchacho. Good, good, you are here. Tonight we celebrate the feast of Saint James, the patron saint of the Basque people. I make piperrada y bacalao. Muy rico." Don Miguel led Jonah to the same table he had eaten at the night before, only this time, without prompting, he returned with a bottle of Uruguayan Tannat, a wine made from an Uruguayan red grape, as he explained while pouring a generous glass. "Compliments of the chef," he said, before returning to his hawkish perch at the lectern. A bark broke through the music and a whimpering short-haired wiener dog came waddling over the tiles to Miguel.

"Garufa!" he said. "Go say hello to the guest!"

When the dog refused, Miguel grabbed the Tannat and walked back to Jonah's table, coaxing Garufa to follow by patting on his thigh. To Jonah's surprise, Miguel took a seat, grabbed himself an unused glass from the table and, filling it, took a pleasured sip. Neither of them spoke. Jonah turned to look back at the photographs on the wall, many of which showed Miguel and Oscar on ports with cities spread out behind them. He came across a portrait of Miguel with Oscar's arm over his shoulder, the two of them dressed in overly heavy coats with the wintry skyline of New York in the background.

"So, tell me about your time in New York," Jonah said.

"Ah yes. The Big . . . Apple. Well, it came about as a result of our both doing a tour in the Merchant Marines," said Miguel, whose decent English now sounded tweaked with a James Cagney-like nasal snarl. "It's how we met, traveling the world together. I would say we've known all the major ports of the world. Buenos Aires, of course; Sydney; Singapore; Shanghai; up to New York; over to Dublin; down to Bilbao—the best of all; down even more to Cape Town, which is on the same latitudinal line as Montevideo, you know."

"Why was Bilbao your favorite?" asked Jonah.

"Have you been to the Basque country? It's beautiful for the people, an unconquered tribe. It's where Oscar and I . . . well, let us say that it has become like an adopted home. We have since been back many times."

Miguel waved his hands at the flag and jersey Jonah had noticed earlier. "That's the jersey for the Athletic Bilbao. Oscar is a big fan, as is Garufa. Aren't you, Garufa?"

Miguel reached down to give the dog a scratch. Jonah noticed that Garufa's collar was in Athletic Bilbao colors.

Oscar came out of the kitchen with the piping hot peppers, set them down, and poured himself a glass of Tannat. "A break now until the next guests arrive," he said, glancing at the door. But no one showed up.

Miguel put in a new CD and returned to the table to pour himself

220

another glass of wine. The restaurateurs listened to the aching voice of the tango singer, and at times joined their voices to his song, gazing into each other's eyes with wonder and an insider's deep satisfaction.

"Who is this?" Jonah asked.

"Carlos Gardel. Uruguay's greatest."

Miguel pointed at a sepia-toned photograph of a man who looked like a South American Humphrey Bogart.

"I thought tango was Argentinian," Jonah said.

"What? Absolutely not!" Miguel hissed. "The Argentines are always claiming things that are not theirs. They even think Gardel is Argentine." Miguel gave Jonah an icy glare. "It's as if all good things that develop here must be taken from us. All our beautiful men leave for Buenos Aires, all our writers and artists leave for Paris, all our riches leave for foreign accounts in Switzerland or Brazil or up north. We were once the richest nation in South America until those Tupamaro bastards came along and ruined everything. And now this country is being run—into the ground, if you ask me, by those crooks."

"Now, come on, Miguelito, you're getting all upset over nothing."

"No! I won't calm down!"

No one spoke for a moment, and Jonah realized that Gardel was no longer singing. His music had been replaced by a song in a language he didn't recognize.

"What's this playing now?"

"Ah," said Oscar. "This is Evert Taube."

"What language is Señor Taube singing in?"

"Swedish," said a female voice. Standing in the entranceway was the woman from the theater, the woman from the previous evening.

"Señora Aussaresses, que bueno verte!" Oscar leapt up to kiss her hand and welcome her.

"I didn't mean to interrupt the conversation with your guest," she said in soft, French-accented English.

"Not at all," said Oscar, also switching to English. "You're welcome to join us if you like."

Miguel was at the table, pouring her a glass of Tannat. Evert Taube's lilting sea-captain Swedish sounded out like a bard's tale, full of roving wanderers and unhappy endings.

"Señora Aussaresses, this is . . . eh . . ." Oscar paused. "You know, I don't think I've asked for your name, muchacho."

Jonah stood up and extended his hand, which she took gently. "Jonah."

"These gentlemen call me Madame Aussaresses, but you can call me Laura."

"Jonah is here from New York City," said Oscar with a boastful note.

"I have always wanted to visit that city. I was once in a relationship with a man from New York, but that was a long time ago in another place. Now I live in Montevideo."

It *was* Laura. C'est pas possible.

He had whispered it softly to himself, but she had picked it up immediately. "Ah, but how are you speaking French?" she demanded to know.

"I'm actually from Paris," said Jonah.

She gave Jonah a look that he found hard to interpret, something between suspicion and relief. "Très bien, then you will understand why I come and eat here nearly every night. It is so hard to find a decent place to eat in this town. All Uruguayans eat is steak, steak, steak. But these gentlemen, Oscar and Miguel, fellow wanderers and exiles like myself, they always make good company and good fun, and they have the most wonderful collection of music. You picked this place out of all others, so you must have an eye for good things too. So, why don't you tell me: What brings you here?"

"I'm thinking now that it must be fate," Jonah said faintly.

"Fate . . ." She turned to the Basques. "You hear that, Oscar? This young man seems to think he knows a thing or two about fate."

They shared a laugh at Jonah's expense. As easily as he had seemed to win over Miguel's approval, now it looked as though he were losing it just as quickly.

Laura stood up again, seeming to take note of the intensity in the young man's gaze upon her.

"Well, I'll leave you to your food . . . and fate."

"Vous devez m'excuser, je suis impoli," Jonah broke in.

"Alors vous êtes vraiment français . . ." Laura said, still skeptical.

"Oui, enfin, plus ou moins."

Oscar and Miguel had to attend to other guests, but Laura demanded to know more. She wanted details, the whole story, and with his permission, she joined his table, poured herself a glass, and listened. Jonah began at the beginning, as he had with Nathaniel. He tried to explain himself as best he could.

"And what about you?" Jonah asked, when he had finally come full circle to the present evening. "What is your story?"

"It's like yours," she said. "Made of so many threads and wanderings I never know where to begin."

19

"**M**aybe with a question," she said. "Because who I am is not so simple, and even very difficult to say if one expects the name of a country to suffice. For instance, I am Armenian by heritage. Born in Beirut. Speak French and Spanish and Arabic. You could say I am a métèque, like Moustaki says in his song. My education was French. I was a student at the Sorbonne before I left it all. I lived for three years in Mexico City where I fell in love with a young lawyer who wanted to marry me. Another man I had to desert. I returned to France to be with my family."

She tended to her father who was dying a long time. And then her mother, who started to decline soon after. She cared for them with the help of Rosemarie, a Catholic from Guyana who came by to help before her night shifts at the hospital. After her mother's death, she fell into a depression. She took up part-time work at a travel agency. They were very nice and did their best but she was a terrible employee and they fired her soon after. She wasn't working for the money anyway. Her parents had left her enough, not a fortune, but more than she had expected, especially once she sold their apartment.

That was the beginning of the second fugue. A flight to Buenos Aires, with vague plans to stay for a few months. The men she met there were intolerable, and most of the women too. But then in Quilmes she met two friends who were different from the others, who she discovered were not porteñas at all, but Uruguayans who lived in Buenos Aires where they could find work. They insisted she should discover their hometown. Her initial impression of Montevideo was that it was the ugliest, saddest-looking city she had ever seen. Nothing in its appearance should make one want to stay. And yet, for the first time in as long as she could remember, she started to feel alive again. Something about the city's unrelenting air of sadness alleviated her own. For so long she had stopped trusting the faces of men. As the fog of depression lifted, she could see them again, but differently. She felt at ease and no longer sorry. She enjoyed defying them. The roughly whiskered drunks in their caps who inched along through the market streets of the Ciudad Vieja or sat on the seawall along the Rambla staring at the long breakers. She felt neither fear nor desire as she crossed paths with young men shouting and knocking into each other. Their world was so gray and melancholy that her own life in comparison stood tall. The weightlessness of afternoons became addictive.

Still, it might not have lasted. She had, in fact, been considering returning to Paris and would have if she hadn't entered one night into a tavern called El Vasco for a late meal. "That was where I met him," she said. Salvador Aussaresses. When she took a table, he was already quietly dining by himself. He was at first glance fairly ordinary in appearance, though she could tell from his brightly colored scarf that he liked to dress. When her food arrived, he rose in a grand manner and approached her without an invitation. "Forgive me, but a woman should never dine alone," he said, in Spanish, and she knew immediately from his accent that he was Argentine. His attitude was off-putting, but charming enough that she felt it unnecessary to dress him down. He ordered more wine for the table and introduced himself as a successful local painter. He was disappointed that this information left her unimpressed. But when he learned that she was from Paris the conversation lit up. He knew it well. Had many gallerists who carried his work there over the years. Had not been back for at least a decade but had an undying admiration and love for the French and their art. He was a man who had been very handsome once, even if something had worn in the better features she could tell he had once possessed. When the proposition that she pose for him came, there was no naivete in her casual affirmation that she would consider it. "Come for a session," Salvador insisted. "If you don't like the experience, you can leave," he added, and slipped her his card. He paid for her meal.

When she decided, two days later, to go and see his address, Salvador seemed to anticipate her arrival. Before she had a chance to decide whether she would ring he had sprung outside coming into the street to greet her. Solemnly, he ushered her inside for tea. The house was large and well appointed. Salvador's taste in beautiful things was refined and one could tell that he took pride in their display. They took tea in the kitchen, which was tiled with smooth warm-colored tomettes like those she had loved as a child in her grandparents' house. Afterward, he took her to his studio. It was a beautiful open space, with old windows facing the inner courtyard. At first, she was very stiff. But the sound of the charcoal became soothing and after a time she got used to it. When the session ended, he pressed a pile of bills into her hand. It turned out to be an extraordinary sum, so much so that her worry about ulterior expectations nearly brought things to a halt. But the experience had not displeased her, and there was something about Salvador that she found unexpectedly attractive, she said. So, she returned. By the third week, she was posing entirely nude. At the conclusion of a long evening session, when he made a proposition, it was not the one she had prepared herself to answer. Salvador said that he was going to be away in Argentina for several weeks, that if she wished she could stay at his place. He would leave money and keys and she would agree to care for the house until his return.

That was how it began, she said. Having such a beautiful place to herself for long stretches of time, totally independent and with no concern for money, meant she could try something she had been thinking about all through her depression: the idea of writing. Now she had the means and a place to do so untroubled, in a city that she had fallen, however oddly, in love with. Salvador was aloof, an aesthete, but mostly harmless. Besides, he would regularly go away for weeks at a time, and when he came home, all he would ask of her was to sit for him so he could paint. She had so much time to herself. In the courtyard she could sit by the lemon tree in the sunlight and read books for hours without hearing a word or a sound besides the chittering of the birds and the lives of the insects. Salvador was often her only regular companion. Despite passing time together, she was never sure she knew him well. She had worried that he would ask her for sex. But he didn't, and after a while she stopped worrying that he would. Sometimes he had other models come to the studio, always young women, sometimes young in a way that made her uncomfortable. But artists are wont to surround themselves with the beautiful. The girls who came to the studio were certainly that. She knew he liked to gaze. Sometimes she would catch Salvador watching her from another room. One time over coffee, he said that she had a mannish quality to her face, that she reminded him of a close friend whom he had lost in the Falklands. She wanted to ask more about it, but the way Salvador spoke she thought it better not to.

Her writing continued to fill up her journals, she said, and the time of the world slipped away. Everything would have been perfect if it hadn't been for the nightmares. They were always similar and very regular now. It started with a conviction that Salvador was at the door watching her sleep. She would feel a deep powerlessness, her body paralyzed, and then wake up in a cold sweat. She always checked to see if Salvador was in the room or lurking outsider her door. But he never was. Outwardly, there was nothing wrong, as far as she could tell. But increasingly, she noticed that people fell silent around Salvador in a manner she had not noticed before. Worse, she said, sometimes she found herself doing the same thing, as though merely being in his presence made her lose her voice. Or she would become uncertain as to whether or not she had spoken. And she began to get visits at night from a tall blue bird. It would land on her head and grip her skull with its talons. She would stay very still and beg that it go away. But the sharp talons dug in. Just when she thought she couldn't take it anymore the bird would take off with a clapping thunder like the sound of a helicopter, and sometimes she was convinced it *was* a helicopter, or a great plane passing low overhead and moving out to sea. Then she would wake. People looked at her funny in the street, she said. As if they knew something about her, as if she was guilty of something terrible. "But all I'm guilty of is wanting time," she said. "Of needing space. Does anyone know how hard it is, even in this day and age, for a woman to live free of any attachments? Free of the need to work? To have a good place to live and write and not owe a man anything, not money, not sex, not the raising of children, nothing!"

There was a momentary quiet. By now the few other diners had long gone. Miguel was standing at his lectern nearby, but Jonah couldn't tell if he had he been listening. Oscar was somewhere in the kitchen, presumably washing up.

Laura was looking directly at Jonah. Their eyes lingered on one another's.

"I'm sorry if I've frightened you," she said after a moment.

"No, not at all."

"I thought, I don't know, there's something about you. I think you remind me of a friend I once knew, a dear friend from long ago. I hope you won't mind me saying this. But I almost never see black people here, you know."

"I can imagine."

"Please, I know it's sudden, but would you come to see me before you leave?"

"I will if you want me to."

"I do. Come see me tomorrow. I will introduce you to Salvador. I think he may like to meet you."

She asked Miguel for a menu and, to the maître d's obvious displeasure, wrote down her address on the back with a rough little map to show him.

"I will see you tomorrow, won't I?"

"Yes, I'll be around," Jonah said.

Satisfied, she left. Jonah immediately ordered another drink. But the bitter sea air in its bite was not enough. The winds had crossed him with Nathaniel's Laura. There could be no doubt. Indeed, he didn't dare doubt it, because it was already as if he had spoken too loudly and been overheard. And now the infinity of the world was answering his rudderless drift by crashing him into the rocks.

20

Jonah spent the next morning anxiously going over the whole thing in his mind. On the one hand, he thought of heading immediately to the internet café to send a message to Nate. On the other, he thought about what the meeting Laura had demanded might promise—what was unspoken but powerfully felt in the way she had looked at him. The thought of her desiring him was troubling in the best and the worst way. Telling Nate would have the effect of collapsing the possible future course of his actions. Postponing that revelation would allow him to make discoveries, to inquire more about Salvador, for instance, which might be important in any report he sent back. But he was sufficiently torn that he made his way to Ciudad Vieja to check his email anyway and at least consider sending a note.

He looked first to see if there was any news from Arna, but there was none. On the other hand, there were several emails from Isaac, one being a short letter and the others containing links to news reports from different outlets. Isaac sounded characteristically grim, but there was a hint of anxiety in his tone that was even more alarming to Jonah than the aggressive graphics in the news clips.

There had been another ugly police shooting, this time in Brooklyn. In fact, it was only seven or eight blocks away from the apartment on St. Johns and Underhill. A team of undercover officers had come up to a young couple leaving their wedding party at a club and for reasons that still remained unclear had shot them as they were getting into their car to leave. The number of shots fired was incredible. As Isaac put it, "They just lit the car up like they were at a shooting gallery, for no reason." The head of the Patrolmen's Benevolent Association had put out a statement to the effect that no investigation would be necessary, it was a tragic incident of mistaken identity, the couple had acted suspiciously and failed to comply with police demands. The man was a local party promoter and the woman a nurse at Woodhull Medical Center. They were both pronounced dead at the scene, but there was additional controversy over whether or not the officers who riddled their bodies with bullets had bothered to call in a timely manner for an ambulance, with some reports indicating that the ambulance had actually responded to calls from others in the wedding party who were in the parking lot and witnessed the shooting. Three of the officers involved were white and a fourth was Hispanic.

There was already a fury in the streets because of the intensification of a campaign to randomly stop and frisk anyone coming in and out of the projects, and the city was now on edge as calls for revenge on the police were being circulated online and peaceful demonstrations in the neighborhood were overtaken by increasingly violent clashes. The police were responding with more brutality, more tear gas, and mass arrests. The images were out of a dystopian nightmare. Phalanxes of cops in military-grade body armor, mounted officers raising batons and smashing their shields into faces in the crowds on the dark streets of Brooklyn. Hundreds had already been arrested, the president had given a speech calling on "the better angels." But the raw anger in the streets and the grotesque disproportion of the police response were feeding a hopeless downward spiral. Isaac was still supposed to go to work and teach his third graders, but many parents were refusing to even let their kids leave the house as long as the threat of a wider riot was still heavy in the air.

By the time he had digested the news and realized he would have to compose some kind of note to Isaac, Jonah was utterly demoralized. What was there to say? Telling him about his adventures and discovery of Laura in Montevideo seemed somehow both unseemly and vaguely unkind. He wrote and deleted and rewrote several times what amounted to only a three- or four-line email, with banal phrases telling his friend to "stay safe" and "stay strong." Any thought of writing to Nate evaporated. He couldn't think straight, and besides, it wasn't the right time. But when would the right time be?

Outside in the cool breeze, he walked along watching the people of Uruguay go about their tranquil lives. How different it would be to live in some small country like this—with its own complicated history, no doubt, but where, at least at present, one might grow up without ever really thinking that anything one's country did or failed to do mattered, apart from occasionally making it to the World Cup finals. No foreign wars. No racial conflict spilling into the streets every day, no mass shootings, no sudden world-altering terrorist attacks would come screaming across the sky. Also, no black people. Which meant no place he could ever really be. Well, almost none. Once Jonah saw a glimpse of what appeared to be a drumline parading down one of the avenues. It was brief. He came around a corner and saw in the far distance a group of black men, one of them waving an albiceleste flag with a black diagonal stripe. But they were walking away from him and the music faded. He had asked Oscar about it, and had learned that there was in fact a small community of blacks in Uruguay, the descendants of slaves who had escaped south from Brazil, where emancipation didn't come until 1888, a full sixty years after the Uruguayans had fought their way to independence from the Portuguese Empire. The diaspora was always larger than one imagined. But whatever the situation of the black folk in Montevideo—and he guessed it probably wasn't magnificent—could it be as bad as Brownsville? As the bloody streets of Baltimore? He walked in a daze of muted anger. At what, he didn't know exactly, mostly at himself. He felt guilty and stupid for being where he was. For having it so easy, but also for not having an answer, something that would justify his trajectory. While in this state of agitation he found himself, having wandered a good deal farther to the north than he had anticipated, standing outside the green entrance of the colonial solare that Laura had described to him. It was late in the afternoon by the time he arrived on the beautiful, tree-lined street, which showed no signs of life other than the occasional car or small truck thudding along under a light load.

Laura met him at the door and led him in through cool dim hallways to a spare living room. A neoclassical mold stood in one corner, a large palm by the window fronded a passage to an inner courtyard, and in the middle of the room a long, heavily worn-in couch, dark and sea green, faced a small fireplace flanked on both sides by towering bookcases. Glancing over them, he noted artist monographs, old volumes of classical literature in Spanish, and moderns like Borges alongside names that Jonah didn't recognize, that he guessed were Argentine or Uruguayan writers of decades past.

As he was taking in the room, Laura brought a bottle and two glasses in from the kitchen.

"Will you drink with me?" she asked.

"Avec plaisir."

"Ah, tant mieux. I've been waiting for an occasion to have someone to drink wine with—you know they love their whiskey here. I hope you will be pleased with the vin de maison—naturally it's Argentinian."

"Honestly, I'm not picky. Besides, I think I can trust your taste."

She uncorked and poured them each a glass, then turned to him again.

"Do you mind if I ask how old you are? You look . . . very young, you know."

"Old enough."

She smiled at this. "Ah! Well, cheers to that. I enjoyed our talk. I realize I did most of the talking. But you put me at ease in a way I haven't felt in so long. I think I told you . . . you remind me . . ."

"Of someone you knew, someone from years ago in Paris . . . a black man."

"Did I say all that? Well, it's true enough. He was special to me . . . Something about him was different from all the others."

"And I remind you of him?"

"In some ways, yes."

He was very conscious now of controlling his voice, every intonation, of the way his hands were placed and more still of how her eyes fell on them at times as though quietly imbibing something there at the surface that she wanted to keep for a later time.

"Do I make you nervous?" she asked.

"No, only a little, maybe."

"I hope you don't mind if I say this. I can't help it, I'm always very direct. But you have the air of a young man who doesn't stay anywhere for too long, or with anyone for too long. Are you still planning on leaving Montevideo very soon?"

"Yes, I can't stay much longer . . . I think I've started to realize that there are a number of things back home that I really need to get back to."

"A girlfriend perhaps."

"No, actually. Not that."

"Are you sure? I would be surprised if there wasn't more than one you might have left behind."

"You seem to see more in me than others. I wish it were true in a way, but it isn't."

"Well, I feel lucky then to have caught your eye while you were passing through."

"Did you catch me? I feel like it's more that I've . . . found you."

"You've found me at an interesting time. I feel more myself now than I've felt in years, almost as if I'm coming out of a deep sleep."

"Tell me, what was he like?"

"Who?"

"The man you knew in Paris."

"He was a beautiful man. Handsome, athletic, darker than you—very intelligent and kind. He knew how to make love in all the ways that matter. What about you? I think you are probably too young to have such experience."

"I haven't got as much as experience as I would like."

"You wish you had more?"

"Yes. If I were with someone who wanted to give me the chance, then yes."

Instead of responding to this directly, Laura rose from her end of the couch and walked into an adjoining hall. He heard the creak of a faucet. A moment later, she reappeared in the living room, lifted her drink, and took a sip while looking upon him, and sat down again.

"I'm going to take a bath. Would you care to join me?"

Her gaze was steady, and he met it as he thought carefully about his answer. She was older, of course, and rounder and heavier than in the picture Nate had sent along. In the picture she still had a girlish prettiness, but also a blankness to her features. Now she was a woman, her body thicker and more attractive, her face more expressive, beautiful in a way that the image he had seen was not. She had grown her hair out very long, and now as she waited for his reply, she had taken some of it in her hands.

"I think I will, yes. If that's all right with you."

"Good. I would like that."

She put down her drink and moved across the couch, leaning in over him so that her hair was falling over his arm.

"Don't move."

"Okay."

She put her lips to his softly. And as he started to kiss her back, she took his hand in her own and placed it against her breast. When she had felt what she needed, she got up and led him to the bathroom where they undressed. She held him against her body as they waited for the water to rise. When it was ready, she turned off the faucet, threw down a pile of towels for her comfort and, having smoothed them to her satisfaction, turned to confront him with her sex. Afterward, they slipped into the hot water; the tub sang like a whale as they slid against its hull.

It wasn't until they were drying off that Jonah even thought to inquire about Salvador, and he was alarmed to learn that the owner of the house had been there the entire time, painting in his studio upstairs. Laura was nonchalant.

"I told him you might come by and he agreed to meet with you if you did. Why don't you go upstairs and you two can get acquainted? I'll be ready and have something for us to eat this evening when you come down."

After he'd dressed again, Laura led him through the inner courtyard, and over to a stone staircase that wound around itself. The air outside was immensely pleasant, and dramatic pinkish light was coloring streaks of high cloud above. She motioned for him to go up, then turned and headed back inside the main residence.

The studio of Salvador Aussaresses occupied an entire wing on the second floor. Jonah found himself on a landing with a small window adorned with a box of bougainvillea. He made his way across a short hall and found himself immediately facing the great open space of the studio itself. The chipped ceramic floor tiles were covered in rust-colored drips, and on what looked like a drafting table there were piles of soiled canvas rags. Paintings in various stages of completion were stacked together haphazardly along the walls. The stinging smell of oils hung in the air.

In the very center of the room, a man sat on a thick wooden stool squinting at the mounted canvas before him. He wore a pair of khaki shorts with a braided leather belt, flip-flops, and nothing else. He was tanned, the effect of his tall, angular build somewhat belied by a leathery neck and tufts of white hair sprouting at his shoulder blades. The column of his spine popped out to accommodate his spry corpulence as he leaned forward to apply the nib of his brush. Directly in his sights was a very pale naked girl reclining on a taupe divan, one arm draped along a wad of ragged throw pillows.

Jonah instinctively froze in his tracks and was about to turn and back out when the artist, without turning to acknowledge him, made a loud snort and motioned him in with the back of his free hand. The reclining model tried to look over at Jonah with her eyes, but at the quiver of her neck Salvador made an abrupt hissing sound and she became fixed in stone again. Jonah could tell that she was an adolescent, perhaps sixteen or seventeen. She had a mousy face, concentrated in an expression that might have been intended to convey coquetry but that suggested something more like masked terror. The artist continued his work uninterrupted. The model tried to sneak another look.

"Mírame," Salvador muttered under his breath. But the incident had broken his momentum. "Please sit down, pull up a chair," he ordered without taking his eyes off the canvas. His English was impeccable, with a touch of Oxbridge in the accents. There was a stool by the wall. Jonah pulled it over and sat toward the quarter of the room behind the painter so that they both faced the scene of subjection.

"So . . . you are the young man my Laura has been telling me about. I'm glad you came. I knew from the moment she told me that you would. As I'm sure you can see, Laura is a beautiful woman. We have a good understanding, she and I. She knows my nature, and I, in turn, know hers."

He paused at this, considering the exposed model on the makeshift couch.

"Tell me, young man, do you care for painting?"

"Painting? Sure."

"What part of her do you like best? What part catches your eye? Do you like her breasts? It's okay, you know, you can say so."

"I like the hands."

"Ah! The hands. Good, that's very good. Did you know that human hands are the hardest thing to paint? One hand alone, if a painter wanted to get it perfectly done, would take a year to paint . . . Even Rembrandt struggled to paint a good hand. But, the hands of the father in the *Return of the Prodigal Son* . . . now *there* is a hand painted in pure truth, the truth of our greatest fear . . . the fear of our own choices. I will tell you a little secret. Do you know which Rembrandt contains the greatest hand of all?"

"No."

"*The Slaughtered Ox*. Musée du Louvre, in the Richelieu gallery. A genuine masterpiece. Maybe his greatest work. True, it not a painting of a human hand. It is far greater, more ambitious than that. It is a painting of the hand of God."

The poor model, who hadn't moved an inch, sneezed. The light in the studio was failing. She must have been getting cold. Salvador dipped his brush in a jar of water and wiped it down carefully in a cloth. With a nod of the head, he dismissed the girl. It took her a moment to get up. Her legs seemed to have fallen asleep and she stumbled like a lame animal to a corner of the room and began hurriedly dressing. Salvador Aussaresses now turned his attention fully upon his visitor.

"Egon Schiele. There is a great painter of hands! I'm very fond of Austrian art, you know . . . Before I found this place, I thought about moving there. Had quite a few friends who left for Austria in '83. But I haven't kept in touch. I just want to paint. I just want to live quietly and enjoy the time that I have left. You'll see, when you get to be my age, you see things differently. I'm more sensitive to time now, how little of it there truly is. And I've become greedy, in a way. I want to be surrounded by beauty. I want to paint the perfect hand, a hand so sublime that one day it will hang in the Museo Nacional!" Salvador laughed, so hard that it pitched him into a brutal fit of coughing. Then he was composed again. "I'll be saved, you see," he went on. "I'll be saved by the curators. The critics. After you and I are long dead and gone, they will need careers and reputations, and then I will be *rediscovered*, celebrated—an overlooked, neglected master."

"Maybe, but then again, maybe not. I don't think my generation even believes in the idea of artistic greatness."

"You're a sharp little monkey, aren't you?"

"What did you say?"

"Don't think you impress me. You're still just a boy. I, however, am a man. I have struggled. I have known what it is to believe in something, to do whatever it takes even to achieve small, pitiful victories. You haven't struggled for anything in your life. It was all handed to you. And what have you done with it? Your entire generation . . . grown up with the whole thing handed to you. The war over, the dust settled. You're decadent, flabby. You forget that you are living in the world *we* won for you. *We* fought the Communists! We were the ones who eliminated them, so that you could come of age with all the world at your fingertips, playing with your new gadgets, shopping, living it up. How old are you? What do you know about anything?"

Jonah got up to leave, but the old man surprised him, crying out for him to stay, pleading with him pathetically over a sudden coughing fit. As Jonah wavered, Salvador fished under his easel amid a pile of rags and produced a bottle of whiskey. He took a couple of jars over to a sink in the far corner of the room and rinsed them out. The studio was getting dark. Jonah felt paralyzed. He looked around for a light to switch on, or a lamp, but there was none. When Salvador returned, he poured them each a large glass and sat down again in silence. Jonah realized he could barely see the painter's face now, just the deep bluish outline of his features, a glint of arctic sheen.

"Do you know what I like about painting?" Salvador began again, resuming his philosophical tone. Jonah put the glass of whiskey to his lips as Salvador continued.

"I like its faithfulness. All a good painting requires is faithfulness. Looking steadfastly at the abyss and accepting the world for what it is. Not just tolerating it. Weak men can do that. But taking it whole, as the greatest artists do. I have struggled my whole life to do it. But I have not yet succeeded. Now I have so few years left. One day, you will understand this. Or perhaps you won't. I was born in a time of war. I lived the wars of my time. There is only one law of human life. The permanence of war. And I faced it. I didn't grow up behind a screen."

Salvador carefully lit the end of a cigarette. The hot eye drifted in the gloom as the old man took a deep drag. He offered one, and Jonah accepted. When his own smoke was lit, he was ready with a reply.

"Maybe there's something more powerful," Jonah said. "Something real in the world, that escapes your law of war. Always and everywhere. And maybe it's just that you need to believe in war because the things you needed to figure out in your life, you've always left empty."

"Ah, you think perhaps I am merely a doddering old man. You have the idealism of youth, and yet your life, just as mine was, will be dominated by power. Even more so, yes, even more so. Ha! Look at you! A Negro, or what do you prefer we call you now? Black? You know, I've always been curious . . . how does it *feel* to be a *black*? I have often wondered. It seems like it would be quite terrible, if you don't mind me saying so. It seems like a cruel joke. One even feels sorry for you, *up to a point*. A people have to know when they are defeated. The Indios, the slaves. You can't unwrite the history, can you? It isn't *my* fault, is it? What has come to pass. You can't fight the nature of men. The war between us is permanent. Look how your towers have fallen. Dirty wars. Who has the dirt on their hands now? We laugh at the pictures of Abu Ghraib because you Americans are stupid enough to take them. You know what has to be done but you have no maturity, no stomach, no seriousness of purpose. I see by the look on your face that you are shocked by my words. But it is *you* who is not living in the real world. The real world is the law of violence: directed, organized by the will of men. The strong take violence into their own hands, lead history like a naked man on a leash—when the man yanks, smack him with the stick, and soon enough he learns. The Arabs are stubborn as mules. I admire that. I admire men who are not persuaded by anything but death. Mark my words, the day the terror stops, you will miss them, your Arab terrorists. War is without end. It is also without limit. You will see. These tools will be turned on you and your neighbors. The soldiers will come home and turn on each other. The drones will patrol Colorado and Texas and Virginia. For the blacks, well, I'm sure you can guess how it will go. I'm not fooled, I can see it all clearly. Thank god, I'll be long gone by then. In my day we fought for principles, for a way of life. But what do I know? I'm just an old painter. I only want the peace of an old man to live out his last days."

The old man drank for a time in silence. The studio had slipped into darkness. Jonah could barely make out his own glass.

"I hear Laura met you over at the Basques'?"

"Yes, Miguel and Oscar . . ."

"Did you enjoy their company?"

"Yeah, sure."

"Did they enjoy yours?"

"I'm fine with where I'm at, if that's what you're asking, but frankly I also don't plan on sticking around much longer."

"Oh no, what about the cuisine—great cooks, eh? Their kind always are, no? Didn't you like their food?"

"Yes."

"Good, I wouldn't want to have to tell them that you didn't. Hah! The Basques—they're liable to blow you up for far less. No, but I like them, I really do. In fact, I fully support them. Lots of good people around here do. They've got no better base anywhere in the world than right here in Uruguay. The Spaniards will never conquer the Basques, never I tell you. Spanish intelligence is a joke. Don't you think so?"

"I don't know what you mean."

"Of course they're a joke. You ever hear of the Spanish Air Force? You can't have good intelligence without a good air force. As an aviator, I had to learn how to dominate my instincts, in an environment where the slightest mistake, the slightest miscalculation, can be fatal. Omniscience is essential. Perfect eyesight, solid minds that stay cold. The same goes for the other game. We got our terrorists because we understood how to handle them. We wiped them out so badly it will probably be a hundred years before they ever come back. And it would be suicide even then. But something tells me they will come back some day. Those people have a death wish."

"No, you have a wish to kill. Because you're not just a painter, are you? You're ex-military."

"And proud of my service. Proud of my country. When I was a boy, even younger than you, I grew up dreaming of Jorge Newbery. The aviators were admired in those days, they were our celebrities. By the time I joined we were already in the process of national reorganization. The Communists were crawling all over the place like roaches. It was our chance to do something for our country. I volunteered for the counterterrorism missions, most of us did. I operated the Hercules, the C-130s, those big whales we got from America. We would fly out of Morón and hop down to Mar del Plata. We would land before dawn and the jeeps and trucks would come out to meet us on the tarmac. The Hercules is a magnificent aircraft. Up in the cockpit the airframe is so wide you feel like you're at the helm of a flying cathedral. At Mar del Plata we refueled, and they loaded the cargo. I was always in the cockpit. It was cold out there with the sun about to rise, and cold gusts from the Atlantic pouring over the airfield. I went through my checklists, chatted with the ground crews on the radio. The loading took a long time. Sometimes I would see a chaplain in black robes walking around, talking to the officers on the ground. Everything was very orderly. When I got the signal to go, we would rev up the engines and barrel down the runway straight for the ocean. I would set a cap due east and we would fly out two or three hundred miles. That's when the second officer would give the signal to take us down on a low pass over the water. I would straighten us out at twenty-five hundred feet. The cargo officer would open the payload doors and then he and some of the Naval Intelligence guys would go into the hold. My job was to keep the plane steady, and that's what I did. We would fly like that for twenty minutes or so. Then the officers would come back into the cockpit and strap in, and I would take us in a long loop, circling back over the drop zone but this time headed back toward Mar del Plata. There were always dark shadows in the water there, and when I asked the Navy boys about it, they said they were sharks. We did the same sorties two, sometimes even three times a week, for a while. It became routine, boring. On the flights back, we would often discuss the Malvinas and how the war was going. Everyone found positive things to say, but we all knew it was hopeless. England was too powerful, and probably the most stubborn nation on Earth, more stubborn than even the Arabs. One day, when we got back to the base in Morón, as I was heading into the barracks, I realized that I had forgotten my sunglasses in the cockpit. Since the hold was open, I went up through the belly of the plane to get them. The belly of the Hercules is like a train tunnel. I found my glasses in the cockpit, but on my way out I stopped in the hold again to marvel at its size. I shouted a little to hear the echoes. Then I noticed something by my feet. Along the bottom of the hold there were locking gears and grappling hooks for securing cargo to the floor. Tangled in one of the hooks was a large clump of hair. I could tell right away that it was a woman's, by the length, by its luster and curl. I'm a painter. I've always been a close observer of these things. I could tell it was the hair of a young brunette. And as I kept walking, looking closely, I found more clumps of hair caught in the riggings. Hair of different colors, some men and some more clearly women. That's when I knew. I mean, I knew before then. But that's when I knew for sure. An officer appeared on the ramp; he must have heard me shouting. He asked me what I was doing. I told him I was just getting my sunglasses and I quickly made some joke and we walked back across the tarmac together laughing. No one ever asked me any questions. Not until years later."

"What did you say when people did finally ask?"

"Some reporter found me in 1991. He came looking for names. He wanted to know about what he called 'the death flights.' I wasn't concerned. The president pardoned everyone. I was untouchable. But that's not the reason I kept my trap shut. The reporter offered me money in exchange for names, good money too. But those people don't get it. They don't understand there's no price you can put on loyalty. I'm not a mercenary. I can't be bought. I faced the reality of my time and I chose sides. And they were believers too. We were all wolves. Was it bad? Yes. They were alive when we dropped them. Drugged but alive. Our will was stronger. We had the virility of youth. We had the great forces of order, the state and the church, and the military on our side. The nation was imperiled. We had to clean our house . . . We had to reorganize . . . We had the will and it was a time of wolves when anything was possible and we were young and history was on our side and every sensation every action was vivid and extreme . . ."

The artist trailed off and there was an interminable silence. Jonah thought he heard the crack of a door slamming shut somewhere in the courtyard, but it could have been a branch snapping from a tree or a heavy book landing on a tile floor. The jolt should have prompted him to get up, but his muscles locked. The old man stared serenely across the darkness, his quivering lips parted ambiguously, expectantly, faintly amused.

21

What Salvador said of him was true. Jonah had never felt touched by the chill of evil. Atrocity and human suffering were spectacles that befell others. They came to him as breaking news, they bothered him, troubled his nerves for a time, but did not even come close to bringing him to the point of naming or even acknowledging anything like a willful, metaphysical malice that might at any moment take the form of a human face committed to irreversible destruction. He had never had a cousin gunned down, lost his family to a local warlord's political ambitions, a passionate campaign of slaughter, a posse of racists on the hunt, or a man so broken he would put you in the dirt for four hundred dollars, for bragging rights, to defend his wounded honor. Yet these were the most obvious features of life for most people everywhere. Far more obvious than whatever enemy he conjured for himself when he invoked the specter of "late capitalism," which was the nearest phrase to which he could affix the largest share of blame for the ills of the world while dimly perceiving that it also assured his own procession through it. The wheel of fortune had spared him from having to do truly ugly things. Many ugly things were done on his behalf. And many had also been endured. His body the gift of colossal, unending histories of violence. Salvador knew this, and he reached through the darkness to take Jonah by the hand and show him.

Before he knew it, Jonah was bounding down the stone stairs and making his way back across the courtyard and into the house. Laura was singing to herself, and he followed her voice to the kitchen where she was preparing dinner. As he entered the singing stopped. She could read on his face the end of a line of thought.

"You're not staying."

"No, I'm sorry, I have to go."

She did not appear wounded, but moved into a suspended pause of judgment, a stay against a blow.

"I should have . . . I should let you out then."

"Laura, I have to leave tomorrow. Could I see you once more before I go? Tomorrow morning. Please. It's very important."

"What for?"

"I have something. Something important to give you. I don't have it here with me. If you can meet me tomorrow morning at the Basques', I can leave it with you. And also, I want to get a chance to properly say goodbye."

"You could say it now. You are saying it now."

"I know, I'm sorry to be like this. I'm confused, really, I'm afraid . . ."

"You're afraid. Well, I'm glad you could at least say it. Go on, then, I have things to finish up here. I'll show you out."

She walked him back out to the front and for a moment stood regarding him out on the street.

"Will you promise me to come tomorrow, at nine o'clock?" he asked.

"You don't have to worry about it."

"So, you'll come?"

"I always come for the men who deserve it."

She had no more words for him, and he found himself drifting down the foreign streets alone, one cigarette after another lighting the way to his relative shelter.

When he got back to his room at El Vasco, he couldn't sleep. He opened a page in his travel journal and started writing a long letter to Arna. When he looked up, pale dawn was already in the window. He went down into the waking streets and made his way to the only internet café he knew in the old city, hurrying in case Laura decided to come early. He wanted to check his mail and look up as much useful information as he could find about Buenos Aires. He wondered how Octavio was doing. There had been no word since his arrival in Montevideo.

His inbox was overflowing, mostly with the usual spam. There were several emails from his mother and one from his father but he did not want to deal with anything from his parents right then, and he did not open them. More pressingly there was an email from Nate and an email from Isaac. With a sinking heart, he saw that Arna had not written him back.

Jonah considered writing her a brief note. He opened Isaac's email instead.

Sorry to break the news this way, man, but I've had to make some choices. With the way things are I've come to the decision that New York just isn't for me. I haven't told you about everything that's gone down at the school but suffice to say I'm done with that. I'm just not happy in the work, and everything with the shooting and the protests and all the crazy shit that's popping off in this city—I'm done with it, man. I don't want no part of it anymore. Also I've been talking for a while now with this sister I met online. She's from Atlanta, works for this label down there and she's been trying to get me to come down and see her for like forever, and last week while the shit was hectic I decided to take off and see her. And, you know, she's right. It's beautiful in the ATL. Reminds me of home, except the music scene is off the charts right now. A nigga could really get somewhere if he put his mind to it and had the right connections, and I'm feeling like I want to give this music shit a real chance. It's always been something I've loved and I feel like I have what it takes to do well in the business, especially right now, working with artists, scouting talent, maybe even producing records. So, I know this is kinda sudden, but I've decided to move down there. I've already put in notice at work. Lease is up soon, and the demand is so high here—I've talked to the management and they can't wait to get rid of my black ass. Not sure when you'll be back, but the one thing I wanted to touch base about is these letters, man. Your French girl been sending you mad longhand correspondence. I know you'll want those so I was thinking I would forward them to your place in Paris. So, send me your address when you get this. Hope all is well otherwise with you. I'll miss our times hanging out, man, I really will. But when you get your shit together, come on down to the real South America to see a brotha. You'll always have a place to stay with me. And I can show you a good time too. There's a whole world down there y'all don't know nothing about.

—Isaac

Thus he learned the friendship he had made in New York was dissolving. There should have been nothing terribly dramatic about it. It was, from a certain point of view, logical and maybe even predictable. Friends moved from city to city all the time, and people held on to friendships as they could. And yet the news brought a rush of sadness to his chest. He reread the email, stunned, and then sent a brief reply saying how cool it was to hear about the move, and that he was excited for him. He gave his coordinates in Paris and hit send. Caught in a blank anger, he went to sign off when he realized he hadn't checked the note from Nate. To his dismay, the missive was fraternal and warm, and it struck like a dagger.

Good brother,

I was thinking about you again today and wondering when you might be coming back. I don't know if you've heard about the shooting and the protests in the city, but you've been missing out on some amazing stuff. Folks are mad as hell and taking it to the streets in ways I haven't seen since like the seventies. I know a smart young cat like yourself could be involved in it. I wish I could be, but honestly, I'm too old for this mess. Besides I got my hands full with my after-school ball program and all that. My offer still stands—would love to have you up here working with me. It could even turn into like an internship, a hoops fellowship. Kinda like the sound of that! Are you still in Montevideo? I can't lie, I do still wonder sometimes if she's really out there. I gotta stop with these fantasies. But what can we do? It's like Janet says, that's the way love goes . . .

—Nate

Jonah felt his head spin. He knew he had to tell Laura to leave Salvador. He had to give her Nathaniel's letter. And he knew that as soon as he did, he would have to leave Montevideo.

Back in his room at El Vasco, he packed his things. Nathaniel's letter had gotten slightly crumpled in his bag. The envelope had not been sealed, and the fold lay flattened on its back, revealing a bit of paper marked with Nathaniel's handwriting. With a flush of shame, he pulled it out. There it was, his silent travel companion. He nervously unfolded the paper.

Dear Laura,

I'll start this the only way I know how. I don't know if you will ever get this letter. Probably not. In a way, it's as if I'm writing to you from the past or maybe even a past life. I want to leave a record of my thoughts, so that if by chance you do read this, you will have some idea, at least some understanding of the man I am now. What can I tell you about that man? I'm writing to you today from New York City. From my desk in the heights of the Bronx, the city runs down the Hudson River away from me into steel and glass and fumes of Manhattan. It's not at all like Paris, which I can recall as clearly as this view. I can still see you standing outside the tabac, your hands moving as you talk at a café table, the shape your body made under the sheets, your books, the smell of cigarettes and plaster on the rue des Cinq-Diamants. That was Paris. It was our city, but it was your home. This is mine.

If you came you would find it's too hot in the summer, and too damn cold in the winter. It's too crowded and too poor and too rich . . . and every year it seems like things are getting worse, although, in truth, things always seem to be about the same. This is where I was raised, not just in the Bronx, but the whole city. I love the sound of a New York voice. I love the sound of helicopters in the sky, tugboats on the river, yellow cabs as they jump in and out of lanes, small talk at 125th Street and Lenox, night games at Yankee Stadium, girls in troupes cursing and singing and clapping, the beautiful sound of Spanish on Upper Broadway where they sell platanos and sandía out the side of a Chevy, players pushing Fleetwood Cadillacs through the projects, bass booming. The smell of garbage and the hiss of frying meats, kids clowning around coming out of the corner bodega, brothers talking that talk on the corner, the subway rolling down the Jerome Avenue line. I love the sound of basketball courts at dusk. It's a sound that takes me way back . . . I'm talking back to the days of guys that used to play there that we gave names like Big Helicopter, Earl "The Goat," "Pee Wee" Kirkland, all these legends that I came up playing with in Rucker Park, a place where if your game was tight you went home feeling tall as Kareem.

I remember kids used to sit in the trees just to watch Julius Erving rise up through the air from the free-throw line, his arm carrying the ball like a torch of liberty. These things are the stuff my city is made of.

Laura, there are things I wish you could see. I have children now. Ones I'm teaching what I can in the hopes of doing something to make things change and come out right for once, to try and change the destiny of the kids who grow up on the blocks where I grew up, blocks where half the kids I grew up with are gone, dead, or doing bids upstate. I want so bad for these kids to have a chance to see what I've seen, to move through the world different, to see more and know more, and taste the kind of living that they struggle to imagine. And I can see it happen before my eyes one at a time. With all the love the folks in the community show me, I get new students to my basketball clinic every day. They come from all over the Bronx to learn how to play ball, how to improve their game. I always tell them: If you want to improve your game, improve yourself. You are the game. They don't know how literally I mean it. Sometimes there are fights, and sometimes the play is too rough. I remember how it was when I was coming up. I was small. I used to get knocked around a lot. Had to learn to scrape, had to be better. The game is intuition. You always know before you let go whether it's going in. You always know when to make the pass before you can think to make it. You know where to be, you feel the ball reach your hands at the top of the key, you fake, you whirl like Earl the Pearl, you open a notch and pop up, the ball is gone, it's over, sinking in, and you turn away because the game has already moved on. Everyone moves on, and the world doesn't slow for none of us.

The other night I went for a walk along the West Side

promenade. I stood at the edge of the Hudson and looked up. The lights of the George Washington Bridge parted the night. The sight of the bridge struck me like John Henry's hammer. I looked up and thought: What is this? What is this giant thing that I am made of? America, wading knee-high in the blood of its own children. Of the African slaves. Of Cherokee and Sioux. Union regiments and Confederate cavalry. Of sharecroppers and lynching blood on the leaves, railroad workers, field hands and migrant farmers, the children of Birmingham and the garbage collectors of Memphis, the people of Vietnam under our napalm and our flamethrowers, the blood of our own sons and daughters. The blood of my ancestors that flows in my veins. All that blood that I know we got to answer for. This imperial force more powerful than Rome. The George Washington Bridge is so awesome, so vast. It's got to mean something, to portend something that's still happening, something so big we'll never be able to imagine the end toward which it is pointing. And then I also feel there's something austere, even lonely about it. A Miles Davis kind of thing. For Baldwin it's where a man goes to jump when he can't take this life no more. I've seen people in my life go that way, and sometimes I've even secretly thought it myself. I think every American comes to that bridge at some point in their lives because how could you help it in the face of the sheer madness of things perpetrated on a daily basis? But I strive to see it otherwise. Call me a dreamer. Maybe, but to me that bridge could be my light, my lonely lighthouse, towering over Gotham, sending a bat signal so bright that you might see it round the bend of the world.

Laura, where have you gone? When will you come flying back to me? Your face peers into my dreams. How does it do that? Maybe because you are the one person I can speak deeply and freely with. I feel totally free when I write to you. Listening to music and watching the hand of time pass over the city. I like to listen to these jazz shows on WKCR when I write just to absorb some of that artistry. It's something in those brothers that moves me. I hear them playing like the only thing that matters is beauty. Even with all we going through. I hear them say, hold on now. Listen. How beautiful we are.

The other day I went downtown, found myself on Sixth Avenue. And truth be told, I had never thought of it before but we call it: Avenue of the Americas. The Americas. We should always use the plural, I think. What a beautiful ring it has to it. A life in the Americas. On every street corner and every subway car in New York City, the Americas. One island in the human archipelago. Headstrong and unstoppable, like the Staten Island Ferry, always chugging headlong into the looming shadows of the white buildings. Some folk stare up from the deck holding a paper cup full of coffee wondering if they'll ever catch a break. Me, I always preferred to stay apart from the crowd, looking back at the way we came over. You see, people always thought of me as just a body, a man they could use. But I got a mind, and my own philosophy. And being in the world a good number of years now, I have come to believe that it's in the nature of the human spirit to search. For a long time, I myself was on a search to understand where I came from and why, and what I ought to do with myself. And when I met you in Paris, I thought that maybe you were part of the answer. I guess I always thought the answer would be something new. But it's not. I understand why you left. I know you're searching for something too. Just remember that it might not be a new thing, but the old one to come back to that drives you onward again. I guess I've gotten carried away. It keeps happening with me now, when I sit down to write you. It's as if I need to get the whole world off my chest, and you, Laura, you are the only intelligent person left on Earth.

I've got to get down to the playground. Late afternoon, low eighties. Perfect weather. The Knicks are playing tonight I keep fixin' to give up on them, but I'm trying to give faith and patience a chance. I got to admit, I still wish it was me balling in the Garden under the big lights, taking it up the floor. Hitting them with a sweet move, the God Shammgod reverse finish at the hoop, taking it back to the old school, when we played the game the right way. But I know it's too late for all that. What I really want you to know is that I still have the passion. The years may be creeping up on me, but I got no plans to get old. There's just too much still to do with the neighborhood, with this city I love, with this mad country I got to live in. I feel a little tired. I guess I'll sign off here as I always do with a wish: to see you again. When you next consider flying across the waters, think of coming here, think of coming back to me

     Nate Archimbald

⌘

Laura met him at exactly nine o'clock on the street outside El Vasco. Jonah suggested they go for a walk, a proposition she accepted without comment. But their mutual pained attentiveness only prolonged the unbearable and she stopped him short at one of the wide corners where they had been waiting for the light.

"Why don't you get to whatever it is you want from me? I'm not in the mood for romance today."

"Well, I have to give you something that won't make sense at first, but I

256

know that it was meant to be this way, maybe not the way I've gone about it, but I know that you need to read this, and when you do I hope you'll do the right thing and leave Salvador. Not just Salvador but Montevideo."

"What do you mean?" asked Laura, suddenly stiff.

"Trust me, promise me, no matter what—that you will at least get away from Salvador."

Before she could react, he pulled out Nathaniel's letter.

"This is from Nathaniel. Nathaniel Archimbald. I met him in New York, and he gave me this letter because I think he knew somehow that I would meet you. It's crazy, I know, but here we are. You should have this."

Laura didn't move. She seemed paralyzed. They were silent for a time, and then she spoke.

"You need to leave."

"Okay."

"Now. Please leave."

He could see anger and confusion cloud her face. He thought to kiss her on the cheek, but she motioned him away, so he murmured an apology and left her there clutching Nathaniel's letter in her hand.

All the way to the ferry terminal in Colonia, Jonah could feel his face burning. When he got on board and took to the rail to look back at the receding shore, he finally felt a terrible weight begin to lift. He was running on his own now. But the new lightness in his chest wasn't better. It was worse. He told himself that he was seasick.

22

With the letter in Laura's hands, Jonah took the ferry across the Río de la Plata. The great avenues of Buenos Aires looked like nothing so much as Paris. Proud, lively, officiously pretentious. From a cheap hostel in San Telmo he went searching for good bookstores in Recoleta. Everyone claimed there were excellent bookstores there. But it wasn't true. Not on the calle Borges and not anywhere else. Palermo Hollywood was teeming with young Americans. He got roped into a conversation with some earnest, bright-eyed banker types. They demanded he talk sports. Then proceeded to enlighten him about the terrific opportunities of sovereign debt. There was no place they could fail to presume they should get what they wanted.

He ditched them and plunged onward, losing his way in the labyrinth of the city. Groaning buses filled the air with diesel fumes. Women with tinted shades pranced through the soot clutching monogrammed bags. Finally, he found a bookstore in the city center. The cool air-conditioning and the quiet were a relief and he idled in the aisles. The shopkeeper, a potbellied man in a gray sweater, came over twice to ask him if he needed help before huffing off again. Jonah decided on a copy of *Los poemas de Sidney West* by Juan Gelman. The bookseller practically snatched the money from him while muttering something he assumed the gringo wouldn't understand. But Jonah did understand. There was no such thing as a good black person in Buenos Aires.

Large demonstrations against the government were taking place on the Plaza de Mayo. Mothers with gray hair tucked into their scarves carried signs demanding knowledge of the fate of their children. They were the mothers of the "disappeared." Over coffee, Jonah deciphered the headlines in the leading daily. The generals said they were sorry, but that they had done nothing wrong. They were following orders. What was done had been necessary to rid the nation of Marxist terrorists.

Back at the hostel, the lady who did the housekeeping and tended the entryway noticed Jonah's book of poetry while he was reading it alone in the common room. She asked him if he liked poetry very much. Yes, he said. She asked if he knew what they had done to Juan Gelman's son. No, he said. They impaled him, she said. Impale meant to stick a rod up through the anus into the stomach so you bleed to death very slowly. They sent his pregnant girlfriend to a detention center in Uruguay. No one ever saw her again. He was twenty-four. She was twenty-three. So many young people, she said. All of us will take this stain with us to our graves. Every day, I ask myself, how could this have happened? Where are you from? America, he said. Why didn't anyone in your country speak out and try to stop it? Because we supported it, he said. I know, she said, I know, but *why*? He tried to think of an answer. He thought of Katrina. He thought of how many images of disaster, torture, and death he had consumed in the relatively few years of his conscious life. I suppose it's because we don't care, he said. No, I mean, we do care, but only about money. Yes, she said, it's the same here. Well, in a way, we are everywhere, he said. It was Burson-Marsteller that made so much money by lying about it. Who are they? She wanted to know. Advertisers, Jonah said. The best in the world. Then advertisers are the greatest criminals of our age, she said. How could they? Our mothers only ask for justice, peace, answers! And they get silence, threats, and lies. All of Argentina is built on unspeakable crimes and indifference. And nothing changes. The people are still in poverty. The same forty families own all the land. The Yankees, the military men, the bureaucrats, they are still our masters. My country is built on lies too, Jonah said. Terrible crimes, even worse. Yes, she said. Yes, of course, it's very true. I suppose that's what we have in common. It was impossible to sleep in Buenos Aires.

Without a plan, Jonah went to Constitución Station and studied the timetables. Finally, he settled on a late departure, a night train heading south to Bahía Blanca. The train went over the sweetgrasses of the Pampas in total darkness under the stars. The conductor wore a green bow tie and drank yerba maté to keep himself awake. Jonah tried to write, but the janky tracks made it impossible and he gave up. In the morning they passed an overturned Range Rover at a rail crossing. The conductor clicked his pen and made a note. At Bahía Blanca Jonah bought a sandwich then boarded the connecting bus for Viedma. As the landmass of the continent narrowed so did his options. At Viedma he saw nothing worth the price of staying a night, so he waited for another bus, this one nearly empty, that took him farther south again to Puerto Madryn, a town that promised whale-watching tours. The town turned out to be only a Potemkin village set up by the tour operators to greet visitors and ferry them out to the whales. After the hours on the road, he gulped in the oceanic air. It tasted like release.

He found himself heading out on a skiff with a young German couple from Würzburg. They spoke excellent English and insisted Jonah must visit their town. The most authentically German town, with the nicest people, the man said. Despite what happened during the war, and the heavy price they paid, the woman said. Jonah was relieved that the ocean was relatively calm. They bobbed about in the hot sun. When the breach came it was so sudden they almost missed it. A terrific snort followed by a slapping slurp in the marbled froth. Then another smaller hump just behind, a hillock soon dissolved. The boatman said it was a female, probably with a young one in tow. The Bavarians shared laconic exclamations as they watched the trail of spume unspool. They all waited, scanning the rolling swells intently in the hopes of another salutation. None came. Still. He had seen it. The Leviathan. Her lungs the size of Volkswagens, hot blood coursing through arteries thick as his thorax, perhaps dim awareness of her fingerbones. The biggest mother out there. Concentrating in her body the inspired will to dive, to undertake those long hours of nightwork in the deep trenches, bathed in sound, seeking out that nourishment so needful for ascension. Why should her mere proximity cause such emotion? Was it a sign? A hopeful nod that he was on the right path? Or a signal that he was deceived? In Milton's poem, mistaking the whale for an island got one dragged down to hell. Was that his trouble? That he could not tell the difference between signs of hope and signs of hopelessness? Or was it that all along he had assumed there *was* a problem? Believed, even before Phineas had made him self-conscious of a desire to pursue it, that he had some mission to fulfill, some heroic effort to discover, when the truth of his condition was that he was the lucky survivor of a wreck, an Ishmael, whose isolated life was defined by the privilege of floating safely shoreward on the tides, a blessing of the gods, a stroke of dumb luck, a fortune inherited precisely because the defining moments of death and destruction had already taken place. What if there was nothing left to do other than tell the story? Nothing to accomplish other than continued survival and a contemplative retelling of the ruinous past? Had he come to the far end of the world in order to learn something that was the biggest nothing of all? These black thoughts? Convinced he was going one way, was he, all along, going the other? It would be in keeping with everything else. The rotten purposelessness of the age. The mindlessness swallowing everything into itself without any possibility of resistance, only horrific jests. Neither progress, nor regression. Only this holding pattern, this undertow of disorientation. The fear of revisiting the past and the fear of the annihilating future holding everything and everyone in a nihilistic torpor, sending out fluxing lines that sparked all manner of derangement and decadence. Including his own. Yet was this anything the old folks didn't already know? Wasn't this what, in their own way, they had always tried to tell him? That it would come down to making a way out of no way, creating a future over and against its absence? Wasn't it ingrained in his impulses, this reflex to run away in order to live? But the North Star in the age of the satellite is everywhere and nowhere. There would be no outrunning in this brave new world; whatever you had, whatever you could hold onto, you would have to make into a home. And he understood that he was looking at what he could not see before. The circumference of his errant life, his ceaseless fugitivity. A line without relief.

At Puerto Madryn, he boarded a bus that cut straight west across the continent to Bariloche. They drove on unpaved roads through the desert. Late in the night, the roar came to a stop in the garish light of a service station outside a Mapuche settlement. The Indians of Argentina. Same story as far as he knew. An ancient people decimated. No one seemed to be present other than a lone attendant at the pumps who laughed with the bus driver as they waited under the glare of the Chevron ensign. In Bariloche the lakes were sparkling. Jonah stayed at a tiny hostel run by a Chilean mother and her daughter who showed up in the evening to help. They insisted he must see their country before he left, and they suggested the island of Chiloé, easily reachable across the border.

The next morning, he was on a bus crossing the Andes along the snow line. On the way down out of the mountains and into Chile, the snow gave way to green pastures, farms, and rows of poplars lining glittering streams. On the outskirts of Puerto Montt new housing developments, still wrapped in Tyvek, were marooned in barren lots. Volcanoes towered in distant otherworldliness. At the ferry dock, he decided to drink to take the edge off. This was a mistake. Later, on the crossing, he thought he saw the Devil or a troll-like person watching him. And he remembered what Orígenes had said, that even the Devil would be saved.

The island of Chiloé was on the Pacific. In Ancud penguin tours were heavily advertised. But when he inquired at the tourist office, Jonah was told the seas were too rough that day to see any penguins unless he were willing to pay a good deal more for a bigger boat. The hills around Ancud were the color of avocados. Large black birds sailed overhead, great black crosses. He was informed that they were condors, a type of vulture. The tourist office turned out to have a selection of books by and about Chileans, their culture and history. He bought a copy of Vicente Huidobro's *Altazor*. He left Ancud penguinless, but on his way found a newly opened sushi restaurant. No one there was Japanese. But they had chopsticks and the fish was fine. Jonah read from *Altazor* and took comfort in its charm. "I love the night," sang the poet, "the hat of every day."

From Chiloé he traveled again, this time straight north up the spine of Chile to Santiago. In the capital he checked into the Villa Gramaldi, the American youth hostel. There was a terrible smell in the bathrooms. Someone said it was something in the drains, an ineradicable stench. Jonah quickly headed out to explore the city but there was very little to see in terms of sights, and he ended up drifting through residential neighborhoods with no distinctive character. He thought of Salvador Aussaresses. He could have lived comfortably on any of these neat tree-lined blocks. In the roundabouts there were bustling traffic and signs for an upcoming concert by Shakira. She was performing at the Estadio Nacional, the stadium where Pinochet had set up his open-air detention center and tortured people in the locker rooms. As far as he could see, there were no black people anywhere at all.

He would later reflect that the end decisively came into view in the cubicles of that sad locutorio in Santiago. He had joined the others plugged in at the long bank of numbered computers with their telemarketer headsets. He gazed into the screen with placid relief, allowing random media to wash over him as he clicked. He had no real desire to check his email. What he wanted was the feeling of being online itself, the narcotic, effortless involvement in the hive mind. Soon enough, however, he had scrolled through all of the homepages for websites that he could think of. He ran a search for massages in Santiago. That led to more links for sensual massages. Cascades of glossy thumbnails, unlikely names, and numbers. He stared at them quizzically, then abjectly. He jotted a few down in his notebook. Downstairs, he used a phone booth to make the calls. The first one was so confusing and aggressive that he hung up right away. The second was a soothing, laughing voice. He asked for directions. He went back upstairs to check the address. It was in a suburb to the north of the city. He went back down and hailed a taxi that took off speeding along curvilinear avenues leading out to the north of the city. They pulled up to a corner in what appeared to be an affluent neighborhood. He rang the intercom in the entry hall of a residential tower. A young woman's voice buzzed him in. It was not the voice he had heard on the phone. A dark-skinned woman opened the door. Venezuelan, maybe. She was in her underwear, a green G-string and a black padded bra. She had a sweet smile and very distant eyes. Her thighs were striated in cream-colored marks. She took Jonah by the hand and led him into a living room. A large black leather couch dominated the room. Facing it was a coffee table with a shallow dish full of candies and a large flat-screen television. An episode of *The Cosby Show* dubbed in Spanish was playing at very low volume. She sat him down on the couch and asked how long he wanted to stay. He said he wanted whatever the usual was. She chuckled and put her hand on his groin. She told him to relax. She kissed him on the cheek and told him to put the money on the coffee table. She was going to freshen up and would be back in a moment. He heard her go upstairs and close a door. The Huxtables were revolving around the studio set warbling in Spanish. He looked around the room. There was a faint breeze coming through the bars of a window full of boxed begonias. He looked at the pile of bills on the table. He heard a sink faucet running upstairs. Then he was up and making his way to the door, to the hall, down a flight of stairs. Outside, he started flat-out running. He ran as fast as he could, until he got back to the large avenue where the taxi had dropped him off. Across the avenue, there was a park with a large public fountain. He stood at the edge of the fountain facing the water. The jet of water clapped and splattered in his ears. The spray beaded in the sun and he put his hands into the fuming iridescence.

The ATM never lies. This one informed Jonah that his money was almost out. All those savings from Uncle Vernon's years of patient, steadfast labor. God only knows what he had sacrificed to get those funds and keep them in his account for his family. What he refused himself. What daily humiliations he put up with. And Jonah had spent it carelessly, without anything to show for it. His head wasn't right. Or was there still time to get it together, to do something righteous? To do justice to Nate's vision. To connect with Isaac again. To make a work of art, to make something for Phineas. To make use of the impasse he had driven himself into. If he could just get around to really sitting down and sticking to it. If he could reach understanding of self.

If it wasn't too late. At Santiago Central Terminal he boarded the international overnight route on the intercity bus. Destination: Buenos Aires. He felt hopeful. Rising and falling, up and over the Andes, the bus lurched and groaned along perilous roads. Jonah thought he heard each soul among them praying for the driver to stay awake, to see them through their voyage to the end of the night.

Somewhere in that night, as he lay balled up and shivering, the feverish questions came circling, wheeling shadows like the condors. What a random place to perish! And if it did happen, what could anyone say? What account could he give for his brief season on Earth? With everything given him, every chance and opportunity, every gift, what did he have to show for it? Nothing.

But it wasn't true. There was one person who could say more than a good word and say it true. Arna, of course. And he could see her in a flash, waving to him in the rain on the rue des Écoles. Taking off her wet shoes, one foot undressing the other, and humming along to the score as Ingrid Bergman wandered through the ruins of Pompeii. Reading on the green bench with a piece of hair in her mouth. The loveliness of her forearms in the scattering sunlight at the café with the terrible omelets. Those moments and others recombine as they ride the Métro together, always to stations near the end of the line. Visit the palm trees in the greenhouses at Auteuil. The book market at the Parc Georges-Brassens. It's summer and they walk together in the dusk as the great murmuring of the city surrounds them. They argue about poetry, about the poem of the future. He says it must be made of the best of the new and the best of the old. Arna says it will be what it always was, a form of music. And he knows she is right. That it could start right here, at a moment like this, in the thick of the midsummer's night when the scent of hidden blossoms pulls an arrow through the spirit and all the songs of the human past seem close, as closely held as a letter in the hand. And set deep in the grain of this poem, she says, is the map of a feeling waiting to be discovered, the keys to our own language, which are always in reality just out of reach, like the lamps of the Luxembourg Gardens after dark. And he knows then, he is certain, that Arna will write it. Her whole life she's been wanting to write songs, not one or two, but whole albums full, with words that will catch all the music she's always carried in her head. They go along together, passing beside an old stone wall covered in ivy. Arna fingers the leaves and they clatter softly. He remembers then that this is the wall of the cemetery, one full of the illustrious dead, where Richard Wright is buried, and one branch of Arna's ancestors shares a dilapidated crypt. They say nothing more until they reach the halo of a subway entrance at a little tree-ringed roundabout. They stay there a moment, inhaling the rank blossoms of the giant horse chestnuts, pulping their flowery, clotted droppings underfoot. The dry five-fingered chestnut leaves form a papery darkness, a ladder of shadows leading up into the unfathomable blackness beyond reach. Let's go home, Arna says. Yes, he says. And they drop down below, waltzing into the Metropolitan's musty electric air.

It was dawn and the bus thrummed along, following a small stream and a rail line that ran beside it. Jonah shook himself awake. He was cold and there were specks of crystallization in the windows. Every five miles or so they passed small clusters of abandoned buildings, sheds, faint chalk marks in the wilderness. The cordillera was long behind them and they had started coming out of the ravines and into the rolling foothills. The bus continued to descend on a long sloping turn into the vineyards of Mendoza. Jonah looked back. The distant rose-tinted peaks of the Andes were glowing in the clear morning air. Then the mountains disappeared, and they followed a river that wound through the plains and larger roads that passed through vineyards and cattle ranches before merging onto the highways where they joined the dusty big rigs and the commuter traffic roaring onward toward the capital.

The first thing Jonah did when he arrived in Buenos Aires was to email Octavio to tell him that he was going back to Paris. To his surprise, Octavio responded immediately, telling him to wait, insisting he needed to come down to BA anyway and that he would arrive in time to see him off. Jonah agreed to the plan and booked a plane ticket for the coming weekend. There were even more tourists than he remembered in San Telmo. He watched tango dancers performing to the music from *The Godfather*. He found a low-key bar where he could drink and generally keep to himself. He was done. He was ready to be home, to get back on his feet, to start over.

But then it was all undone. It was terribly wrong. The day before he was to leave, he learned that something had happened to Arna. He was getting a flood of emails about it now. The actual accident had happened several days before. He had sets of forwarded emails, and updated notes from his mother. Basically, they all told the same story. A bad collision, heavy impact and trauma. She had been stabilized but they needed to operate again. Her parents were insisting they bring her to the American Hospital in Neuilly where they had specialists.

Jonah tried to find out something more. But naturally there was nothing really to be gained by it. He circled the block. All day he was in and out of the cybercafé checking the emails again. Updates. No updates. The time he had paid for was up. He felt drained and consumed with rage all at once. The faces of perfectly ordinary people looked hideous, detestable. He tried to gather his thoughts rationally and calm himself. Of course, she would pull through this. But constantly the awful sense of falling backward returned. Arna dying was impossible. The universe would never allow something so grotesquely unfair to happen. For some inexplicable reason it seemed to him important to think it aloud. So, he said it, even as he grasped feverishly at images, memories, words.

Octavio showed up the next day as he had promised. They met in a café in San Telmo. There was just enough time to have a coffee before Jonah had to head out to the airport. Octavio was looking great. He was animated as usual, and he had a healthy glow about him. Immediately, he was catching Jonah up about his time with Francesca. They were really clicking, it seemed. And Jonah asked him if he thought it would last. Octavio shrugged it off. Who knows? Probably not, in the long run, he said. But this was about the present, the extraordinary intensity of all that he had been learning from her about how to be a dad. Not for real, of course. But it was wonderful in ways he hadn't thought of, and Jonah could see that he really meant it. If they could figure out the visas, Francesca might try to bring Paolina to visit him in New York one day. Jonah was overjoyed to see Octavio. But he was embarrassed at how hard it was for him to make that even somewhat apparent to his friend. He found it hard to talk. He kept trying to think of a way to tell him everything about Arna, but for some reason he couldn't bring myself to. "What's next for you, caballero?" Octavio wanted to know. He evaded the question.

Now he suddenly wished that he hadn't waited for Octavio. It was so good to see him, but it also felt like somehow his being there was making things worse. He had botched everything, even his own departure. They tried a neutral gear, talking sports, and Octavio noted that his beloved Vasco was performing horribly this year and was in danger of being knocked out of the Brazilian Série A altogether. They tried to talk about New York, but the news about the aftermath of the riots there really didn't help. Actually, it made things worse and Jonah started to feel slightly ill. He had to get to his flight. Octavio helped carry his bags up the Avenida 9 de Julio. There was sadness in his eyes. Jonah felt stupid for not thinking of something better to have done with their brief time together. But then a cab pulled up and

Octavio was yelling at the driver in Spanish, beaming with his usual fire. Jonah got in and Octavio came over to the window and they clasped hands. Jonah was mumbling something about seeing him around, but Octavio with great dignity and noblesse, cut him off. *"Avant tout, la liberté!"* He was still shouting in his awkward French and making grandiloquent waves as the taxi pulled out into the main lanes and Jonah lost sight of him in the heavy traffic.

23

While he had been away nothing had changed, but now everything was different. The first decade of the new millennium was winding down and headed into troubled waters. The television screens in the waiting area of the baggage claim oscillated between coverage of a potentially historic American election and an economic crisis of devastating proportions. But the anxious hope and breathless panic saturating the airwaves went beyond the question of financial catastrophe or politics. It seemed to encompass a whole new way of being in the world, as if everyone had stopped to peer collectively over a cliff, allowing the new normal to momentarily come into view, or at least the outlines of its major patterns, which promised to be glittering, swift, and cruel. The France Jonah had left behind was doing its best to keep apace of the times. At the airport all the business-class types were following the bad news on their new portable screens.

What chance did Nate's injunction to do good, or the work of a few teachers at a high school, or Uncle Vernon's hope for him to do something righteous have against all that?

His mother was waiting for him under the gray high arches of the terminal at Charles de Gaulle. She looked older, more delicate and frail than he had remembered. But the deepest lines in her face hadn't changed. Not a drop of clarity was missing in her eyes. She wanted to help with the bags but he insisted he was fine. As they weaved their way through the terminal, he struggled to hear her voice over the clamor of announcements. On the RER train the fatigue caught up with him in heavy waves. They passed the suburban stations in procession. The housing projects loomed on the horizon. His mother was happy because he was home. She was talking about things that he had missed while he was away. His father's health was worsening, she warned, worsening every day. He leaned against the window. He couldn't stand it anymore.

"Mama, I'm no good . . ."

"What do you mean no good, sweetie? You're tired, you're jet-lagged . . ."

"No, no. You're not *listening*. I'm no good at anything. My life hasn't worked at all. I feel like . . . like all I've ever done is waste time."

"You've been out in the world, exploring, learning, teaching. Right now, you're hungry, you're pooped! Look at you! You probably haven't eaten a proper meal in days!"

"No. No, that's not it. I feel empty inside. About everything. I hate everything, and nothing even makes sense anymore. I'm nothing. I'm nowhere."

"Jonah, listen to me. I'm your mother, I know what I'm talking about. What happened to Arna isn't your fault. These things just happen . . . they just do, and you can't take it all upon yourself, it doesn't mean the world is against you or hates you, it's just that, I don't know, it's the way things *are*. But it's going to be okay again, I promise it will."

"Mama."

"I'm so sorry about Arna, Jonah. I'm so sorry."

He waved her away. He didn't want to talk about it. The train plunged underground, racing to the platform at Gare du Nord.

"You know she sent you all these letters. Your friend Isaac forwarded them all from New York. I've been keeping them for you in your room. I brought them with me. I thought you might want them right away."

The stack of envelopes was addressed in Arna's unmistakable hand. His mother had tied the packet together carefully with string. He thumbed through them, checking the postage stamps. Arna had sent him letters from every corner of the new Europe. He took them and closed his eyes and waited for the pain to pass. It did not.

His room hadn't changed. He put the letters on the bed, walked to the window, and opened the shutters. The accordion wings swung open with a dull thud. There was a gray, empty sky over Paris. The motor of a moped went snarling by. A car was honking. Downstairs on the corner of the rue de Tocqueville, traffic was piling up. Two black men were operating a municipal truck as it lifted a green apple full of jingling recycled glass to be towed away. Jonah went back to the bed and sat down by the pile of letters. He looked up at the big map of the world on the wall. Rio de Janeiro, Montevideo, Porto Alegre, Santiago, Buenos Aires, New York. Places and people went spooling through the projector, their memories played to the inner eye. The distance between life and inner life, as between life and its sudden evaporation, a leap incalculable. Inside the names and the abstract points was a tangle of stories, and more than that, a string of choices that led right to his very last footsteps, to sitting on the bed, to his room with the window open onto the gray afternoon. If he were a wandering poet, perhaps he would have known to make something of it. But he had always been a terrible poet, a wannabe poet, worse than corny, a phony. He felt very small. He thought of what Isaac had said, and Nathaniel, and Uncle Vernon. And he wondered if he had done the wrong thing.

He also knew it was a stupid thought. For him everything was still possible. His privileged path and all that he might do with it was just beginning another cycle full of abundant second chances. His life was not the one that hung in the balance.

Tomorrow, he knew, would be an important day. They would move Arna into an operating room sometime after noon and then she would go into surgery. In the morning he would have breakfast, then go out to Neuilly to meet her parents who were staying overnight in the neurology unit of the American Hospital. If all went well, by midnight they would know.

He heard the muffled sound of his mother coughing in a far room. He cut the string, and Arna's letters fanned out on the bed. He ran a thumb over the stamps, over his name in her writing. Her handwriting. Her hands. His mother was calling from the kitchen. He could hear her opening cupboards, pulling down pots and pans. She was making something to eat. He looked at the letters. *No*, he thought. *No. Not now, not like this.* It was impossible. But he didn't know. He heard his mother coughing again, coughing, coughing. He opened the first letter and began to read.

ACKNOWLEDGMENTS

This book would never have seen the light of day without the belief, courage, and brilliance of my editors Michael Barron, Julia Ringo, and Alyea Canada. A shoutout to Anitra Budd, who saw what I was trying to do and encouraged me at a crucial time. I could not write without the love of my entire family, my dear friends, and fellow travelers along the road, who inspire me always. The earliest draft of this novel was completed during an extended stay with Ingrid Formanek and Brian Puchaty in Villanueva Mesía in the spring of 2008 and I thank them for their hospitality. Special thanks to Namwali Serpell for reading the manuscript with such care and providing invaluable suggestions, to Joshua Cohen for his encouragement, support, and advice, and to Jamaica Kincaid and Teju Cole for their example and camaraderie.

ABOUT THE AUTHOR

Jesse McCarthy is assistant professor in the departments of English and of African and African American Studies at Harvard University. His first book, *Who Will Pay Reparations on My Soul?*, a collection of essays, was published W.W. Norton & Co. in 2021. This is his first novel.